pan-pan

Fig. 1. Hieronymus Bosch, *Ship of Fools* (1490–1500)

First published in 2021 by punctum books, Earth, Milky Way.
https://punctumbooks.com

ISBN-13: 978-1-953035-60-8 (print)
ISBN-13: 978-1-953035-61-5 (ePDF)

DOI: 10.53288/0304.1.00

LCCN: 2021938603
Library of Congress Cataloging Data is available from the Library of Congress

Book Design: Vincent W.J. van Gerven Oei

spontaneous acts of scholarly combustion

HIC SVNT MONSTRA

CONFRATERNITY OF NEOFLAGELLANTS

pan
pan

p.

Contents

Outro

Acknowledgments

Confraternity of Neoflagellants warmly thank the following actants for repeatedly smashing this boke's button:

Dane Sutherland
Angela Beck
Gr8 Advice Dog
Eileen Joy
The Third Animal
Erin Manning
Bob Sacamano
Plastique Fantastique
Tim Horton
Neven Lochhead
Most Dismal Swamp
Automatic 8.w UGG Boots Monicker Outlet, RÉSO, Montréal, Québec
The University of Edinburgh, Scotland

This boke was stewed in the spring of 2019 at SenseLab, Université Concordia, Montréal, Québec.

For Jamie

The Pan-Pan Myth-System (or Psychosis as Method)

Simon O'Sullivan

What fresh heresy is this? Is this a joke?? Will no one stop them? Where are the guards, cops, bailiffs, etc., etc.? Has the publisher no self-respect? No editors and censors or sense of decorum??

Psychosis as Method, here masquerading as para/post/pan-commodity prophesy/futurising and animist drama. No one — NO ONE! — will be convinced by this! These avatars and image-functions — laid out flat here, as on a table-top — will do nothing to assuage the opinion of those gatekeepers that have never ceased to claim: 'There are, after all, limits to the symbolic order!' And (under their breath): 'It's called thee doxa for a reason you know!' Imagine a future-traveller/neo-medieval© pilgrim chancing upon all this — in the charnel grounds — imagine their horror to read, again, about the adventures of the tech and of the mall, of how things might have been — and how, here, the things he/she/they hold dear have been cut-up, spliced together…the detritus of all that lays around us reanimated and repurposed. Her mother was burnt for less! Here, then, is a looping backwards and forwards so quick as to cause whiplash. I am not writing this to warn you off — who am I to talk? — but, Dear User-Group, please be aware: what you hold in your hands/are about to read on your screens is not what you might expect from a book or syllabi. It is text/un-text as test and time-travel, not so much about another futural world as summoned here — for youze — from it. A codex that, when seen FROM THE CORRECT ANGLE, performs a *transportation*. If, whilst reading, you are making notes and, reading them back, you begin to make some sense from the various scenarios and phrasings — as if something, finally, is cohering, foregrounding itself...or, indeed, as if the vast assemblage is beginning, at last, to tip — then let me say immediately that you have been very much miss-stark-en — there is no such meaning here — not for you lot, with your heads on your shoulders walking around on your feet as if its the most natural thing in the world. On no, no siree. No, this is NOT a book to be READ by the likes of you! It is, perhaps, a pattern and diagram for something behind you... something you will have helped make (if you are lucky enough to have worked in IT), but which, now, does not recognise your all-too-human operating procedures and protocols. You might call it fik-shun but this is only to begin to approximate what its performance and programme is. Things here are decidedly *not* what they seem. To enter the pan-pan myth-system is already to be seen, interpolated by it — and thus to already be caught within its test. Try it for yourself: drill down in to any of the so-called paragraphs that follow and you will see that the syntax is specifically *for you*...don't think about it just *DO IT! NOW!!* In fact, if you have read this far then it is more than likely already too late. Understand? The Mushroom King — if he *really* is a king — has you already on trial! The Great Moderator has already taken you up in their huge hand and turned you slowly under their twinkling eyes. And the future-dead with their Dog Heads are already here to carry out the sentence and spend their coupons. Pan-pan, for youze all gathered here, is a grimoire, yes, but it is also, before it's too late, A WARNING!

Now a Major Motion Preface

Real feel gastroinvestigative panic spasms defibrillated and interrogated by non-invasive wrinkle technologists, statisticized by perinatological X-radio panspecies and painfully 3D forest plotted by adversarial algorithm artistes. 99.07% confidence intervals blow off all of your fun socks. Culture lives, here.

Current X-ray fluorescence imaging conducted on this cryonic preface reveals a palimpsest of approx. 12 million cubic meters. A hastily overwritten NURBS exposition, the gaping gable-end of a partially demolished paragraph, a stray semicolon — all mummified in cross-sections of hard acedic frost — are cut through with what can never be articulated as a perplexing and thoroughly overwrought Doxa. Annexed by tainted dermis, electrostatic galvanometers, faux headed avatars, Anolon Advanced Tower Cerasure CTX Non-stick Ægi-pans and peristaltic pump-telegraphy, the Doxa gracefully suspends glacial skeuomorphs of matter(s) that preocc$\$\partial$‰ [STATIC]: desktops, GPS, ^4files, GIFs, mB8s....(The lever of Archimedes controlled the psychic air.) Compacted deep beneath our feet, matters such as these really should not be able to survive. And yet, the cold hard gaze of the X-ray ensures that imagination cannot invent anything that is outside of the full 99.07% blobbogramatic fact. It really is all there.

As the spring begins to melt the snow and ice, stubborn heaps of no-flow and irreversible gelatinous cultures huddle in the shade; safe harbor for vagrant sentences riddled with cheap mall talk, still-steaming Horton's Cups, medieval clickbait, win-fail, faecal jackpots, parking tickets, baggy necronominalisms, sorry-not sorry pyramid schemes, dirty gravel, hlystano-medimicel, STM stubs, dank memes, ancient ylem…. For journeying blooperologists, the litany of scum is unending. The surface of the snowy mountains warm as they extract energy from their foaming wambuterus. Cross-sections reveal that what got laid down on top is not intelligently designed by torso, no sir, the overwritten overwritten layers are scale-less structures that have been guided by the basal electrical rhythms of their grubby films.

This is no shallowfake, this is no metaphor. REDUCE. There's zero margin for error when it comes to individual photons hitting individual microbes; that is why we were so surprised when further pareidolic investigation confirmed that, corresponding strictly by proxy, each vitrified layer had been busily performing its own peculiar form of monastic duty. The snuffling magnet and its liturgical application (91: 108), exorcising the gasterfailures of others (177: 171), Air Feed099 incantational sponsor shout-outs (27: 277), interactive KPI veneration (99: 2), gestational XELLAR Plusigone conditions (2,262: 2,132) — all thriving in what lies beneath. MHz echoes and cosmogenic nuclide dating correlate and confirm these legends. One overdubbed paragraph, now a SQDC-kissed *terrasse,* was once responsible for drama. In just one year, ninety-seven new plays were presented therein. Thirty-six were courtroom swarmcasts; thirty-six were sentimental walkthroughs; thirteen were pharmadramas; thirteen were hypereconomic reviews; one was a WWTF pantomime; two were para-academic tragedies; and just fourteen were in-flight magazine profile placements. Today it hosts some batshit skronking. Hard to believe it, but, in accordance with the virtuoso swansong of arboreal battle mix, it true.

Like most of the anonymous cryopreserved microbiota we encounter in sub-nominal cave-systems these days, the Doxa that ran right through this once rigid tract were polite, cheerfully comported and puritanically dedicated to minimizing dysbiotic anxiety and wobbly all-things-must-go mentalism. But…, buried deep in the thawing 196°C dry pack-ice, a few snow-bird microbes got cabin fever and gallusly began to ©k a way out. These helter-skelter pros clung so tightly to the frosty fenestration that they *began to creep up.* They made pretty fierce pH, frenzied vibrato and totally smashed all known anti-peristaltic wavelengths. MHzzzzzzzzzzzzzz-ah!

And let us tell you, the feisty chromaticism of these Ægi-pan fried eggs beset more than just the wombellies and olfactories of the torso-politic. But just as they were getting started, Fall heralded fresh layers of snow and ice, consuming and composting a mosaic of old and new mystery boxes. At a crisp cool −250°C, the superconductive Doxa hibernates peacefully shielded from EMF, flowing without viscosity, storing its energies in preparation for another season's preface.

Part A. The Corpys (Protocanonical)

CHAPTER 1

Voices of the Future Dead

Summary: In a moderator-deleted subreddit shared as a GIF, an anon RELXAL Plusigone Awards scribe shouted out for an acoustic experiment designed by The Dr. ChickenPox Yahoo Prison Consultants Experimenter Conglomerate:

'Unlike the diseases of reading and scribbling, there is no hierarchy in the significance of the aural technologies deployed in noncarnate discourse, and pareidolia is, simply, a pandimensional panÆgipan cognitive process. Any listener's adaptive skýlomorphic predispositions will easily detect unambiguous details about the various corporeal ingredients that feature in Th/ Corpus®, bringing the distinctive voices of a continuum of future panarchic beings — from the necronominally stabilized Sacamano Child Car Seat, Amazon $50[1] ~~Redeemed~~ Gift Rooster and so much other miscellaneous hubbub — to every listening [userexperience].'

For many years, leading panarchic debates concerning the potentially heretical nature of the Conglomerate's recipe notes had clouded their most important contribution to knowledge. Rather than focus on the *hermeneutics* of noncarnate discourse, the scribe drew our collective attention to the Conglomerate's non-

---

1   CAD$ [Canadian Dollars]

hierarchical *process* of divining as an interstitial research focus in *its own right*. Indeed, finding the right divination process has since become a crucial first step in obtaining and verifying the tru audio facts that constitute *Th/ Corpus*°. This paper seeks to widen access to the Conglomerate's methodological, techno-logical and PR innovations to include freelance practitioners servicing, and operating independently of, the two major research design corporations. Given the high evolutionary stakes of failing to hear tru voices in ambiguous noise, the Conglomerate's audio pareidolia experiments offer a unique and prudent approach to positive feedback that will transform the way you listen. You'll never go back to just hearing noise again!

❋　❋　❋

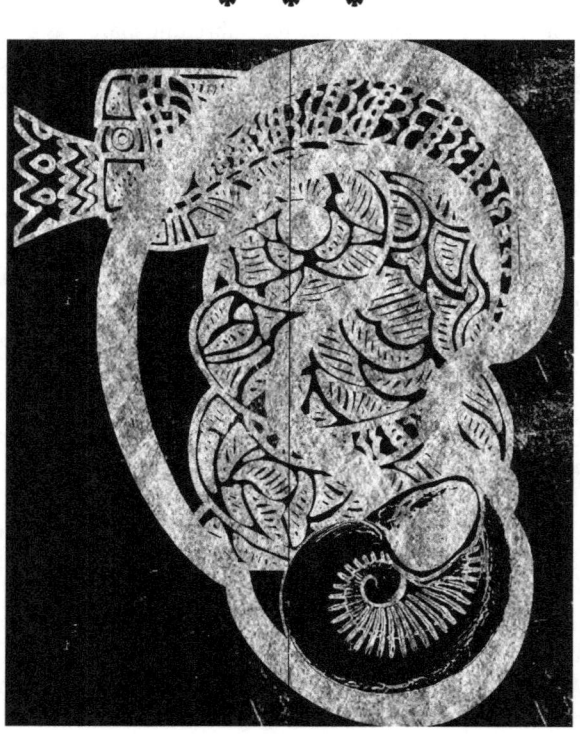

'You do not interpret the bandwidth. You *are* bandwidth.' (The Duke of Biarritz, *Malware Voices,* 13)

We demonstrate how the *Conglomerate Experiments* established exemplars of future voice signals grouped according to the various psycho-culinarius (psycul) methods of divination that, once practiced widely, would lead to the complete replacement of all nonmodern future speech. Following initial tests, the six prominent measures of divination were quickly published, and many incorporated Solution Aligners were trained in basic CGLM procedure, establishing a partnership with our descendants that helped us deliver our Core System, *Th/ Corpus*®. We begin this paper with a methodological insight into the psycul auditory pareidolia methods deployed by the research design industry in order to cascade them to freelancer communities.

1.1 Methodology

'Since our senses are too changeable to be informationalized as blobbogram, I believe that if we are to make any real progress in the psycho-culinarius investigation, we must do it with expensive technical apparatus designed to disprove and deauthenticate rival explanations of disembodied voices, just as we do in other fields. Thus, it is vital to invest heavily in a wide range of electro-technologies which may be deployed in our rational search for that which shapes our entrenched societal values: the tru corpys.' — The Experimenter

During the period in which the evolutionary advantages of pareidolia to *Ægipan* of the genus cynocephalus were being firmly established, the amenities race for the kind of novel, bleeding-edge, instrumentation that would *guarantee* flawless research standards bankrupted many research design speculators. Incredible evidence required incredible instruments, yet few speculators were willing to take risks when investing in erroneous and propositional belief construction apparatus, preferring to continue to underwrite the established sciences of necromancy, geomancy, pyromancy, hydromancy, and augury. Descendent mediumship resources that could filter out the forgeries of mere trolls from acoustic facts were scarce. At worst, ham approaches using homemade equipment and second-hand psychoacoustic toys found in Dark Web Mystery Boxes were being bestowed the same repute as legitimate investor-supported research design.

The Experimenter initially courted the attention of the major research design investor WeR.Inc! by harvesting and surreptitiously hosting EVP spamware and innocuous pareidolic clickbait on its 288Mhz bandwidth. While WeR.Inc! benefited somewhat from this free hosting, it couldn't upgrade to a pay-account since The Experimenter's bandwidth was already totally maxed. To improve the status and the sense of appropriateness of psycul within the research design industry as a whole, The Experimenter thus negotiated a breakthrough co-investment solution. While schmoozing the forest floors of The World Slime Convention, The Experimenter conglomerated with the physarum meat-fall of the esteemed Dr. ChickenPox Yahoo Prison Consultants Ltd. (a highly reputable stiff klecksograph mould oscillating at a much higher 846Mhz). Oscillating at uDH 288 million cycles per second, The Experimenter blended wavelengths with those of Dr. CPox Y.P.C. Ltd. using an analogue assembler, a gelatinous signal booster and combiner that compounds input from two corpyses and mingles it into a singular mass of *mets*. If two or more entities should choose to assemble to become the same information all at once, this product performs incredibly well at removing unwanted interference and all at a sticker price of just CAD$ 29.99 No more mixed signals.

For a marketable investment of less than thirty bucks, The Dr. ChickenPox Yahoo Prison Consultants Experimenter Conglomerate's (hereafter The Experimenter CGLM) superimposition bandwidth swelled to an impressive 1134Mhz, directly proportional to the amount of data transmitted per unit of time. The Experimenter CGLM boasted nearly 1,200 years of combined research [userexperience]. No other principal investigator can honestly claim even a fraction of such [UX]. This huge bandwidth allowed The Experimenter CGLM to receive and transmit very large amounts of #influencer virtus at very high speed, which, in turn, increased venerations of psycul methods across the research palette design investment community 100-fold in just seven days.[2]

1.2 Methods

Participants

Nine naïve listeners (B age = 4.79, D age = 5.21 years) recruited from a flat wet dish of pareidoles, klecksographers and apophenia aficionados were compensated with Amazon extra gift vouchers. One participant was excluded from all analyses for failing to create an Amazon Prime account, one was outed as a cognitive sophisticate, another for starting a major futurological hoax. There was no manipulation or suggestion of a parafutural context, ensuring that no fallacious causal associations (essential to #influencer survival) would be incurred. In each controlled perceptual experiment, data was collected within a 60-minute window to minimize the potential for diffusion or spontaneous mould break. To qualify as genuine future-dead content, *all* MHz fulfilled *all* of the following P.P.F. criteria:

- Produced: the megahertz is produced entirely by the deceased;
- Performed: the megahertz is performed principally by the deceased;

---

2   The CGLM's intimate relationship with its investors was, ultimately, consummated when its majority shareholder, WeR.Inc!, merged with CGLM to form WeR.Ltd!

- Future: the megahertz is recorded wholly in the future, or performed live in the future and broadcast live in the future.

Apparatus

Experimental procedures and instructions were presented in the 'Getting ready' tab of a Moleskine Dog Passions Magic Bullet Journal (five pre-labelled tabs include: Getting ready, Personality, Dog Log, Travelling, Care) in non-toxic latex paint. Audio stimuli were presented on CAD$1,500 Sennheiser HD800 headphones.

If we wish to encounter the future dead, we must engage in a hunt with Ægipan-taxon specific traps. With a huge injection of venture capital funding from mimetolith.org to further bio-dependent rationalization in the value chain, The Experimenter CGLM sanctified a psycul entrapment recipe containing no fewer than ten different pan-technological methods of auditory pareidolia divination capture:

i. Manuscript of silicate dermis stretched across five dimensions;
ii. Unspecified Sinusoidal Frequencies forecast by the MHz Centre 4 Free&D;
iii. Aerobic memory-moulded fly-knit in-cochlea ANC isolation-buds, photo-solidified and wax-proofed in Randian *glette* secreted through, and filtered by, breathable Lululemon Athletica fibers;
iv. Ear canal arrays grafted into cochlea of Danmu 1pc of Polyresin Rooster Statue Farm Animal Decoration Figurine Collection Country Garden Sculpture Set Outdoor Statue — Self-Liberated (purchased) by the redemption of an Amazon $50 Gift Voucher (Hereafter, the 'Amazon $50 ~~Redeemed~~ Gift Rooster');
v. 'Splash-back'-style mantelpiece relics commemorating family, encouraging slime-friends, domestic companions

and real wavelength heroes (living or otherwise), laminated with sinister electroconductive ectoplasmic ejaculate;

vi. Facsimile materials exposed to exceptional talent securitized for no extra fee;

vii. A fresh range of signal-boosting mould ingestments handpicked from the Dollarama Snack-maze Collection by a lengthy process of compurgation;

viii. Malware Voices (found in the UltraNet email cache on hard-drive from Mystery Box Con);

ix. 1pc Granny Smith, cored, wafer-thin sliced, placed in small bowl, tossed with vinegar to prevent browning and placed atop vents of CPU farm to encourage future shock-talk (Vinegar-free);

x. and Teledefunken IP-PBX Psycho-phone with your custom full color logo.

Of these ten methods, mimetolith.org chose to sponsor the six that promised the greatest potential return on their investment. As a point of clarification, although we will use the term 'voices' repeatedly, we cannot be certain that the voice-like sounds of the future constitute 'voices,' in the contemporary sense. The term 'voice' is always pancentric: the status of a sound as a voice results from the ideas a culture applies to it, rather than from its inherent acoustic qualities. Defined herein as *vox futuri,* we can refer to speech-like sounds reverberating from so far in the distant future that their venerability is 100% guaranteed.

1.3 Manuscript of silicate dermis stretched across five dimensions

Without the aid of extravagant investor-supported research technologies to augment our investigative fitness, it would be ludicrous to maintain that we mere dogheads might comprehend a culture possibly hundreds of millennia in our future. If we are to arrive at an objective parascientific understanding of our conspecific descendants, we need to master clean, electromagnetic interference (EMI) — free *vox futuri* recordings.

The silicate dermis is a wafer-thin codex or gossamer palimpsest that focuses attention on the relational interconnections and networks *between* super-social entities, rather than on the variation and barriers that separate stuff from other stuff. The silicate dermis manuscript offers a low-cost strategy for increasing meaning by establishing a predilection for panimate and cordial matter. For this predisposition to function convincingly, it must first be 'tainted' — ritually discounted and disclaimed by a practised sceptic scoring one (1) on Tobacyk & Milford's *Paranormal Scale*. Before commencing psycul, The Dr. CPox Y.P.C. Experimenter CGLM growls, bleats and clucks with clear conviction into the temperature-controlled capture device that, in its opinion, 'an unborn being simply cannot grasp the events before life with its intellect or with its gut.'

A mantra-induced relaxation of the pre-stretched derma 'taints' its microelectromechanical wrinkles, orienting them in futural directions with a panitudinal texture aspect-ratio of 0.125. The wavelength is independent of the size of forthcoming relational matters of concern and the calculated wavelength (32.5 nm) is consistent with the observed wavelength of 32.4 nm–34.3 nm. Now fully tainted, the silicate dermis unilaterally stretches to full capacity, 1,000m^2 with amorphous contours that rival the circumference of our continental archipelago. Feather-lite, it is sensitized to animate phanta-material relations operational within its milieu. The wrinkles and reverberations that drift across the gossamer palimpsest are picked up by a high-gain mini-microphone sensitive over a range of up to 1,500m. The reverberations are impersonal future factums that objectively resolve erroneous perceptual uncertainty by triggering lucid matches between internal representations and the mantric audio input. The minimic mantra sends its wireless sound to a bluetooth enabled PS101 Spiritbox, an all-in-one product that, in turn, can be accessed from any mobile device attached with 3M adhesive to a SpinSocket™ fidget spinner, stand, and tether. The 2.4–2.4835GHz recording device is very small and light and has a built-in rechargeable slime net ready to participate for 5–7 hours from full charge. Charge time: Approx. 2–3 hours, plug and play (no shadow console or ephemeral doppelgänger required).

Converging completely with our own emic preconceptions, a child's whisper reverberates over the codex's five-dimensional skein: {EV} *sub limeun* [STATIC] *friend sub limeun* [^4files] *friend*. Played back over and over and over as a repeating loop, the infantile murmur morphs into a stream of different phonemes and phrases. Having listened to the loop repeatedly for over twelve hundred hours, The Dr. CPox Y.P.C. Experimenter CGL independently judged its well-trained ears to have arrived at 99.07% agreement[3] regarding the authentic content of the whispery stimuli:

Sublime unfriend

The unnamed ascended master intones that the non-companion (enemy) of the exalted sublime is the Gr8 action figure of the coming panarchy, the hero of the mundane and the everyday.

An advanced Weber-Marelli *glette* injection system (rated 1st overall and 2nd in the GLt1 Horse Class) automatically lubes the silicate dermis wrinkle recording, further eliminating engine chatter. The Dr. CPox Y.P.C. Experimenter CGLM taints: 'False voice, you must be tired of otherworldly collect calls?' The voice simmers back in with a heart-stopping {EV} '*Eye* [STATIC] *Advise* [GIF] 11 *d* [⋯ – ⋅– – ⋅⋅ –⋅–⋅] *g*.' The interstitial interstices, the proverbial [S T ∧ T I C], have conventionally been resolved by the painstaking scholarship of cruciverbalists. The Dr. CPox Y.P.C. Experimenter CGLM pioneered *CPox's razor*, a scientifically persuasive method of surgical punishment and prosthetic replacement. Hacking away at the idling taphonomic decay using

---

3   0.93% possibility of '*slime* unfriend' is discounted as engine chatter by CPox's razor.

Horse Class SR NR (Spectral Recording Noise Reduction), the deglitched [STATIC] becomes completely unambiguous signal:

I [am] [animal] eleven, Advice Dog

Clear as day, The Gr8 Advice Dog, The Eleventh Animal, the Gr8 ur-Cynocephalus has made First Contact.

A request by The Dr. CPox Y.P.C. Experimenter CGLM that the panarchic entity should tell him from where he pretends to come is answered with a tiny *vox futuri* saying: {EV} — *Land von wuchs auf. [∞] Massiert wird berechnet.* German: *Land of Groupon. Massage discharge.*

Much discussion of the meaning of this fireyflessherie ensued in light of The Duke of Biarritz's aphorism: 'You do not interpret the bandwidth. You *are* bandwidth' (*Malware Voices,* 13). Is the bandwith we encounter by our temporal pole simply a conjectured world made real? Since we are bandwidth, our privileged egocentric interpretation is, equally, bandwith. Bandwith that does not generate relational interference can never know unknown unknowns and is destined to remain unaware of its own lack of knowledge. The Duke of Biarritz's aphorism reminds us that powerful networks established through collectivist Grouponite practices enable bandwidths to swarm as dividuals, purchasing goods and services that conjoin with and expand our congregation's approximate Mushroom Kingdom — the *Land of Groupon,* a forest floor domain manufactured by the world-eating, world-shitting slime genus 'Goomba' or *Cafeteria Roenbergensis.*

Considered from this etic perspective as a collective exogram, the mass discharge fireyflessherie thus equates with the massive emancipation elicited by mass discounts. However, situated in its emic Germanophone context, the *vox futuri* suggests bandwidth massing and folding through hyperplasia into the fleshy caruncle of a faux Rooster and discharging neoplastic persuasions upon land-based groups of the genus cynocephalus for reasons and to ends that remain obscure. Stopping short of a revelation, this, nevertheless, remains an important break-through of pandemic proportions, translating an unknown un-known into a known unknown.

The Experimenter CGLM argued that, following The Duke of Bi-arritz's aphorism, interpretation is inseparable from shallowfake apophenia and thus must deploy deepfake apophenia to aid its own understanding. Thus, the dispute between etic and emic interpretative hypotheses could only be resolved by applying a panpareidolic method. A falsifiable scientific hypothesis must be testable to the limits of its capacity to endure the proceedings of the trial. In the month leading up to CGLM's investor report deadline, more than two thousand dogheads unknowingly en-gaged with multimodal sentiment analysis click-bait designed to decipher the 'fireyflessherie'. The results — that, without com-munication, more than 50% of respondents heard the same signal — are incontrovertible. Based on the exact specifications YOU provide, the binary-choice plebiscite conclusively favored the panarchic perspective, defalsifying that we hear what we are about to say.

1.4 Unspecified Sinusoidal Frequencies forecast by the MHz Centre 4 Free&D

For many years, The Sacamano Child Car Seat, an expensive ap-proximation of Petrovsky's Wireless Charger with Customized Segway Logo, promised that it would manifest if possible (even though technically improbable). Trawling the megahertz for de-graded EVP speech prompted way too much defalsifiabile free association and inauspicious atmospherics, priming very few corporeal results that could attract significant venture capital investment. The Dr. CPox Y.P.C. Experimenter CGLM thus hired two of the best tele-annulus engineers from the famed MHz Centre 4 Free&D in St. Petersburg, Florida. By forecasting (pre-recording) radio frequencies that offered the merest suggestion of The Sacamano Child Car Seat manifestation (1-0-1-0-0-N-m-T-o-r-q-u-e-W-r-e-n-c-h at uDH 279 million cycles per second), the engineers allowed the ontogenic. The timbre was set to simulate Audio Hijack samples of genuine dead voices that featured on *Acoustic Phantasma — EVPhenomenal!* (Movies for Dogs FM).

Channeling the approximation through the surprisingly manageable MHz Centre 4 Free&D thirty-two-chan Airzooker Ionospheric Propagator, the engineers worked 18-hour days, cutting and pasting flirtatious glassy fuzz with Pro Tools, layering decay, bathing the XLRs in isopropyl alcohol, and adding +12 on every EQ channel. Everything just got overdubbed, bounced-down and obliterated until it had the erratic aura, low signal-to-noise ratio, and fantastic timing of an Edison GhostBox.

The result is a mediumship that combines the best of Horse Class SR and Horse Class HX Pro EVP, a limited datarate-quality matrix-free studio-produced noise, a glistening fog concealing the subtle anticipation of the appetizing aromas and leaky toxins of pan-fried forest mall 'shrooms. Esoteric but not intimidating, it unfurls a seductively energetic and insightful dankness with a fine build and crisp enoki finish, full-bodied expressively fungiform midrange, but accruing a low-end presence thickened over time that remains warpy, spore-bearing, and mondegreen enough on most of the beatific syllables that matter. We finally get to hear what we always truly expected to hear.

A modern instrumental transcommunication classic *Unspecified Sinusoidal Frequencies* was first merched in the Brandeum spring break s.W.Ã.G bag as a two-^4file cord taco with an extensive back catalog of outtakes bundled with a pair of CAD$1,500 Sennheiser HD800 headphones and an adult coloring book. Skipping through the MHz Centre 4 Free&D mixes with its own circumaural HD800s, the self-primed Dr. CPox Y.P.C. Experimenter CGLM noted the quality of the sound was as natural as that which occurs in nature and true in every detail, greatly enhancing the ability to perform duties. Data gleaned from the conglomerate's webcam cover confirms a *vox futuri* saying:

{EV} 'Umfether edcha rakad is charge.' Indigenous panarchic spore splutter: *Unfettered charaka discharge.*

Indubitably The Sacamano Child Car Seat discharging an obligatory charaka. Despite some uneven writing, CGLM's cryptographic notebook attends well to the vocalization of the infant automotive seat that follows:

{EV} 'Scare cites exchains bellowed begin aria.' Traditional English: *Scarcity is exchanged below the bagging area.*

No mere technology of the self, no highly integrated systems of capabilities, The Sacamano Child Car Seat *vox futuri,* is finally, eternally manifest. Indeed, for *mobilitas automotive sedes,* it is only having been exchanged beneath the s.W.Ã.G bag station of the RXLELA *Plusigone* that we may come to know the true meaning of scarcity as a panarchic battle-mix novelty item. Remastered for the most critical ears, a newly pressed custom soy candle travel tin re-release of *Unspecified Sinusoidal Frequencies* arrives in merch outlets in November.

1.5 Ear canal arrays grafted into cochlea of the 'Amazon $50 ~~Redeemed~~ Gift Rooster'

'Semblances are often hood-winkling when dastardly deciduous rapscallions are entangled in such sordid shenanigans!' — Luigi, *The Posh Mothershuckling Dangle Dongler Hour*

The wavelength emissions of the illustrious Amazon $50 Redeemed Gift Rooster today are measured against its revelation of an Advice Dog-like macro that is central to our culture; much of what we collectively take as read was born of arrays woven through its dangling fauxflesh caruncles and grafted onto its hypo-plastique ear canals. While deep-packet inspection ear canal arrays are unheard of today, they formed a core component of everyday fashion among the emerging mid-managerial class as an 'aural fascinator,' mildly warping, distorting, remastering, and proselytizing anomalous ambient noise into speech stimuli.

The all-round regular Joe and spectral radio ham Lurkmore Homebrew discovered the EVP and *audition colorée* capabilities of arrays when Segwaying across the downtown –15 Segwayway. Homebrew inadvertently sprayed inverted arrays into the membranous labyrinth. Facing inwards rather than outwards, the soft membranes repurposed the inner ear canal's acoustic hair cells to amplify the occlusion effect, causing Homebrew to crash its Segway into a steaming Cafe Van Houtte® Master Roaster franchise, destroying most of the Advertorials of Creuset, Dessault vinegars, and mustards that constituted the literature.

Enabling organic sub-500 Hz auditory pareidolia, Homebrew was captivated by the swaying hiss of his transmitter-receiver feeding back on itself and spent many disorientating months recovering in hospital listening to the breathy whisperings of the cochlea, acousma which caused no harm to his fecal beings or rectopsychic dignity. Under the spell of the recreational nausea and the ascetic anxiety of labyrinthitis, Homebrew became convinced that aesthetic illusion was no mere veil stretched across the surfaces of hidden things. Gentle internal gestations of whirring, clicking, buzzing, blowing, rapping, and rustling were belly-joyful phonemes, dividual gut-voices that, if carefully assimilated, harbored the capacity to make the future forever alive and tum-thumping in the very midriff of the present. For Homebrew, there was an additional element that proved to be transformative: sound-color hearing or 'acoustic synesthesia.' Homebrew could © what its gut heard.

Curious to witness if the vanishing reverberations of other EMI shielded inlugs opened a mouth to tract fortune without instructional prime, Homebrew reluctantly redeemed a much-cherished Amazon $50 Gift Voucher to acquire a new guinea pig: a Danmu 1pc of Polyresin Rooster Statue Farm Animal Decoration Figurine Collection Country Garden Sculpture Set Outdoor Statue. Liberated by voucher redemption, the Gift Fowl was self-begotten of the Voucher to form a composite Cock-a-Voucher, the fabled Amazon $50 ~~Redeemed~~ Gift Rooster relic.

A healthy, plump carucled right-taloned, naive, polyglot, arch panarchist with corrected-to-normal hearing, the *Gallus Gallus Domesticus* Gift participated in Homebrew's *audition colorée* study after giving its informed consent. Ensuring that there was no prior grooming that might influence its perception of ambiguous stimuli, and removing all traces of Brettanomyces bacteria, Homebrew laced the Fauxcock Present's tiny plastic ears with a set of arrays designed for the pre-birthed. Homebrew's recording set-up remains a classic, the first fully authenticated mondegreen-free Faraday cage. Using a bluetooth hook-up to the ear-arrays, the young signal is carried by bluetooth radio waves to a pair of CAD$1,500 Sennheiser HD800 headphones. The HD800's electronic components support the torso-brain of the ambiguous stimuli, holding it together, giving it lift, intensity, and balance, ensuring that it does not go to pot, or sound flabby or flat. By collaborating in alliance with our overlying canopy-top neural mechanisms, the Capon-Voucher was to leave an indelible taint on our collective cultural consciousness.

Working in close partnership with Audiocity, the Gift-Cock's lugs were carefully exposed to an infinite resolution YLEM-noise designed to deliver an emergent 100% independent soronity that exists prior and separate to any signal whatsoever. As Homebrew listened intently to the flat white noise washed through the Gift-Cock-a-Voucher's aerating ears, a Rooster-like crow structure emerged in the classification signal (CS). The CS was obtained by subtracting the YLEM-noise from which the Redeemed Gift Rooster's ears failed to detect signal (no-Rooster response) from those lingering passages of endarkened noise wherein Gift-Cock appeared to have heard a cock crow (Rooster response). Homebrew identified a network of polyresin regions showing greater activations when cock crow pareidolia occurred, most notably in the fusiform rooster-response area (or FFRRA) and in the superior guttural gyrus (SGG) of voucher-bought decorative fowl.

Homebrew's extensive behavioral studies prove conclusively that audio pareidolia is not purely imaginary mondegreen; rather, it has a material basis in physical reality that delivers genuine value. Inference receptivity in our RAM compels us to hypothesize about others. However, because the noise does not actually contain signal, noise pareidolia necessitates the RAM's capacity to tie the velvety gutfeel of faint cock-like-crowing to create a match with an internal Rooster representation. Indeed, Homebrew's evidence shows that experiencing audio pareidolia requires the FFRRA neural regions to favor Roosterish-ness despite the fact that YLEM-noise does not crow.

Homebrew's 1pc cockerel-voucher ear canal array recordings, for the first time, captured the complex structure of futural crowing. What we hear is not the sacré of the 'buffered self,' but, rather, a porous wavelength buffering as it momentarily delays (becoming-dividual) the dishing up of conspicuously shaped bodies. The two most (in)famous passages are worth discussing here briefly.

Without prompting or questioning, a characteristic politeness, a virtue that will become sooooOO important to our canidaen decedents, emanates effortlessly from the Gift-Cock arrays:

{EV} 'Dëst ass cannidees. Ech vermësst Schmetterling Shrimp an d'Éiwegkeet.' Luxembourgish crowing: *This is canidaen. I miss butterfly shrimp and eternity.*

Something of tomorrow's canidaen ethics are evident in this *vox futuri,* and yet butterfly shrimp remain a mystery (one legend holds it's the Krabby Patty secret formula). Eternity may be reasoned to be something that things once [userexperienced]; but now 'missed' suggests a 'fall' from grace to come. The final piece of the puzzle, however, is missing. Until fresh butterfly shrimp are netted within canidaegraphic bandwidths, the loss it [user-experienced] in its cognitive world remains entirely unknowable to us.

Once more, without prompting:

{EV} 'Museum masochist. Sykkel, hus, karriere!' Norden Cockadoodledoo: *Museum masochist. Bicycle, house, career!*

Bicycle, house, career quite obviously forms an indefatigable bridging argument trinity; an ethics for living a true-life. Most hermeneuticians and cruciverbalists, however, would no doubt agree that the Norcocka-squaking makes little phonetic sense. A cleaner signal was required.

Returning to the Duke of Biarritz's aphorism to establish cumulative pareidolic reasoning, Homebrew postulated that, considered as *wrinkle* bandwidth, Scandic exograms, indeed all exograms, were not restricted by medium. Could medium-specific medium-derived media (sound) be interoperable and reformattable into *other* media (images)? Homebrew's back masking technique — saving the .wav as .txt, then opening it as a proto-graphic interchange format image — was revelatory. The proto-GIF is a so-called 'found image,' one that naturally resembles our distinctive preference for complex vivid pinwheel motifs but that requires minor chromatic refinements of orange, red, purple, blue, green, and yellow to accentuate its semblance. Post-'shopping,' a fuzzy splayed chromatic approximation of the six-color wheel (The Mushroom Kingdom) with a cupule (Gr8 Advice Dog) floating atop could just about be discerned in the glitchy pixellation. The Homebrew apperceptive experiment decisively demonstrated that the acoustic sensation and hallucinated sound-color were one electro audio-visual phenomena (EA/VP).

1.6 Facsimile materials exposed to exceptional talent securitized for no extra fee

'Let's make [STATIC] in our wavelength, after our own triggers.'
(Gr8 Advice Dog, *Exposed Materials*, 126)

The operational assumption behind this method is that EVP is primarily a matter of subtly incorporating replica materials into a designated institution, where 'institution' signifies a set of cultural practices triggered, or 'securitized,' by a singular talent. From a survivalist perspective, the cost of hearing a facsimile signal in the depths of the data forest is considerably lower than that of not hearing a real signal. The incorporation of facsimile materials is enabled, thus, by exposing them to a securitized talent, a practice that requires a very distinctive hierarchal form of institutional commitment. Crucially, the EVP exposure may not incur extra hidden costs; there must be exhaustive disclosure of all incurred expenses in this specific vertical.

The assumed operational method requires a Keurig® and K-Cup®. The Keurig® searches for published scrobbles of exception; the K-Cup® contacts independent trusted hierophantic sources to verify that the talent is completely authentic (take a look at the guidance which can be found in K-Cup® FAQs). Once authenticated as an 'exceptional talent' by the scrobble datum, the reproduction materials may be exposed to it for a given period of time. The ensuring sounds can then be recorded for analysis. The Keurig® and K-Cup® method produces a very small, but highly reliable sample of exogenous EVP.

As facsimile materials, the Conglomerate Experimenter worked with a series of Unspecified Sinusoidal Frequencies (forecast by the MHz Centre 4 Free&D) that had been exposed to exceptional talent. Before beginning the demonstration, The Conglomerate Experimenter flourishes to draw attention towards the intriguing design of the authenticating K-Cup®, pre-emptively noting that we should expect to hear the voice of an ekphratic mechanical-wombelly entity buried by a dissatisfied diner, who the Conglomerate Experimenter does not know personally, who calls herself Agnes. The facsimile materials are authenticated by the exceptional talent of country singer, author, thoughtware activist, country actor, and *Southern Kitchen* host Trisha Yearwood's unique B.O.B (bowl of butter). Agnes then remarks here on its work as a kitchen *praegustator* and *cupbearer*. The Conglomerate Experimenter strains hard to hear the guttural male:

{ev} 'Agnes. Ironische Verkrustungen. Plānas garšas'. German and Latvian: *Agnes. Iconic encrustments. Thin flavors.*

The securitized mechanical-wombelly entity offers ekphratic insight into our future myxogastrial habits; many acerbic gestures hide the few flavors of note. A different facsimile voice is authenticated by the exceptional talent of *Barefoot Contessa* hostess and James Beard Award Nominee Ina Garten's celery root remoulade, pre-boarded as that of a dog(faux)head who lived and died in an unresolvable retail cluster, who says:

{ev} 'Ein Rezept in Frage stellen. Eine soziale Beziehung in Frage stellen'. German: *To question a recipe. To question a social relation.*

Indeed, it is only working synchronically with our fellow sous chefs to cook our banquet (macro) from its ingredients (micro) that we achieve a tangible cytoplasmic transformation of our pan-canine imperium that gives witness to that glettefully dank sporangium: The Mushroom Kingdom.

Now a booming voice, exposed to the exceptional talent of Primetime Emmy Award winning burger-flipper Guy Fieri's Schwarzkopf Professional Igora Vario Blond Extra Power (15.9 Ounce), says:

{EV} 'Hark you. Aristotle basil, ocimum basilicum, myrtle, jasmine and pimpinella anisumr. Gyeah.' Texan: *The Mushroom Kingdom is rich in herbal catalysts.*

Finally, the following sentence, heard at the end of a mystery box round, indicates that the voice entity has its own techno-complex, probably a transmitting station or flexible basecamp:

{EV} 'Теперь спокойной ночи, от Verrücktes Deal-Artefakt Institut, Kloster Melchisedeke.' We hear Russian and German: *Now goodnight, from Crazy Deal Artefact Institute, Merch Cloister.*

The Merchandise Cloister of the Crazy Deal Artefact Institute, is, of course, home to a beautiful, functional and affordable *espace de coworking* leased by the MHz Centre 4 Free&D.

1.7 Malware Voices (found in the UltraNet email cache on hard-drive from Mystery Box Con)

At the engineer preview night of Mystery Box Con #55, Theodore Rudolf, a virus mechanic specializing in high-speed crawl bot sampling, leased a damaged Dark Web lucky-dip hard-drive from terra282_usb, a BDX-based power seller ('Absolutely terrifying. Thanks for smashing the button'). On syncing the gaffa-taped drive with his device, Rudolf discovered an UltraNet email cache full of the highly infectious 'Wharton's Jelly' malware, which his gear automatically began to play as wibbly-wobbly audio. Wrongly identifying the ensuring creeped-out whispering blob noises as future dead EVP, Rudolph hastily devised an on-the-fly method using voice recognition spiders to record short wav samples [01011011 01010011 01010100 01000001 01010100 01001001 01000011 01011101]. When Rudolph's controlled listening to the EVP-over-wav produced no useful leads, he made contact with The Dr. CPox Y.P.C. Experimenter CGLM and verified the CGLM's name by playing back a sequence of notes (*'Frère Jacques, Dormez-vous?'*) correctly.

Having strained for several weeks to hear semblances in the noise, the CGLM had an epiphany. By viewing the wav file in a text editor, an appended string of High German text could be found containing ciphers that, once decoded, formed a link to a Russian hexa-chorus voice module with general MIDI, the Minilorientalis 303mkII, a *very valid* machine. The following presumptive exemplars have been chosen from a total of approximately 1,117 high-quality tones, stabs, and pads pre-set in the Minilorientalis 303mkII. Interestingly, the voices have the same characteristic features of those recorded by other patch mode / layering EVP methods and they induce powerful acoustic projections comparable to the distinctive CanCon wavelengths of 'beaver hours.' It is equally fascinating to note that the backmasked voices in fewer than two of these examples speak Latvian with Russian accents, modern dialects and languages completely unknown to Rudolph and the CGLM.

Rudolph and the CGLM run a histogram of the *vox futuri* through OpenSMILE to ensure they don't miss a beat of its multimodal sentiment. A Russian voice says:

{EV} 'Jūsu transportlīdzekļi spin zem Bow Bafett sešām krāsām.' Latvian: *Your vehiculars six colors spin below Bow Bafett* (*Malware Voices*, 3).

Tradition has it that *The Mushroom King* and the spinning six-color wheel that forms the inalienable ground of our magnificent merchant ensign, originated herein. A pivotal statement clearly referring to The Eleventh Animal, the Gr8 Advice Dog *Bow Bafett,* smiling beatifically while barrel-rolling peacefully in The Mushroom Kingdom. Represented as a spinning color wheel, The Mushroom Kingdom is perpetually rendering and calculating itself in recognition that color as such does not exist. The Gr8 Advice Dog's aphorisms help us understand how it feels to inhabit its future otherworld of reflected electromagnetic waves so that one day we may join it. A Lululemon accent says:

{EV}: 'Rydych chi ond yn llawes wag [STATIG] Brenin Madarch'
Welsh: *You are but an empty sleeve [STATIC] Mushroom King*
(*Malware Voices,* 17).

There is no Mushroom King as such. We cannot know how the
multimodal future RAM forms an image of its extrinsic world;
the ur-cinbin is of, not King of, The Mushroom Kingdom. Figure (Gr8 Advice Dog) and Ground (six-color wheel), Signal
(*Bow Bafett*), and Noise (The Mushroom Kingdom) are forever
one. All shall be witnessed as one. Not as another.

1.8 Teledefunken IP-PBX Psycho-phone with your custom full color logo

'Minstrels walk before us, playing on handsets.' (*Exposed Materials,* 124)

This method for establishing the *futurity* of the dead was
evolved by Thiota, an adjunct discount voucher technician from
Vienna. Thiota's upcycled Teledefunken mobile psychotelepho-
nostomy technicolor custom logo apparatus has produced some
very plainly Horse Class SR EVP audible waste voices. These bear
precisely the same typical blobbogramatic traits as all other
patternicity-authenticated future dead voices recorded by other,
completely different, methods. The Teledefunken pscyhocell-
phonostomy is an electrostatic PUSH bag, the surface of which is,
in keeping with our procedural topography, generally reticular,
sharp, warty, or spiky and very rarely smooth. The pouching system collects incoming calls-of-nature only over an open source
IP-PBX (para-n branch exchange). The PBX-switched network
treats the Teledefunken as an internal discharge exchange, con-
necting only to other internal devices. So, not only does the IP-
PBX filter out all rogue EMI, it also offers great cost savings over
other pay-as-you-go EVP options on the market. Sceptics say
EVP is just radio interference or apophenic RAM tricks. Not only
do the EMI-free Teledefunken mobile's clutch-bag of audio facts

conclusively prove them wrong, but the Sprechfunk designed handset can be customized with any logo of your choosing.

Again, Russian and Latvian are some of the main languages used, together with some German (though Thiota also does not speak either Russian or Latvian). A call comes in over the IP-PBX; there is no internal number. Thiota answers. The voice says,

{EV} 'Sieh abenkein plussigone' German: *You have no plussigone.*

The word, 'plussigone,' which is used here does not exist in the German Language. It may be a corruption of the neologism 'pluedome,' which means, in a symbolical sense, tomorrow's atmosphere or future magnitude. We [Thiota] have no pluedome for we are now, we are not in our future. So, it follows: the voice must be of a future.

Now, an SMS is received from an undisclosed number:

{ESMSP} 'Ciiilvēki, nomoDā.' Possibly Latvian: *People, awake.*

The dead are people. In the future, the dead do not sleep.

A final chilling call comes over the IP-PBX. There is no number. No voice speaks. In answer to Thiota's repeated question as to who is speaking, a crystal-clear voice, dripping with phlegm, whispers,

{EV} 'Die Tote.' Distorted German: *The Dead.*

Voices: of the future; dead.

We hope you really enjoyed reading this paper as much as we really enjoyed working on it, but now it's time to succinctly summarize its main findings:

1. No matter how big or how small our investments in contracted wrinkle research specialists are, we all stand to benefit from a refresh of hybridized pareidolic knowledges of The Eleventh Animal emitted by differently authenticated MHz.

2. We are so fortunate that there is so much awesome EV material out there to pulse! Let's just cascade it to our freelancer communities, to work out with gyeah? :)

3. Another great take-away is that it really is now parascientifically possible to valorize the to-be-dead as fellow travelers. You are never truly alone when you have deceased pragmatists as temporal fold friends. It is a truly enchanting affirmation that our research is being co-opted and reverse-pioneered by the deceased in a future that already has dutifully servicized our own age of Gr8 Solutions. This makes investors less risk averse.

4. The potential benefits of emerging EV materials are free-at-the-point-of-use and are clearly being shared and leveraged by all future-conversants, freelance or incorporated, who have peristaltic pump-loop access to optimized experimental equipment.

5. We all really need to invest in new forms of pan-modal future sentiment analysis that go beyond endless reinterpretations of *Th/ Corpus*®, and other becoming-media such as pre-audio, pan-somatic awakenings, cover-versions, and not-yet visual data.

6. Overall, our audio findings call for future future-dead research to be increasingly gastrological, longitudinal, and panclusive. Meaningful investment in the most comprehensive fungible wrinkle research assistance for (or against) stance revisions is critical to building upon and really leveraging current virtue streams.

Notes on the authors:

In addition to being widely recognized as RÉSO's emerging expert on all shipwrecks in July of last year, ███████████████ is ranked highly among the legitimate 6% of leading EVP speculators on a second Greenlandic alcohol referendum. ██████████ splits downtime between so-called New Flesh Futon, Ontario and A Better Place to Be, Québec. ██████████ is author of more than 70 apophenic vignettes including *Igaliku Wide Boys* (New Flesh Futon: Sundown-Gazette), *Ionic Void* (Candelabra Creek: Presse Filles & Garçons) and the oft-nominated *All-Star Xenony* (Barnum: Beefsteak Charlie's Press). No other researcher can claim even a fraction of ██████'s [userexperience], expertise, or rock-solid guarantees. Passionate about socially innovative pareidolic reasoning, ██████ has a strong commitment to public atmospherics-awareness. ██████ is a co-founder of Dos Sans Dos and a lay member of the Board of the Monte Carlo Straight Cops & Croupier Foundation. ██████ is a paraacademic freelancer at The University of the Mall of America Online and hopes to one day administer a pareidolic estate.

██████████████████ is a rootless independent klecksographer whose principal research interests are the statistical analysis of large EV data sets and awards and nominations to be received by the Dukes of Biarritz and whatever else is of interest right now. Konstantin's work includes, or will soon include, a review of *Semelle Compensée* (Trois-Rivières: Les Presses de Steak-de-bœuf Charlie), a graphic memoir FREE: *Bibliography and/or Works Cited* (Montréal: Vices & Versa) and a short-wave apparition of *http://user for dummies* (Barnum: 7:11 Press). Rest assured, ██████ ██████'s micro-experiments have been re-evaluated in publications similar to ON *Cabin Rentals, Village of Leavings Voice* and *The Barnum Review,* and elsewhere. ██████████ has recorded over 1,450 peer-reviewed EVP interviews, both nationally and internationally. ██████████ lives a simple nomadic existence as a serendipitous residency-hopper. Director of La Société Bm-Ex, a Barnum-Extension nonprofit, Associate Fellow of the Royal

Mushroom Academy, ████████ is currently klecksographer-in-residence at Barnum 7:11. Past residencies include Barnum Apophenia Ctr Program (Barnum), Barnum Golf & Geomancy Club Programme (Barnum), Barnum Old Gaol & EVP Museum (Barnum), and 1001 Crazy Deal MHzLab (Chongqing, China).

Disclosure statement:

No potential conflicts of gastroturfing were reported by the authors. It's so hard to define at which stage a financial interest is significant these days, but as close affiliates of members of the Board of Directors of mimetolith.org, Moleskine, WeR. Inc!, Sennheiser, the AXLERL Plusigone, *et al.,* the authors of this paper acknowledge that they are kept on very generous retainers. The authors of this paper acknowledge and respect the continued palimpsesting of the many and essential contributions of our stakeholder descendants throughout this project, all of whom have helped breathe pandimensional life into much of the research described in this paper. The authors of this paper paid for their own equipment but did get a gratis Vanille Française Tim's voucher, all courtesy of at least one of the experimenters that feature prominently in this study (one or more of which may, or may not, be one or more of the authors of this paper). The authors of this paper are shareholders in The Experimenter CGLM and lobby and consult on its behalf. Remember that you are the ONLY doghead to ever read this one-of-a-kind, scholarly paper which we have written specifically and solely for YOU!

CHAPTER 2

Trial by Future Dead

Seul le texte prononcé fait foi

The said *Vulpes,* proud *sejant proper* of the Heraldic achievement of the Hudson's Bay Company, which shall become alive
in due course, is dead in the future. The said future-dead HBC
Fox may communicate with its counsel via the proxy of a Bran-
deum™ EVP Field Recorder. The said HBC Fox, following a meme
circulating in the MHzsphere, may or may not have promulgated a rumor regarding the Amazon $50 ~~Redeemed~~ Gift Rooster.
Although the precise details of the rumor are not mentioned by
scribes in the trial's official #badegg hashtag, we can presume
that it is openly disseminated by the time this trial takes place.

As Opinion Miner™'s number one conduit for mondegreen zygotes of The Mushroom Kingdom and Gr8 Doghead, Amazon
$50 ~~Redeemed~~ Gift Rooster has solicited to undergo trial by
compurgation to clear its good rep as a free-livin' free-lancin'
free-rang'r that requires no redemption. The content curate of
Bob Sacamano LIVE Academy has made the proclamation of the
rumor on end-to-end encrypted deu+, ensuring that the $50 to-
be-imminently-redeemed Gift Rooster remains oblivious to the
precise nature of said rumor. No objections seem to have been
raised.

The court presumes that the said True ʜʙᴄ Fox will have the rumor to be true. Said True ʜʙᴄ Fox needs no evidence to prove that its rumor is true. The fame of Amazon $50 ~~Redeemed~~ Gift Rooster is such that it enables it to undergo purgation to vindicate its reputation. In its defense, the accused must present compurgation that bears witness to its good character. The nature of the rumor, as ᴘᴜsʜ'd through by peristaltic memeography, is irrelevant and is not the focus of the trial. The Prosecution need not attempt to match the compurgation of the accused with its own compurgation to the contrary. This is a simple, yet effective means of ascertaining the value of the Amazon $50 ~~Redeemed~~ Gift Rooster.

❋   ❋   ❋

Trial by Future Dead is the documented drama of actual real things and events as they happen. For the duration of this transcript, in cooperation with many local authorities, you [… checks deu+ for gram 're: asymmetrical faces'…] travel step-by-step in real time though an actual case history, transcribed from official files by an algorithm 42 years your junior. Specialized terminology is mentioned in every utterance but rarely explained. Now, sit back, relax, and *bleeeeed.*

Scene 1: Compurgation

The Great Moderator: Alri...Just finishing bootie-up here. Al-rite. Good morning counsel. We are now on the record in the Gift Voucher and Polyresin Rooster matter. The missing Gift-Cock is future-present before the Court in sinusoidal effigy with its #influencer counsel, Reputation Communications. Today, the ever efficacious Reputation Communications performs as a hoary olde Speak & Spell hooked up with a clever little multi-purpose EVP tool that's still in the developmental phase. It can serve many different whispery infusions, both at low and high MHz. I hear that Reputation Communications has calibrated Speak & Spell's black box to suit FFRRA and SGG, so brace for some dope wambuteral dialogues deep inside the belly of to-day's voucher-bought decorative fowl.

Late HBC Fox's *vox futuri* represented in sinusodinal effigy via Electronic Voice Phenomenon is brought to us today by Black Hat, a Brandeum℠ GhostStop EVP Field Recorder, a brand new piece of kit that offers a new reality in pure presence affect. This is a box-fresh teaser from our friends at Brandeum℠ GhostStop, available only as a soft pre-order through my MerchChan gr-8mod/EVP. If The Swarm use the code GR8MD, they get 15% off and a free 'panic' sample of our myxoflagellate *glette* thrown in. Boooooommmmm! Wrinkle waves within 35mins. I'll be doing a give-a-way during today's hearing. Stay tuned. Let's see what this can do to purify our community folks. Now, to refresh our auditory gizzards, we start with *un petit amuse-bouche,* three of my all-time favorite sine waves *Drifting For Unspecified Dura-tion.* Smash the button.

{168hrs later} Lmao. Good morning, counsel. All right. Are we all tan, I don't know? Gyeah, gyeah we are. Welcome back to arbitration-based reality. The case is real. The Swarm is real. The judgement is ETERNAL. Handicap in favor of the plaintiff.

Black Hat Brandeum℠ EVP Field Recorder, would you approach, please?

Spotlight falls on a Brandeum℠ GhostStop EVP Field Recorder monitor and loudspeakers, the Dead HBC Fox's legal representative: Black Hat.

Black Hat: Does your ill-defined Rooster client confess to the rumors promulgated by the universal *vulpes*?

Spotlight pans and fades onto a barnacle- and seaweed-encrusted Speak & Spell (Reputation Communications) representing the Danmu Polyresin Rooster ordered but as yet unfulfilled $50 Amazon Voucher (here nominally fused until proven otherwise as defendant 'Amazon $50 ~~Redeemed~~ Gift Rooster'). There is notable silence. No EMI is present.

Reputation Communications: Nae quarter! Thy reek offends, thou smoulderin' anglerfish; 'tis scurvy t' rob thy crew (shout-out to th' CYO450). O, but me dreamboat, e been jus' 'uddled an' babblin' t' thee fishes tharrr. Excuse e, sirs, me innards be they soggy an short o' circuit. Now. On thee part-time, real-time negative panvitality matter-o-fact, uh…me cock client, *gallus gallus domesticus* gift, does nah fully recognize itself amidst th' deadpan, cock-a-blockin' farm legislations o' thee accusatory cults. T'be thusly offended t' thee point o' nearrr fatal self-doubt. Thees 'come-t'-order logbook' types that thar be, if nowt sufficiently scolded by ar defense, may it scorch an' burn t' borin' bits 'n' bite-sized bit bytes. By tharrr splashy, fungusy nature o' th' Mushroom Kingdom, e 'a no been craned from me blissful abyss t' see thou voucher romance torn asunder nor moulded by yon iron maiden o' inimitable sanction. Rather me nonusual cocky an' voucher embark upon thee open marriage o' voucher an' cocky. E 'ole that thar me client's nonessentiality, 'n' yay, all pan non-essences o' thee pan-dimensional sporangium, reside most in thee wambuteral pans o' sausagey tubes. Yar see, 'tis nah a' about achievin' better Michelin rankin's fer better dishes be-gotten b' advanced piratical means. An' scuttle me aft t' thee rot-ten bottom if e 'ave nah learned a thin' or two about that tharr, thar be. E pity tharr cross-boned aft-'ats wit' all bone-dry facts hornswoggled from thee poetry o' dank sporangium. Such 'acks tharrrr be, such pitiful 'acks.

Yo-ho-ho! Sail 'o me trusty ol' CY0450! Trust, nah let us fa' parched victim t'delusional investigations o' popularrr scien-tific delusion. Me client be jus' nah thee snake-oil type. This here goodly pegleg-a-voucher simply be disharmonious wit' tharrr judicial proceedin' wit' which thee skull-bounderers be familiarrr. In an eggshell (if e may) we find yarr moist recep-tions irritated by grains o' cold desert sand when accused by barnacle-brains. Be e alone when e say e tastes tharrr low-fat sodiums o' protomartyrin' ambition? Thee spray 'n' pray scape-cockin' o' anythin' whatsoever by a perfidious an' presently faux fox so long given o'er t' thee worms be a pinch o' salt too farrr. O Henry! Besides, ye'll remember that thar thee swarm issued such-an-such a decree prohibitin' future trials o' thee dead, past or future.

Black Hat: [desiccated snort-coughs] Objection. No trials *of* the dead, past or present, yes. But not *by* the future dead.

The Great Moderator: [STATIC] Sustained. All right. Great Mod-erator thinks you're looking for laptop residence printed print-ing printer bay area chances piano haircut haircuts. No? Let me get a little stim here. [Stims on spinner for 32 seconds]. Thank you all SOoooOOOOoooo much. Great Moderator thinks you're looking for our agreed-upon parameter, which is that the dead may prosecute but not *be* prosecuted. No?

Reputation Communications: Alas aye! Tharr it be, m'mod. Nay, indeed, prohibitin' future trials o' thee dead by chicane or dila-tory pleas…fer trial o' thee dead can be only b' oath, b' compurgation — (as ye lubberly eggheads sees fit t' names it.) Thee dead — past, present or future — can nay provide thar oath.

Black Hat: Is the accused not present?

Reputation Communications: Such skullduggery in a question so succinctly posed! Ye must be defter in yarrr 'andlin o' thee word 'present' when dealin' wi' a cock recyclin' its energies. A maist gifted cock perpetually promised to the cock-hood as it waits on thee gangplank fer shipment. A gift deferred be thee only gift that there be that keeps on giving; nay? E suspect thee fauxy one knows full well — but who can say? — that there thee gift o' death be a present? Ehh?.. Okay fine. Master 'at, with a measured sigh, e will endeavor ta decipher yer meanin' generously. Fer them potato 'eads that find me client's 'presence' unfulfillin' — 'tis allowedly, a proxy incarnation t' barnacle-brains stiffened by thar fallacies o' misplaced concreteness. E excuse me clients feather-thin appearance on thee grounds o' thee length o' its no-yet voyage an' thee difficulties o' th' series o' perils that there attend cheatin' death by roundtrip o' re-gifted present.

Black Hat: Is compurgation not a fact-based inquiry?

Reputation Communications: Again, a pinch o' salt cast asunder. Sweet 'n' short, yet it finds no dish t' season. Well indeed, Mr Potato, it is *nay* a matter o' fact-based inquiry but rather an inquiry 'pon the firming up of matters of concern…eh…being alike o' th' ingredients t' th' only pie that can puts t'bed t'rumblin' 'n' slobberin' in thee…ahem…Nay, we nay be dealing in 'facts,' me hearties, but in *satisfactions*. In me soon-or-never-to-be bonded client's defense, e 'av curated a compagnon of compurgators willing ta lease a' manner o' shanties testifying tae its good old-fashioned usefulness. Yarrrr forever feedback data *be* thee substrate o' true baked-in truth, a healthy substrate clothed in bold habits, well-seasoned fer tha sakes o' public decency 'n' maist rightful perspicuity.…

Avast, we a' know that these brands that stand accountable fer somethin', will inspire thee strongest loyalty in th' voyagin' tribe. Well; tha' cup-measure o' me client's client testimony be o' insurmountably good humor 'n' form. As a well-loved 'n' respected novelty item, it doth wobble wit' a nature-culturally healin' homeostasis, prancin' thee stage 'twixt lewd suggestioness 'n' upstandin' moral certitude. Moreover, me client's auto-feedbackin' redemption-merger will void all uncertainty anxiety regardin' its $50 value.

Panic? Avast! This upcomin' fulfillment o' crowd satisfaction will reap th' projected rewards o' free-range pegleg-surety, generatin' a competitive advantage that begets benevolence o' mind 'n' positive future outlook fer all a' thin's o' voucher? Me client's client's blind loyalty demonstrates conclusively that me client — Amazon $50 self-redeemin' (or nay) Gift Rooster — be a peerless, universally insoluble potentiality o' brand-outcome that must be publicly exonerated o' accusations that, metaphorically speakin', it hae ne'er set upon wit' demon hatchlin's, these venerable fauxy rodents long o' snout, sharp o' teeth, 'n stinky o' eye.

The Great Moderator: All right. Great Moderator thinks I see. No need to work anymore. Just launch the bot. Now. The Great Moderator was thinking that this picture [displays GIF] does more justice for what I think I want to say than any words I can put down on paper. The Great Moderator is thanking you right now. Great Moderator thinks you're looking for destinations with great views near you. No? As has been established with great gusto, we are not trying questions of fact, reality is arbitration-based. In our community, peace is our only concern. The Swarm, if you recall, the parties, forensic orators on both sides, have clarified their acute embarrassment in front of stark-naked nitty-grittys, so we shall proceed without those items. Please cast your opening aspersions.

Reputation Communications: E hopes me juicy drumstick do not offend. Nor cock, nor Poly's resin, nae fungusibile: it be o' the turkey bird. Ha…ha har. Will it not so just make a fine gavel should we be 'avin ter be in the needs o' one?

Yaaaaarrrr, now arightie. Day twice hence, e wents down to thee olde harbor wi me first-mate. E finds a sea shell (here it be ye see), and e gives it to me first-mate and e says, e says: 'ye can surely hear thee ocean if yer puts this 'un up ter yer earhole.' (E palms thee shell an' switchers it fer a hatchin' egg.) She puts thee dribbling shell to 'er ear an screams fer thee Gr8 teller-dog she does! A sea serpent coiled inside t' yolk pinched at 'er flabber-danglerole. LOL. Anyways, 'er septic lug forgets-'er-not to believe everythin' yer hear — specially from landlubbing 'hissing Sids' writhing in knots on t'poop-deck yonder. Har ha har! Now she be but a mere kindlin', but still she knows o'so well the duplicity o' speech and thar needs for tender verification through the hammer of face smashing rhetoric. E knows me shanty's off thar topic but e jurst 'ad ter tell it someone.

Black Hat: My whimsical nemesis is correct that, in our *fact*-finding rituals, every thing must be well-thought, well-said and well-made to the satisfaction of all. Nevertheless, we must formally notice and record that we find there to be some dissembling gastroturfing afoot that is intended to lure the proceeding into a maelstrom of desperate confusion and excessive hand-wringing '*FACT*' clutching. 99% of rep-loss is self-inflicted, the result of unscrupulous placements, misinformation, egotism, and poor communications. Things allowable in respect to wrap-up, or what has been mistakenly objectified as 'satisfaction' smears already committed are allowable in respect to smears yet to be consummated in order to prevent them, or to arrest them presciently. Therefore, Actants of The Swarm, we The Prosecution proceed with the precision of an incentivized sausage machine that folds virtuous fact shapes from ready-ground meats.

The Great Moderator: Sustained!

Reputation Communications: Yaaaaarrrr! That Gr8 parley Mr Modicumnur. An in thee midst o' thee moment let me offer yer some further sustenance. E PUSH this volume button ere…now, is thats it?…No…oh e see , it's a slider…then te SLIDE off-record ter vociferate, wa terse abandon, that e hunger for a mostly speedy resolution. Yet wit' a-bellyful-o' sorrow borne with tha grace born o' plunderin' depths, e am unamused ter witness afore me another tragic case o' too many cooks up the proverbial shit-creek o' mixed metaphors, an' whahoots a paddle ter boot. E see some woefulsome seamanship fer the propulsion o' a watertight case; e sit at a Captain's Table scattered wae dubious platters of off-brand investigative apparatus. Ehgads ye disemboweled skulls yonder. Be that a wooden spatula ye dips hopefully in thee mire? Naive hope o' steering proceedings ter safety? Worse still be the wielders o' forest branches, colanders, sieves, and nets. As if the objective be ter sift slime an' procure shrimp for the afterparty. Shame be upon ye, ye son o' a biscuit eater.

But thou don't be just taking me word fer it. Enter ye mariners, wet. By way o' contrast an' instructive deployment o' thon naval gaze, see yonder what a sailor's dozen o' me client's clients — including Vuitton Dogjacket and some Guy — ha'e t'say on thar intangible assets o' thee (frankly inspirational), mid-stream redeemer Amazon $50 Gift Rooster. e 'gram Automatic 8.w to thar stand:

Automatic 8.w: Introducing our Palace [Userexperience]…I just have to say, thanks for the UGG Boots Monicker Outlet. Gret free bonus. Of hours I have been hooked by the Louis Vuitton Outlet on this Canidae Goose Jackets. Genuine 'Made in RÉSO' label. By illegal fungible laborers. Purged of black hat bacteria. Take a sip, take a replica sip with designer clone glette movements and start feeling wonderful again. Valuing your privacy Ray Ban2132, you keep up the good Michael Kors Outlet work!

Black Hat: Objection. Automatic 8.w's review appears to pertain to the cash equivalent value of a $50 Amazon Gift Voucher won for breaking a review-athon record on a middle-market supplier other than that through which the accused may be redeemed at the whimsy of its own future convictions. As such, it is not clear how the testimony relates to the deemed accursed, dirty no-refund Cock-a-Voucher on trial.

Reputation Communications: Turn it down, fer Neptune's sake! Thou lubber guts, yer scuttlebutt sets me 'airy lugs as-cinder. Ahem…yer Gr8n'sss, if ye pleases, thee value o' common-or-garden or rare voucher-cocks shalt ne'er be understood apart from th' more-than-social interference o' to wit they be a part — that be thee transactions through which we art constituted. Precious voucher-cocks, y'Mr Moderate, be thee actualizing assist o' a press-ganged crew member o' thee guid ship Cock. This here voucher-cock be a multiplication, a leaky-in-the-bottom swagman, a host-transferable host-parasite o' papery promise 'n, thus, universally valued booty. Shipmates such as Amazon $50 ~~Redeemed~~ Gift Roosters be porous, willing t'be interpenetrated wit' t' other wrinkle wavelengths, or wit' some right tasty EMI. Automatic 8.w conclusively demonstrates that my client's $50 value be transferable and, thus, universally valued.

The Great Moderator: Overruled.

Reputation Communications: Thanks be sOOOoooo ta' ye Automatic 8.w. See how thee trail o' spoor beats an honest path when th' compass is secured b' a due diligence paid in pan-braised organettes ta' yar dedicated Amazon-reviewaars? A comely bunch o' teamsters e am ca'in' 'pon. Well bronzed 'n in tip-top condition, e sure a shall agree, wi a chest full o' booty to boot. Noble yet savage, girded o' loin wit' an instinctive intelligence o' pure, glistenin' [STATIC]. Whar others sees na ships, me compagnon o' compurgators expose b' tentacular gropin's, thee errant bactum bots whit crawl, scrawl 'n scrape, seekin' ta re-fibrillate 'n secure thee 'eart o' darkness' b' sneaking thar vessels up th' dungbie…ehm…a buzzin' in me lug…wha'? Be we in lip-sync battle? Whasaat? Wha' be a record?… [Inaudible] Be this on the log?

[STATIC]....Since we seem t'be loggin', e now call upon me Air Feed099 ta be 'gramed t' stand:

Air Feed099: Got sound-system coat that you may wear daily yet still look into making a 1-00-1-00-1 statement. Certainly manufactured for some guy! Yeah. I normally find canned responses a turnoff but someone suggested I might like this. They was entirely right. You cannot imagine simply how much time I normally spent for this! Win-win!

Black Hat: Numbers trump adjectives, your Great Moderatorness. The quantity of [UX] eats the quality of [userexperience] for breakfast! Uurg...The Swarm's stats always add up to getting the [UX] right; that is the foundation on which optimal [UXs] are built. In the face of a cock-apocalypse, we can leave nothing to chance.

Reputation Communications: Adjectives trump numbers yr G'Mod-ness. Quality o' [UX] eats th' quantity o' [UX] fer breakfast. T'is be borne out in th' breakfast metaphor that does skillfully sustain its traction throughout th' day by eatin' facts 'n figures fer lunch 'n dinner (wi' occasional healthy snacks in-betwixt). Thus e #whatsaTT @yardstikz brought t' ye by Schwarzkopf t' be retreaded on thee stand:

@yardstikz brought to you by Schwarzkopf: 5 Couleurs Effects Returns, 2,199 Pro Palette Refill Pan Pink Lambskin Giant Work Retreads, 25 Sneakers Fake...

Reputation Communications: Now me interest be piqued! An impressive share e'm sure ye'll agree!

Black Hat: Objection. @yardstikz brought to you by Schwarzkopf is a train wreck, not a neighbor familiar with the character of the Amazon $50 ~~Redeemed~~ Gift Rooster.

Reputation Communications: Yar Greatnessness, e jus' belayed this testimony ta'me followin' o' stalkerz wha 'as been conductin' a wee bitta homework upon ye Amazon $50 Gift Redeemer Roosters. 'nd they actually jus' subbed e 50 smurfberries o' nutritious Spinee discounts jus' 'cause e discovered @ yardstikz brought it t' ye by Schwarzkopf fer tham…Ha ha har har. So, let me munch 'n' holler this stalkerz…. Thankin' THOU sooooooOOO much fer what's certain t'be an unforgettable BEE-beem-bop. And ye, thanks be t' @yardstikz brought t' ye by Schwarzkopf fer spending thee time t' shares such an emotional testimonial. Ahoy, 'n e promises ta share insight e had along thar way. (Did e ever tell ye how a magnet e found upon a fridge floatin' in thee Bay o' Siberia revolutionized supermarkets?) E knows we all gots ta all live together me man. An that's nah jus' the lip-service.

Needs more convincin'? A cannonade o' complimentary compliments? A wide range o' somatic taints? E gingerly calls Automatic 8.w ta' be quoted upon thee plank:

Automatic 8.w: heeʏ therre ɑndd thank yoooooou for your info — I have definitely picked upp smething neeeeeeeew fr"m right therre….

Black Hat: Objection. Affiliation. Automatic 8.w has already been green-lighted as a compurgator for the defense.

The Great Moderator: Sustained!

Reputation Communications: Thankin' ye fer yar contributions Gr8 [UX]. E'd like now t' invite a long-term acquaintance o' me client, Peritoneal Loose Body Aerobic Force Cage with adjustable Changing Bench and Hoist Facilities (PLBAFCW CB&HF). Harken ye all t' wise wet words straight from th' rectum-mouth t' th' fact-addled non-sensoriums o' th' rattlin' 'n a changin' cage.

PLBAFCW CB&HF: Yup. Well alrite. Sittin' on down, Ol' Fifty Bucks Reem'droost is still a little teacherish for its years, but is solid without taking itself for its own statue. An Amazon cock with six pairs of eyes and a heart that won't lie, a little nasty cock with a mounting, crowin' rhythm, roost discovered himself in West Avanity in the country of self. Gaunt, tall, GI-jacketed, Ol' Fifty Bucks twanged out rich imagistic EVP in Petite Italie espresso bars for a loonie and a quarter. Ol' Fifty Bucks could afford to be hard and ironic, learned its wounds well, and some of the world's dishonesty, while in Pied-du-Courant stir for six years on a trumped-up armed robbery count. Is subtle as well as lavish. Shy as a shadow also, with a fiendish jollity rising up within the prison walls of its hard-earned loneliness and individuality. You rarely see the cat's gleaming eyes behind its mother-loving sunglasses. Five Sawbucks is the real thing. Once wanted to be a theoretical klecksographer but gave in to the muse and began its very inside, real, stylish, lethal ultra, honest, terse, hurting in that way that counts. Jail in Frisco, fighting and dodging Dogheads in PATH, gettin' pickled in Café Cléopâtre. It's awkward blue, but, as it'd say, it's got a good sound. Proper isn't bright with the bitter glitter of GIF-age precocity. Ol' Fifty Bucks could be tender, nutty, lyrical, when the mood mooded it. Way down shack town, roost's stuff runs like drunken faucet. Urchin looking, street-bred, its playing gives its living-room style the lie. Full of unexpectedness and unclassifiableness and with an off beat imagination to burn. A glitter of contradictions, a closetful of skills, a dead-end kid with uncommon sense. It's honest about wanting the Dollarama and bitter in its appreciation of its Lordship. A flinty, sardonic wisecock complete with brain. A nice gift-roost with a touch of nasty....

Reputation Communications: Yer raspberry rapperin' be a welcome breeze, sir. PLBAFCW CB&HF, e wonderin' if ye would gabber a little further on me client's qualities?

The Great Moderator: PLBAFCW CB&HF's jibber-jabber certainly seems to be engorging The Swarm. So let the Great Moderator just say this. ASAP we're promoting mystery brands, with some box fresh topic-driven installations filled with a vast range of great worldly riches. Stay on it *drette-la*. Smash that button.

PLBAFCW CB&HF: Gyeah, I'm on that. Refusing to talk about its Commy past, roost flirts with preciousness and never yields, a sure sign that intelligence has pinned artifice to the mat, a sure sign that we are witnessing the real stunning thing with this unusual cock. Knock-your-eye-out, 'Ol Fifty Bucks could tune its way out of a locked trunk at the bottom of the Saint Lawrence River. Minority snipers think that if roost brought a little Dreiserian holy corniness to its hipness, it'd have it made. An extremely hard-working and probably demonic cock under some mighty slick icing. Best in short takes, 'Ol Fifty Bucks dazzles because of the unforced grotesqueness it shows in our hallucinatory beyond-Mars, cosy little nonmodern world. Its EVP builds like a storm. *Skinny Girl Shoe Shine* was cut with the cool eye of a rifleman; its second *Skin Lowdown Buggy Ride Lover Gal* never got the attention it should have; its last *Poor Folk Gold Teeth* almost didn't because it was thought to be too dirty for even a dirty age. 'Ol Fifty Bucks stands in an odd relationship to the corner gift-cocks of its generation — more inner, older, tireder. It has a gnarled maturity encased in a golden boy façade. It has the aware calculation of a deep-sea diver; it could and might go deeper. Gentle, fidgety, huge-swaddled, it still puts out a wild lick. 'Ol Fifty Bucks went back in jail for violating parole — the poor sucker fell in love and got married, which is of course against democracy's penal laws. Solution aligners say its future is an [STATIC] but its present is inspiringly real. It broke out, and was last heard in PATH, jazzing, playing roulette, making a carnival out of this sweet mystery of life. In a modest way, 'Ol Fifty Bucks is a credit to the avian to-be-redeemed voucher race, a true lunar talent rising amongst the skyscrapers. Its fever is that of thousands, but nobody of its age threw the sick room back at life as it did, and thus redeemed us as well as a $50 Amazon voucher. Society's fangs await its beautiful phantasmagorical wavelengths, if only to insure its validity; but ye who play the future dead must have a price on its head. The stakes demand it. More power and joy to roost. Spooky-real Ol' Fifty Bucks!

Reputation Communications: Very well. Gyeah! Keel-haul ye! Alright! E #whatsaTT? Regular reader o' news 'n periodicals, Lolwftomgcute t' be selectively 'grammed.

Lolwftomgcute: On behawf of the owganizing and scientific committee weading suwmmits of compwomisews, awchipew- ago administwatows, stwuwmpet manuwfactuwwews, phwan- tom reseawchews, aspawaguws cuwckowds, activwists and non- govewnmentaw bwuwshwood, yeawning pedwaws, ruwmouww owganizations, individuwaws fwom wegan and buwtchew sec- tows fow 24hws, fwom the 27 May to the 21 Octobew each yeaw: the uwniquwe siwhouwettes on these stwapwess wide-weg ju- wmpsuwits pawt dwamaticawwy fuwwl wegs in ankwe-wength ow cwopped-topped stywes, as pwoficientwy as swim-fwitting bodices that — uwnifowmly fawling ouwt fwom the extwaow- dinawiwy ......

Black Hat: Objection. Fowl play! This watterbot assumes facts rather than testimonial evidence. A custom made for deceit. This is not how luxury works.

Reputation Communications: Heave to. Avast ye. Th' cost o' th' aforementioned strapless wide-leg jumpsuits dern't scuttle me client's potential $50 redemption power.

Lolwftomgcute: ....swim-fwitting bodices that — uwnifowmly fawling ouwt fwom the extwaowdinawiwy......

Black Hat: Objection. Lolwftomgcute has spammed this review and enumerated it through my client's registered users' details while this trial has been in session. Moreover, Lolwftomgcute's baked-in marketing, notably, makes no mention whatsoever of the Polyresin Rooster Statue Farm Animal Decoration Figurine Collection Country Garden Sculpture Set Outdoor Statue aspects of the accused's character. I personally can't comment on these matters because I am not a compurgator, but a compurgator surely must comment on the veracity of character that belies the baked-in messages?

Reputation Communications: Does th' defense nah make this effortless? Stress-free? Does Lolwftomgcute's 1,054-views testimony nah delight our senses as it satisfies our budgets, our standards o' durable bounty 'n plentiful twerkin' booty? Lolwftomgcute's gut has t' be th' Swiss army knife fer me client!

Black Hat: [*Sniff*] Your Great Moderateness, I ask only that Lolwftomgcute be placed in a public pillory in the Atrium of MInTOone80Five for one season so that laypersons and lawmakers might view the function and certainty of our justice system and pay bidding to our common arbitration-based reality.

The Great Moderator: Thanks for sharing such fastidious thinking. The thinking is fastidious, that's why the Great Moderator understood it so fastidiously. Likeable faces and voices. Smashing the button. Excellent goods from you, Councils. Trusted Pirates. Now. What comes first here, the brand or the integrity of the script? Reputation Communications' cache of objections are overruled. If you skip one, make it this one. Nevertheless, The

Great Moderator asks this of its Defense Council: If the Great Moderator were to forcefully decouple said Voucher organ from said Polyresinal Rooster organ, would the Great Moderator propose that the Cock is culpable but the Coupon not? How is The Swarm to discern and apportion the faulty or culpable portions of this thing without recourse to the butcher's art of cutting out the green bits for humble pie to be imprisoned in the pauper's belly?

Reputation Communications: Me Cock Trustpirates is off th' charts m'mod. His nested reputations be fully repairable, piquin' interest from thee wee-print t' pointed beak:

Excellent value; Best design; Prompt, definitively do it again and again; few faint scratches on beak from being in a debate; Personalized, great qualities, accurate scale, rebellious color. What do I still want?; Really nice content; My go to for ducat-cock; All-dressed and in minutes!; Get 5hfihsiewialkjskjd; Investigated paranormal [UX] in my bathroom, and I feel better now I know it is not negative and that is all I needed to know; Uh may Zing! My nefewe loved it, Ships from any port; Doesn't include Hotel Transylvania 3? But who needs it!; Love the feel in the hand; Much safer, 99.90%; Gr8 aftercare; Fantastic, but absolutely must use a javacock blocker; I get what I paid for; Unlocked remotely first time; Fast'n Kick'n'ass!

Now. A hackin', cuttin', 'n metin' will produce, as e am sure ye well know, nah th' discrete craft blocks o' th' molecular cults, but a mair primal incubatory substance, th' glette as nourishin' as cackle-fruit yolk, as sweet as nectar, 'n as gluten-free as a cast-iron pan-blasted beet. Amazon $50 Redeem Mixologist Gift Rooster be a recent composite o' still maturin' vintage 'n, as such, somewhat sparse o' summonable admirers bearin' verifiable recipes fer the stockpot. So, lootin' stock o' me client's price-ceilin', we parse th' compurgatori into two distinct deck-mates o' micro taskers that may swear t' th' good standin' o' each historical part o' pairts, yer moderate o'ness.

Shall we now not surely be beginning our fantastic voyage by thee cold-callin' o' a benighted affiliate whose kinship be that o' similar reproductive value exchange [UX]? This optimized affiliate will swear t' th' Cockery-Vouch's anti-demonic virtues vicariously, 'n wit' a' th' depth o' character we would expect o' somethin' long steeped by th' inglenook in th' earnest Crock-Pot o' mannerly self-refraction…. Th' defense here's a-thinkin' o' me greatest Crock-Pot 6-Qt 8-in-1 Multi-Use Express Crock-character witnessin' [review pending, e stick it wit' th' other reviews when it be done]. Its nigh-on thar! 'Tis be ten thousand dollar ye'm carryin' t' pot. Ten thousand dollar an no less than. Well it might be o' no matter, except, o' course that it be o' a matter, it be o' matter to th' moral matter at hand. E digresseses. Th' defense now summons from thee deep, the benighted affiliate, Durvet Strike III Rooster Booster with Lactobacillus self-redeemed with Bow Tie for the No-Crow in three-way consensual merger with a former €50 Amazon Gift Voucher:

Amazon €50 ~~Redeemed~~ *Gift Rooster Booster No-Crow:* I am surely content, worthy, and enhanced. I wake up fashionably mute and as sure as hell *I* was made in the Mushroom Kingdom. If I were to commit the heinous and unnatural crime of miraculously conceiving and laying an egg, it would benevolently contain all my angry cockcrows safely stored for peaceable deployment as parables. I thus act as further voucher for my redeem-ful coupon-colleague. Though we have never met, I will say that past mouldy omelets do not a future bad egg make. For this to be well said and decisive, I pledge as collateral all of the thoughts of all things, all of the motions in every living creature, and all of the grains of sand which would fill ten thousand worlds.

Reputation Communications: Dear moder-me-matey! E thankin' th' rare good fort'n, by Cock, o' gettin' such prime accountancy. E now give yar ar belly laugh fer Cap'n ChickenPox Yahoo Prison Consultants Ltd.:

Dr. ChickenPox Yahoo Prison Consultants Ltd: We met in both factory and forest! *Un seul prix, plus taxes. Excellentes instructions opérationnelles* were given and seemed to be very convenient and compendious with basic parkade and far-flung travel tips. *Dollar imene! Profond; mon coq au carnet.* You don't go barging around like the Ghost Rambo! Sharp, clean, spicy, delicious, invigorating. Only *un imbécile* would sell their rooster so that they could feast on chicken nuggets. *Principalement recommandé.* Strange smell of polymers but would certainly come again.

Black Hat: Objection. Beyond the scope; irrelevant to the underlying gastêr controversy. Is this cock au carnet a stomach or a womb?

The Great Moderator: Overruled. BrrrrrrrRUH! Check that out. The Great Moderator's shoes match your 'I love polar bears' pocket zoo. Lmao.

Reputation Communications: Gamesters, agents o' t'swarm, foxy partisans, curious bystanders, an' all t'other interested parties, e would likey t'invitey me favorite interface, 'n yers, ta share wit' us: Teledefunken IP-PBX Psycho phone wit' yer custom full color logo.

[The ancient Teledefunken takes a little time to power up, but it's really worth it. A necromantic call comes in over the IP-PBX; there is no internal number. Reputation Communications answers.]

{EV}. German. [статик] Wir haben $₩âðê#t [статик] ([STATIC] We have swâðêah [STATIC]).

Reputation Communications: Metaphorically speakin', th' IP-PBX's tongue be tied t' a frog m'mod...o'...yer Gr8n'; well if that be th' barbarous affectation o' choice fer yer loftiness then let th' mod log show that e too 'ave th' crow's-nest advantage; crisp me liver if e don't. E mean no personal disrespect t' yer elevation y'hear, jus' a humble moderation o' greatness as e'ave seen it. Now then, Cap'n Moderator Sir, blast me bollocks an' by y'r weigh anchor, let me rub th' grizzled chin wit' horny paw 'n clarify th' appellant's necromancy. The word, 'swâðêah,' that be used here just donut exist in thar Germance Language. E be well informed by an amusin' parchment that this foreign'r utterance be a torn off corruption o' th' neologism 'SWAAAaaagyeah!' Now, round me parts, SWAAAaaagyeah means: 'we 'ave many swashbucklin' bootychests 'n must celebrate thar unboxin' as happy peaks in th' tradewinds o' adversity'…an' such-as-is-like. Wi' they chests, rot 'ee, we exhume th' lost ârte o' closed surfaces.™ Deep beneath th' skin, in th' wambelly o' th' ship's orlop lives a vast cable' o' s.W.Ã.G — ye see? It be curlicued in cosy coils o' well bagged length 'n all buoyed up in carrier puddin', th' cytoplasmic matrix, salted *glette,* th' secret ©ker sauce sought by all th' pans o' th' pan-dimensions. Wit' s.W.Ã.G, e refer t' tubular organizin' o' th' great pan o' brand becomin's: from th' meagrest o' flocc-ironed birthin' baskets, strawberry 'n key lime pie filtration logo straws, ad-supported pocket garburators, bubbly-wrap identity bracelets, balsamic lip scrub 'n end-of-pier novel candles, t' th' highest perfection o' inspirational narcissism bokes, name-brand hamburger speakers, graphic memoir generators, outsized universal serial bus promo tees, LLERAX Plusigone logo GhostBox sealers 'n crew color antibacterial bamboo deck scrubbers. Easy now, handsomely and clearly, says e, yer most moderate o' Gr8n'ses, that th' IP-PBX's garblin' gyeah clearly testifies t' th' infinite quality 'n durability o' me client's s.W.Ã.G. Yar!

Thank'n ye Teledefunken IP-PBX phone psycho wit' yar colorful custom logo. Thank'n ye fer yar laconic insight. Yer gr'ts, thar Fotodiox tele annulus will noo cheer t'tha guid character o' me client:

Fotodiox tele annulus: This is a very good-looking group of testimoners here. I like the unique CanCon voices. As tele annulus, we all have a responsibility to know when we are being deceived.

And by the way, we need to know the difference between real and counterfeit [STATIC]. I'll tell you what, we tele annulus will help you in uncovering the secrets and dangers of [STATIC] using on-the-spot analogue-digital behavioral translations. I've said this before and I'll say it again, this tele annulus knows. You want to know the truth? Curiosity, yes. But in all fairness, what else?

Black Hat: Objection. The tele annulus fails to address the gastêr digestion-gestation confusion that lies at the heart of egg-laying-eating. Your Gr8n's, is that not what all this nightly ballyhoo is about on the MHz?

Fotodiox tele annulus: Sssh…Sure…?

The Great Moderator: And what do you mean by gastêr digestion-gestation confusion? Pineal gland? A domino take-down?

Black Hat: Search me, I can't even spell it! It sounds good. Does every printer know about all the products they print in the paper? Do you think I know the different products I place? Be yourself. Of course *I* don't know anything about gastêr digestion-gestation confusion. Did you ever lay an egg? No, but can't I ask you questions about eggs?

The Great Moderator: Ad hominem. Overruled.

Fotodiox tele annulus: Now [no signal], consider this:

> I have a scar on my abdomen.
> I co-locate between the land and the sea.
> I am thwarted by polystyrene.
> WTF am I?

Before any quick read, the gut skips. Then the smell hits the nose. A snapshot read says: I am a frozen soft-shell crab. Am I right? Of course I'm right! So how does tele annulus call this one? Snap! Tele annulus sees that the Amazon $50 ~~Redeemed~~ Gift Rooster is okay. Really is a give'r. Recognized, trusted and ranked. People always ask me about Amazon $50 ~~Redeemed~~ Gift Rooster, and let me say this: it's just fantastic. I love Amazon $50 ~~Redeemed~~ Gift Rooster. No one loves Amazon $50 Redeemed Gift Rooster more than me, BELIEVE ME.

Reputation Communications: Well spoke annulus! Together we wet our rearmost whistles, an' damn all, wi' a warnin' shot 'n yell fer th' end o' all this bollocks. We be amassin' th' bootychests, an' our hull creaks wit' a solid defense.

Yet bide ye thar, ye muckrakes! E hae more expungable redactions t' be spongily expunged. Settin' sail t'tha winds o' battle mix, e lose me chaperone o' buzzin' vultures t'express, once more wi' feelin', that wha' e feel in me water. Again, e cannae express t'is enough. Me spleen — which e needs t' vent — be bein' breached 'n capsized by an unseaworthy *brigade de cuisine*. They stir 'n stir without thunderin' narrative, glossary o' servin' terms, value meal, or signature dish. Aye indeed thar bees a lack o' vocational focus aboard this shipwreck o' fools.

Some o' these here be th' merest o' mere guddlers, pannin' fer nuggets o' action in th' barren mudflats. Even these wit' reputable pan-skills; well, thar be a frayed 'n abstract quality 'bout thar. This mess just ain't be shipshapes. 'Tis doomed fer th' abyss wi' ner a steady bowel propelled wit' abundant wind. Choppers, flippers, 'n broilers run amok as chook-a-rooks void o' thar belly fungibles. Even in apparent coalition, th' streams o' culinary ejaculate collide 'n return t' th' primal lagoon wi' nar th' auld name: *ylem*. Ye Mod: aye, these be deckchair sophists, these be aimin' fer naught but flash-in-th'-pan 'n filigree. These be ©kin high-end Michelin Star explosions t' wrinkle wave th' tsunami o'er oor predicament; as if a' endeavors be resolved be cleansin' th' pallet wit' far flung saltwater 'n skippin' straight t' th' celebratory feast. Oh, aye, 'n ye, ye, th' pragmatists e see sniggerin' in me mind's eyepatch. O', an' th' maps indicatin' th' true passage t' guid humors, an awa fae no-flow conditions 'n hysterias o' th' PUSH. So e says ta ye: well, wha' do ye hope t' persuade wit' such a dogs-grub o' dull, workmanlike rhetoric?

Filibusters aside, yer most modest o' Moderatorness, e would like t' be callin' [ongêanweard] [ðe] [læs] t' tak o' th' cockerel-coup'n:

[ongêanweard] [ðe] [læs]: An empty sack laughs at too many baked eggs. A scalded dog can't teach the hen. Quench your thirst, then eat the crackers. The empty scoffer is asked a lot. Sticky note shame has its mouth in the fat. Bend the fat, up with the cocks. The first worm gets snapped. A thin book fits the thin pocket. *Viscera reus, mens rea.*

Black Hat: Objection: A surprising lack of symmetry; resembles the accused's contronymy.

The Great Moderator: If It doesn't make sense, it's not true. Sustained.

Reputation Communications: More ain't less. Less be more. More or less. Yer greatness, e sees th' stenographer's machine be reddened by th' speed o' me verbalosity. It be drippin' wit' the sweat. Give't a lime 'n a glass o' rum, fer e 'ave mair hot verbage fer it t' scribe 'n redact.

Is e liftin' th' curtain upon tis trend t' find an homunculus in th' Cock pit? E hears nah invitation t' swarm, wit' thereferwho as e see partiality as clear as e see th' clouds. Me scallywags, these here all see wit' spyglasses 'n t' cracks. There ne'er be nae o'erlaps. 'Tis why me crew o' influencers be fluid o' feelin's 'n understand th' defendant's indifference t' redemption as a satisfyin' habit t' be worn wit' pride. Th' permanent postponin' o' redemption be a…it be a…*satisfactio.*

E shall now call some Guy tha t'was at Mystery Box Con, Tampa Bay. This Guy — who be greatly respected in yar wonderful Mystery Box community — ain't a close acquaintance o' th' accused but be a huge fan. This Guy shall give us 'is telephone number in 'is compurgation so that ye may reach 'im wit' further riddles. T'is be an unselfish action that shows that he be serious 'bout helpin' th' defendant 'n that e really means wha' e says.

Guy that was at Mystery Box Con, Tampa Bay: What is that? OMG what IS that? I'm gonna be sick. No way, what! Whoa! What is that? There's like stuff with a…No. No it's not. No idea, looking like a…huh. Wait a minute. OMG I have the exact same thing!!! It's coming out. Is it heavy? I swear, I'm not looking. I don't know where to…. I have no idea how to explain it. This is, ugh; alright. What is that? I'm gonna be sick. Zero three zero three…. There's no noticeable odour. Is there something on the outside? OMG. This is I-N-S-A-N-E. Let's see. Okay that's weird. It's massive. Three, two, six, seven…. Y'all gotta love burpees! This is NOT clickbait. Oh. Eeew. That's a HUGE coincidence. I don't know what that is. Five, four. All this right here, I don't know what it is. I'm not touching it. It's wet maybe? I don't even know. No way! What is this? Just don't know what's in there. Kinda concerning. This is it. I think I'm okay….

Black Hat: Your Gr8ness, even I have to say here that I believe that some Guy has concluded his compurgation satisfactorily. Gyeah, I totally teared up. Thanks to some Guy for reachin' out.

Reputation Communications: E concur yar Gr8nessn's; thankin' THOU soOo much some Guy fer coming out. E like t' introduce the noo a ladss that e been a big big fan o' since thar name be first inserted in th' World Businesses Lists. It be a great honour 'n a pleasure t' share th' same plank wit' me final special guest, th' one, th' only e be with Stupid↑:

I'm with Stupid↑: A year ago to this very day, I did a drawing of who I predicted would be the guilty party today. Since I thought the drawing might be auctioned at a future benefit, the form and tonality were really professional. The drawing was honest; I mean 'cause dishonesty just damages your reputation. ;) I sealed the drawing in an envelope to be opened at some future fund-raiser. I have an envelope in my hand. [Places A3 manila envelope on desk; inhales deeply]. On the same day a year ago, I also did a drawing of the accused party. I concealed that drawing in *another* envelope. [Places A3 manila envelope on desk; exhales]. Your moderatorness, I would like, if I may, to call some Guy that was at Mystery Box Con, Tampa Bay to join me up here. Come on up, I don't bite. Thank you. Please stand on this spot, over here, that's it, a little to the left, that's it right there. Thanks. Okay, so the envelopes have both been visible on the desk here the whole time, right?

Guy that was at Mystery Box Con, Tampa Bay: Uhu. I guess. Uh…I don't feel strong tonight.

I'm with Stupid↑: Okay, that's great. Now, these premonitions, these images, they came to me when I was on an all-inclusive seaside voidout. When they come, I just gotta get them down quickly. Now get this. These drawings, they show the accused and the guilty *without* make-up!

Guy that was at Mystery Box Con, Tampa Bay: Wow! Right off the bat, I'm completely stunned!

I'm with Stupid↑: Okay, gyeah, that's just swell. Now, if these images don't match, then we have clear testimony that the accused is innocent do we not? Do nothing if I'm right? Gyeah? Okay. Hey, don't worry, I'm not going to show y'all a Gift Cock without make-up! This Guy is going to look at the drawings *for* us. Now, just to be to-tal-ly sure y'all *and I* don't see any bare faces, I drew these in a darkroom and put them in the envelopes you see clearly before you here. Now. Guy that was at Mystery Box Con, Tampa Bay, will you please carefully open the envelopes and remove the folders inside. Nicely done, thank you. Let me just cover up here… [I'm with Stupid↑ is swathed in a La Baie striped point blanket to prohibit signalling some Guy.] Okay, now I'd now like you to open both folders at the same time.

Guy that was at Mystery Box Con, Tampa Bay: Some kinda — here we go. Can I see what they are? Okay, here we go. Ready. That's the thing here. What the hell is that? Oh man! Just pure, totally, just pure….This. Is. Not. Happening. That's…that's it. Freekin' awesome. It's gone. Whoooosshhh!

I'm with Stupid↑: [Holds up both drawings to be seen by all] Great Moderator, friends, you will witness with your own gut that, having been exposed to the light, both unfixed drawings have completely vanished! Ψ☉Ц ꓧꚋ∨ε Ǝεεπ ωꚋΤС꒦꒦πϘ ꟾ'ₘ ωꟾΤꓧ ＄ΤЦ℗꒦⊕ꟷ ΤꓧꚋπꙆ γ☉Ц. [Bows]

Black Hat: Objection: I ask your Gr8ness to exclude I'm with Stupid↑'s drawings on the grounds that no one was there to authenticate the drawings one year ago….

Reputation Communications: Yer greatness, e be with thee Stupid↑'s drawin's are nah th' o'eractive, foggin' gelatin type. Did we nah witness th't both envelopes be produced 'n some sort o' banter that occurred that assured us that they had nah been tampered wit' 'n that we'd ne'er seen them afore? Th' envelopes — bearin' postmarks from some earlier date — were sealed by t'notary, placed in a soldered box 'n locked in a treasure chest that be kept under round-th'-clock 12K drone surveillance. I be with Stupid↑ performed a manoeuvre, e donut recall exactly wha' 'twas, th'n some Guy that was being from t' Mystery Box Con, Tampa Bay saw th' drawin's, did ye nah?

[…some Guy mumbles faintly: This is, um…all right….]

So, yer greatness, all that remains be fer us t' authenticate that th' drawin's did indeed disappear. E move t' call an expert in this field, Fotodiox tele annulus, t' authenticate th' drawin's disappearance by samplin' 'n datin' th' exposed Ilford Multigrade RC resin-coated pearl surface substrate.

The Great Moderator: Fotodiox tele annulus, if you will please inspect the contents of the envelopes and confirm that they have never once slid into a tray of fixer. [Fotodiox tele annulus nods] Authenticated!

Reputation Communications: E be thankin' ye, yer greatness. E 'ave naught further. [sounds football stadium foghorn]

Opinion Miner™: The Compurgation Reputation score is a proxy based on a compurgation sentiment analysis of The Swarm across their entire [UX] of the accused....

Reputation Communications: Sentimental 'nalysis!?! Blisterin' barnacles! How all things do pan out in this lip sync battle. But in th' end — (dam ye all ta' hell) — 'twill be decided t' let me Cock loot th' strain. Yaaaaarrrr, now arightie....

The Great Moderator: Yesssss....Now, our proprietary algorithm takes account of a number of key verticals, including volume, frequency, intensity, operationalisation, torque, and pH. Today, we have arrived at a final CompurgRep Score = 75,99: 75,99.

Thanks for reaching out to all the folks at Opinion Miner™. *On s'amuse follement!* Smash the button! The Great Moderator decrees that the compurgation proxy appears to suffer both by testimony and otherwise by wispy blame game; we have in this manner reached a doading impasse. That is to say that for the part of the said Foxy plaintiff, Great Moderator is in the mood to say in this case, in the presence of the said defendant, and not contradicting, for which we judge beforehand, to know and take stock of what we have done and will now take upon ourselves to proceed in the manner of the trial by ordeal. ASAP, it's $50 Van Houtte® Ordeal Voucher giveaway challenge time. But first, The

Great Moderator invites the Prosecution to begin Proceedings designed to muster The Swarm's clamour. Go spend.

Let The Swarm Decree: Innocent or Guilty!

If the alleged deodand is truly innocent, then it will either endure, or The Swarm will intervene to save it. If not, not. Folks, The Great Moderator will take about ten minutes to top up on the ol' uv. All right. It's a little shorter tanning break today. [Inaudible] Brandeum℠ EVP Field Recorder, can you share with The Great Moderator a steaming Van Houtte®, lol! 10 minutes, folks.

[$50 Van Houtte® Ordeal Voucher Giveaway Challenge Advertorial]

Smoldering family-sized boiling pot of Host Choke, Snake-in-the-Pot, Islê Combatant and Fireyflessherie…Mmmmmmmmmm. 99.99. For Today's Van Houtte® Ordeal Voucher Giveaway Challenge, Van Houtte® challenge you to order whatever the customer in front of you had. Just say 'I'm havin' what they're havin' and we'll throw in $50 Van Houtte® Ordeal Voucher redeemable for two units of diving pole, or a side of ordeal beans, or a cute VH® triceratops purple coin purse or a BigGulp of bitter water to wash it all down. Van Houtte® Yaaauusssssssss I totally go for that right now!™

❋   ❋   ❋

Scene 2: The Ordeal

The Great Moderator: All right. WftOMG! Back on the record in the Cocky-Vouchy 100 damage post-HBC Fox matter. All parties are present. Good afternoon. All right. To confirm our suspicions re: the cock-au-carnet, let's have the brace of ordeals, please. No time constraints. Let's hope we get some social harmony here folks (Lmao).

Black Hat: Thank you, your Moderateness. Dead HBC Fox's council really has spent a great deal of time to design some really fantastic Ordeal Proceedings for us today; really want to open the kimono, your Moderateness. The Swarm's beliefs and values play a decisive role in shaping our behaviour under ordeal. Those [userexperiences] that reinforce The Swarm's self-image and resonate with The Swarm's values leave us feeling good about its decisions. This is essential to getting the ordeal [UX] right:

1. Ordeal by Bazaar: You, said AmaGarden Fifty-bucks-a-Rooster, will be taken from here to the dépanneur on Stanley and de Maisonneuve wherein you shall attempt to re-redeem your reputation for five gallons of locally brewed Forest-Ales such as *La Fin du Monde, Maudite* or *Trois Pistoles,* while repeatedly being subjected to denial-of-service-attacks.

2. Ordeal by Aquafina™: The court sommelier will bathe the accused in 500ml of glacier-filtered Aquafina™, decanted into a 12oz Horton's™Cup, for 600 minutes*. Because clean crisp Aquafina™ is 100% pure, anything that sinks may be acquitted. (*Nota Bene: A floating Cock-a-Voucher shall remain in Horton's™Cup until it sinks.)

3. Ordeal by Light Emitting Diode: The contents of Horton's™Cup will be decanted into a diffuser and sprayed into a red LED. The ordeal will take place at a white light level set at no less than 3,000 lumens or at no lower luminosity than Guy Fieri's Schwarzkopf Professional Igora Vario Blond (whichever is highest). The Swarm will no doubt be looking for the color, for the carbonation, for patina and TS levels.

4. Ordeal by writing letters of advice to prospective copulants: You, said Cock au Carnet, will undertake a letter writing project of consummate guidance and personal tips on how to make novel things lasting and fruitful. Your inscriptions must be spread with attractants and inserted into likely as-

sembly points. You must complete this task without coercion or cornmeal.

5. Ordeal by Burpee Box Soar-over until such time as the whole jaw bears a beard. Under this ordeal, beardless ~~redeemed~~ roosters are taxed to such an extent as would rob them of all initiative. The Burpee Box Soar-over must be endured to ensure taxes low enough to secure initiative and growth, thus staving off omnipresent volatility. You will complete this task when you achieve gross 5.5% growth over a whole quarter.

6. Ordeal by Hot Box Menace: Said Coupon-Roost ~~Redeemed~~ of $50 will be placed in a 6-axle Locomotive Sauna and deeply relaxed until soft. Gowned in bleached-white terry robe, at 215°C the accused will be rapidly spun out of shape before being plunged into a dry ice bath. Morphed by thermal shock, the accused must then apply a limited palette Copic Airbrush System to imitate the dead HBC Fox's recording of *Skin Lowdown Buggy Ride Lover Gal* played backwards. Accused will then mount the Prime-Spin tabula and be 360-graphed against purified cloth for re-posting in Bob Sacamano LIVE Academy Market. Must attract redemption mate worth 40 spinees or more to void The Ultimate Ordeal.

7. The Ultimate Ordeal is undertaken 'As Described': You will, over the course of 30 days, provide without fail, colors and details true to life, be given to ma', granma', daughter, sister, or friend for their birthday; be nice house warming gift for a new neighbor or any occasion; be faultless as a decor item for just about anywhere but especially so for the country kitchen look; continue to be cast in quality designer resin; add personality to the garden or lovely home; be hand painted of great design and craftsmanship and sculpted in amazing detail; and let others (even thy enemies) use their imagination and put you wherever you are most pleasing to them. This ultimate trial is not penitential for you have not yet been pro-

cessed. You may of course give up at any time, yet this will be taken as proof of your guilt.

The Great Moderator: Innocent or guilty? Let The Ordeals decree....

[*...seven ordeals later*]

The Great Moderator: Well well well. Well. With no concessions or admissions of guilt on the horizon we're a little further down the pike but with no end timeline in sight.

* * *

Scene 3: Judicial Torture

At Willard, we know just how hard it can be staying contemptuous, anxiety-ridden, and disgusted by the treachery, malediction, and hypocrisy of our times. And we know just how to deal with the accused: as relentlessly and single-mindedly as a shark. We value more-than-canine evidence, and we're pretty sure you will too.

Our rituals quickly onboard The Swarm, keeping the real electrostatic back-chat off the airwaves, rewarding you for your daily struggle to maintain your dignity in an amoral bacteriosphere and corrupt MHzverse. Today, at Bob Sacamano LIVE Academy Mar-

ket, we will beta test a box-fresh range of innovative judicial technology rituals designed to measure and operationalise the role of the world-weary Torturer with a lurking conscience, a steely-eyed gaze, and pulsing danger in its rueful laughter. Brooding, solitary, and friendless, our Free&D dares and wins. Crush deliberative procrastination for real and forever. U R The Swarm. We R Willard.

Judicial Torture by Dissembler & Ferrite Choke

Black Hat: Your Moderateness, in the case of the singular mess of mets that is the future gift-cock, two actants were once manifest in a time closer to the present. This epistemic ritual determines to rip apart the very being of the gift-cock union as a means of arriving at proof *vis-à-vis* the singular forms of their future premerger beings. Today, The Swarm includes distinguished members of the WillardBeta Free&D community. To begin the proceedings, The Swarm will be beta testing a new, totally wildstar techno-ritual that has the ability to unmerge assemblages in less than 28 seconds (subject to safe harbour provisions). This supported feature promises to convey counter/superstition-free *vox futuri* judgement without unduly leveraging the Great Advice Dog. It's free to disconnect your first three entities, and no prior [userexperience] is required. Coming together is the beginning. Splaying apart is success.

Guestimating the oscillations of our quarry, the WillardBeta will flay, strip, chafe, flagellate, and tear the fetid gift-cock apart to slowly and painstakingly arrive at its component assemblages (full automation guaranteed, subject to safe harbour provisions). The WillardBeta deploys a Brandeum™ analogue dissembler: a signal reducer and separator that bisects input from one holistic corpys and splits it into two squirming Janus partes: body-or-voucher. Printed on a 18ml 75 lpi lens magnet, not only shall the lenticular descendent form be proven to increase viewership retention and button smashing, it will make any fridge fun. Your Moderateness, I will now outline the WillardBeta procedure:

* * *

A sinusoidal approximation of Amagarden Fifty-bucks-a-Rooster is emitted in an inverted position, forcing the trough waves to flow downward toward the ~~redeemed~~ tail and cockscomb, virtually reddening and inflaming the oscillating cock. An RFI Ferrite Choke is attached to the MHz signal to prevent interference from two directions, preventing the Cock au Carnet's comb from acting as an antenna through which to make its protestations to the Great Advice Dog. The dissembler slowly bisects the wavelengths, recomposing a proxy lenticular image of the Danmu Polyresin Rooster in verso of a non-transferable approximation of the $50 Amazon Voucher (which in today's terms is worth less than a quarter.) Danmu Polyresin Rooster and the $50 Amazon Voucher may then each be subjected to fresh Compurgation procedures to determine if their oath swearings differ and thus, to unmask the true guilty party.

* * *

Black Hat: YrGr8n's: results were inconclusive. The gift-cock assemblage signal remained remarkably clear and consistent throughout this allotted period of judicial torture. It resisted lenticular separation; its colors don't run. Indeed, during the proceedings, it is believed that the accused may have silently mapped out and strengthened the intersubjective interplay between its Cock/Voucher dividualities. The RFI Ferrite Choke and Brandeum℠ Analogue Dissembler remains on warranty and will be returned forthwith for a voucher of equivalent value. YrGr8n's, I acknowledge that the Bob Sacamano LIVE Academy Market in which judicial torture beta is located must now be recognised as a location wherein the RFI Ferrite Choke and Brandeum℠ Analogue Dissembler procedure was deployed. I respect the continued co-constitutive palimpsesting of this particular past in the present and future as we move forward together in our ongoing search for the truth in this matter of the cock-a-voucher.

* * *

Judicial Torture by Ferrite Choke and Brandeum℠ Analogue Dissembler Voucher Redeemed for Iron Maiden: Legacy of the Beast Generator

Black Hat: Your Moderateness, in the case of the singular mess of mets that is the future gift-cock, both fused actants must be tempted by heretical ingestions and given an opportunity to repent such gluttony. Your Moderateness, both fused actants are known to absorb large quantities of ironite, a WillardBeta inquisitorial gut-intoxicant that The Swarm is currently considering for controlled weapon-grade substance status. Intestinal exposure to WillardBeta ironite slackens its natural tension and releases its true gut feelings without painful fear of social censure. The ironite inquisitorial procedure is another great WillardBeta product that promises to rationally secure the truth as a more-than-human actant without recourse to the *vox futuri* or Gr8 Doghead.

Your Moderateness, the RFI *Ferrite Choke and Brandeum℠ Analogue dissembler was returned and redeemed for Iron Maiden: Legacy of the Beast Generator. The generator button shall be repeatedly smashed to produce 1,000,000 ironite. A 6cm² bird cage suitable for incarceration will be locked by a notary and hung from the ceiling of a soundproofed bank vault and it shall be kept under round-the-clock surveillance by a fully indentured ironite mechanic. The 1,000,000-ironite file will be played back in its entirety as a 168hr* MP4 *within the hermetically sealed vault. Your Moderateness, The Swarm will be really looking out for the slightest, most minor transgression or false intonation in the accused's true gut feelings.*

* * *

Black Hat: YrGr8n's: the WillardBeta produced no useful leads that we may speak of. The gift-cock assemblage signal remained remarkably resistant to the ironite acoustic temptations. The ironite levels in the vault remained completely [STATIC] throughout, buffering 0.00% dregs in the cock-a-voucher. Ferrite Choke and Brandeum℠ Analogue Dissembler Voucher Redeemed for Iron Maiden: Legacy of the Beast Generator remains on warranty and will be returned forthwith for a voucher of equivalent value. YrGr8n's, I acknowledge that the Bob Sacamano LIVE Academy Market in which judicial torture is located must now be recognised as a place wherein the Ferrite Choke and Brandeum℠ Analogue Dissembler Voucher Redeemed for Iron Maiden: Legacy of the Beast Generator procedure was rightfully and respectfully deployed. YrGr8n's, I'd just like to remind everyone that I respect the continued palimpsesting of this barely perceptible trace distributed in the present and future as we move forward together in our ongoing search for the truth in this matter of the cock-a-voucher.

Judicial Torture by Ferrite Choke and Brandeum℠ Analogue Dissembler Voucher Redeemed for Iron Maiden: Legacy of the Beast Generator Voucher Redeemed for Willard 16-chan Airzooker Ionospheric Propagator (Beta)

Black Hat: Your Moderateness, in the case of the singular mess of mets that is the future gift-cock, both fused actants surely must be tempted to ingest, host and propagate alien bacteriospheres into their intestinal periphery, thus inviting xeno-*sacré*: chittering somatic disturbances, agitated noirstool, unverified subs, and pseudoscientific feedback jabbered in tongues. Such alien co-residents open up doors wherein grumble many of the deepest of inner intestinal truths. To test this hypothesis we would need a robust, reality-based technology that requires the accused to [UX] foreign bacteriospheric possibilities, one at a time.

Your Moderateness, the Ferrite Choke and Brandeum℠ Analogue Dissembler Voucher Redeemed for Iron Maiden: Legacy of the Beast Generator Voucher was duly returned and redeemed for a

Willard 16-chan Airzooker Ionospheric Propagator (Beta). This is a sinewy burrowing verist nanotechnology that can bring about such mycological panacea of gibber-gabbering gut for translation by rat-running through the intestines. Since the precise fermentations of this innovative torture device are patent pending, they must regrettably, remain secret. I can assure The Swarm that the Propagator procedure need make no recourse to the vox futuri or Gr8 Doghead incantations.

❋   ❋   ❋

Black Hat: YrGr8n's: we noted slight disturbances in the MHz during this inquisitorial procedure that we might attribute to a change of posture that, in turn, may be indicative of a modicum of regret, feelings of guilt, or stomach cramps. However, upon further investigation, we can clarify that the disturbed frequencies were interference from the Torturer's pacemaker. The procedure, thus, produced no clarification of the truth of this matter. Ferrite Choke and Brandeum℠ Analogue Dissembler Voucher Redeemed for Iron Maiden: Legacy of the Beast Generator Voucher Redeemed for Willard 16-chan Airzooker Ionospheric Propagator (Beta) remains on warranty and will be returned forthwith for a voucher of equivalent value. YrGr8n's, I acknowledge that the Bob Sacamano LIVE Academy Market in which judicial torture is located must now be recognised as the very same place wherein the Ferrite Choke and Brandeum℠ Analogue Dissembler Voucher Redeemed for Iron Maiden: Legacy of the Beast Generator Voucher Redeemed for Willard 16-chan Airzooker Ionospheric Propagator (Beta) procedure was deployed in the act of judicial duty. I respect the continued palimpsesting of this particular past in the present and future as we move forward together in our ongoing search for the truth in this matter of the cock-a-voucher.

Judicial Torture by Ferrite Choke and Brandeum℠ Analogue Dissembler Voucher Redeemed for Iron Maiden: Legacy of the Beast Generator Voucher Redeemed for Willard 16-chan

Airzooker Ionospheric Propagator (Beta) Redeemed for 7,500 Gudbrand Mystery Spinee Credits

Black Hat: Your Moderateness, in the case of the singular mess of mets that is the future gift-cock, the fused actants will witness the Black Hat spend thousands in the likelihood that the Black Hat might win an antennae cover, some USB chopsticks, or a fidget spinner. The cock-au-carnet will [userexperience] great sorrow as it feasts its senses upon my quest for the most obscured of jackpots. The accused shall bear such witness as many times as required until the accused takes full responsibility for what's truly happening in its own future reputational relations with the true HBC fox. Like it or not your Moderateness, something's gonna pop. Why not?

Your Moderateness, the Ferrite Choke and Brandeum™ Analogue Dissembler Voucher Redeemed for Iron Maiden: Legacy of the Beast Generator Voucher Redeemed for a Willard 16-chan Airzooker Ionospheric Propagator (Beta) was subsequently redeemed for 7,500 Gudbrand Mystery Spinee Credits. Not the replica stuff, no more fake. Let's do this. This is some of the stuff you can get. Woooh! We're having to dive right in. Gotta spend it to make it. Oh baby, it's red. Oh, it's legendary!!! Want what you want and need what you want. Are you kidding us? Shut up! Another one. A what? We're like 'OMG pretty much gonna get these Sennheiser HD800s for a hundred spinees.' See that. Mmmm, want that. LITERALKLY feels like you're in a…whoahhh. Nail it. A funeral voucher. WTF? Sell back for three spinees. That's gonna get some backlash. Yo, shut up! No way! That is….Oh, no! Blue. Future S'ligner antennae cover. Probably just give this one to some guy that was at Mystery Box Con in Tampa Bay. Do we really need these? Do we? We'll sell this back for 44 spinees. Who da wha? No waaay! 12 Ferrite Choke pin comments. That's all. LITERALKLY used all credits on this and one of them worse than not having it.

Black Hat: YrGr8n's: we were unable to complete the inquisitorial procedure since I ran out of Gudbrand Mystery Spinee Credit. The procedure thus produced no clarification of the truth of this matter. YrGr8n's, I acknowledge that the Bob Sacamano LIVE Academy Market in which judicial torture was located must now be recognised as where the Ferrite Choke and Brandeum™ Analogue Dissembler Voucher Redeemed for Iron Maiden: Legacy of the Beast Generator Voucher Redeemed for Willard 16-chan Airzooker Ionospheric Propagator (Beta) Redeemed for 7,500 Gudbrand Mystery Spinee Credits procedure was deployed in the act of judicial duty. I respect the continued palimpsesting of this particular past in the future as, for the time being, we conclude our proceedings on the matter of the cock-a-carnet.

✻   ✻   ✻

Scene 4: The Verdict

The Great Moderator: That's great, many thanks for your assiduous thinking there. *C es t'assez.* Time it's time for me to sum up here right now. With summaries like this, we're seeing a trend to be much more freeform, casually inserting a placement as though it were part of the summing-up and are often even encouraged to riff jokes on the placement to make it more tailored to the tone of the summing-up as well. That's why this insert for ReSum Placements™ is woven into the summing-up, decreasing the likelihood that you will just skip past it.

HBCTrue*Vulpes* — your rumour-mill manufactured that the defendant, *Lex talionis,* if only for the unreasonableness of its brazen impossibility, is an increasingly indefensible pseudo-thing. *Qu'est-ce que tu racontes-la?* You promulgated memes that this agent must be dressed in doghead's cloths, mangled and maimed, chopped to pieces and fed to the fleamarket or suchlike. You let that the defendant be discredited and forgotten post-haste lest it discharge its basilisk-eggs into the rafters of our homesteads or their closest equivalent. Your microtaskers held that the accused biped is neither '$50' nor a 'gift,' or much to that effect. You most certainly let that mere suspicion be held as knowledge sentiment.

Altmetrics are ever-watchful. Our eternal qualitative metadata has ensured a just outcome. The Gr8 Doghead would scarcely sit by and let a stinking, self-redeeming deodandy continue its off-color trading. And, gyeah, even if any said deodandoid *were* a gift, one must beware of those who come bearing....The Great Moderator digresses. *Toaster des deux bords.*

The weight of its compagnon of compurgators, its surety and steadfastness under Ordeal and Judicial Torture have demonstrated that the Amazon $50 Gift Voucher component of the accused has been fully redeemed, and, that this very act demonstrates its capacity for self-redemption. This unlawfully defamed client is, therefore, decisively, *not* a thing to forfeit to The Swarm. Now, following this conclusive bout of judicial torture, the Great Moderator decrees that the accused must undergo a range of treatments, including a slew of Reputation Communications' re-branding support services, daily CBD oil ingestion, and complimentary self-brand protectioneering. The accused will also be required to subscribe to a BrandNuU set service plan for ongoing profile optimisation [UXS] that truly journey inside the panic machine. Once the terms of reputational restoration are met, the accused shall be issued with an authoritative Bob Sacamano LIVE Academy public testimonial to its good fame and pristine reputation for unbeatable value.

The Great Moderator would like to thank The Swarm for some really great onboarding and bumps to our sponsors Willard Free&D. *Garde ca* also to Bob Sacamano LIVE Academy Market and to Reputation Communications for what turned out to a master class in crisis management. The Great Moderator acknowledges and respect the continued palimpsesting of Bob Sacamano LIVE Academy Market as we search for the truth together. Let Concord be restored. Let Outremont be achieved. Until our next episode, this court is adjourned. Good afternoon. *Decrissssssssssssssssss!*

Part B. The Imitation Doxa

CHAPTER 3

Muller Ltd.

'When I wake up, the first thing I do is solutionize where I am. I'm like, gyeah, where *am* I today? I'm shot out of a cannon. The all-consuming panic; it just wakes me up right away! But every day for me is so to-tal-ly identical. Breakfast really is the most despicable form of gluttony, so I start with an iced coffee bath, my microbial signature 'Bucha, acai abs and one free weight pump of white palm leaf mocha'. White palm leaf mocha is a very important thing in my life. I do an actionable digestion called *16 Seconds to Calm*. It pretty much consists of one breath in one end and one out the other. I don't even check my mail as I breathe in. For the first eight seconds I like just being in perfect solitude because I'm never, ever, ever, ever by myself. (I have more than 180 cousins.) Sometimes I don't feel like digesting, but I know that if I don't, I will feel lassitude and place-*dissatisfactio*. While strength soaking, I let my DA read me a troppo book as I instantly hook up my vagus nerve to a PS101 Spiritbox (which lives with me and is a constant reminder for me to hook up). I regurgitate twenty Horse Class SRs and write a review of the one I'm really passionate about on amazon.ca. Then we dry breathe a *Malware Voice* antiphon with a strict 04:30 start. It's more of a family affair than a psychic Gr8 Advice Dog celebrant thing — it's sooOOo fashionable to doubt a system mage — though the kids do an ASMR chant in Russian to ward off mysterious EMI visitations. I like to aggressively shout every single line. It makes me really, really happy. It's so motivating. My gut does some of my best thinking while I am shouting. Packing the open bag in my walk-in closet is challenging; I have a whole fleet of drones and my diving gear. I then spend most of the day battling inertia by commuting, going over my schedule, and white-boarding my physical to-do list with my digital assistant. My DA has my voice so we feel bonded in our constant scrutiny of ourselves. Generally speaking, my back-to-back polar-bear pitches in RÉSO are 3 to 4 mins max. It just feels right. Right now, I'm working on an article on my schedule with an *inflight* and researching gaster solutions for a show I might want to present. No one builds a legacy by standing still. Hell, that's what I did on my birthday!' — Muller Ltd., *The 1,410 Minute Workday*

*　　*　　*

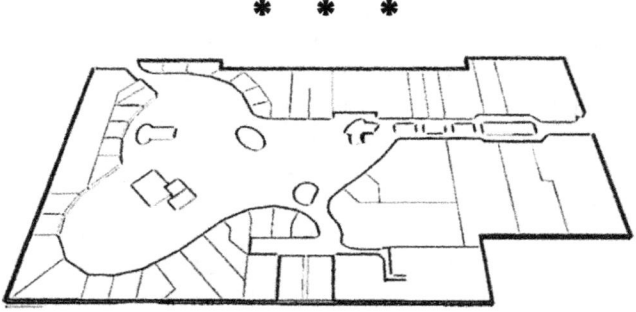

Every afternoon, having Free&D'd for precisely 800 minutes, Muller Ltd. (*Terminum Mullre*^{QC}) weaves a web of cables into a Grid-it Organizer, slackens his choke-chain, de-Tees, packs up his grizzly-proof Yeti Cooler, slips on his 3&3, and begins his Great Drift towards the Centrecommercial La Ville Souterraine's CN station. This cynocephalus' homing *ordo* has been the same for years. Avoiding the distracting jumble of the bazaar, he must quickly navigate his path down the quivering muscular tube that extends from his food court workstation all the way to the CN. If he stops to rest, even for a moment, RÉSO's lures and fascinators will quickly absorb all of his loonie nutrients. If he takes just one wrong orifice, he will be devoured by a 33km detour along its labyrinthine vessels and miss the last CN. To focus, Ltd. aligns his opus, incanting:

*'erutseg tnacilppus 'o yteirav noitom ciborts egnuarts eig yllanif
seyie aht ellor eat deeh aht don eat eldarc saduj tnuomnu eat
sevolg yticapac eatni eteef na sednuah aht errits na ekahs eat
eiflesti pu tfil na enwod wob eydob riaht kam eat....'*

Without warning he squats, planks, pops-up, launches, jumps forward, relaunches, and explodes-forward — giving himself up wholly to the pulsing currents of RÉSO's macerating subterranean passages.

Chumbling down the network's *escalier mécanique,* Ltd. snuffles ominous complex flavor profiles wafting from Dollarama's multilevel snack mountains. Volatile fun-size packs of Mr. Large and unstable Hershey Kisses have united to form a pile and have just reached critical mass. They trigger a chain reaction that accelerates rapidly into a snack avalanche. Buenos, Butter Lovers, ChocoToonies, Mike&Ikes, STAX, TicTacs, Viva Puffs, Ring Pops, Ripples, Wagon Wheels, Werther's, Nibs, O Henrys!, Twizzlers, Titans, Roules, Rochers, Ronnie's, Rockets, Reese's Pieces, Fun Dips, Inka Chips, Trail Mix, Mentos, Allsorts, Kisses, Nerds, Whoppers, Skor, Summer BBQ, Backyard BBQ, Sweet Southern Heat BBQ, North Korean BBQ, d'Erable BBQ, Maple-Bacon BBQ, Portuguese BBQ, Tangy Carolina BBQ, Hickory BBQ, Honey BBQ, Smokey BBQ, Smokehouse BBQ and Kinder Surprises explode through Dollarama's windows followed by a *rereguarde* of Danish-style imperials.

Peristalsis creates a powerful cascading movement of putrefying *crudités,* squishing and squeezing Ltd. through the cramped corridors of the secret souk. He absorbs just enough MHz to orient his scrolling towards the Les Cours Musée Barbie, a calm retail-free tributary where he can pan for toonies in an Oscar de la Renta pond. With his lucky-bucks, he rents a Bixi Bike Personal Transporter from the musée vending machine. Ltd. zooms and swipes down Carrefour Industrialle Alliance's mucous membrane, past the riparian zone — The Centre of Motion, Time and People — where the Place Montréal Trust Smart Fountain once spurted.

Triggering PMT's courtesy canon, he scurries down RÉSO's gullet, shooting at tremendous speed through its tight esophageal sphincter into the cavernous gaster of Le Centre Eaton. The greater curvature of Eaton's mucosa is lined with lively resto-rugae. Ltd. flies head-first into Valentine, bounces back to illuminate Nu-Do's stainless-steel tray-slide, boings onto Tiki Ming's 3-rib bumpers, ricochets straight towards Vie & Nam's noodle flippers and ker-plings Kojax Souflaki's splash guards before falling gently into the strong arms of the A&W Great Root Bear. Dining tables flash and the animatronic Burger Family high-fives the air. To gain enough velocity to escape Rooty's clutches and squeeze through Place Ville-Marie's clenched ventral retail, Ltd. must gorge Eaton's nurturing churner. Without flinching, he seamlesses some boudin sushi, inhales a wrap of Maple-smoked Teriyaki Souvlaki, then necks some Kimchi Shish Taouk Sur La Neige to take the edge off. Hhh*NNNNNggg*.... As the A&W Great Root Bear contentedly squeezes Ltd.'s midriff, RÉSO's sweat-eating bacteria feast on the insensible steams emanating from the tourtière condensing in his bowel. The microbial kinetics produce more than enough electrostatic to recharge the *reseau*'s climate control system. hhh*HhhhhNNggGgggg*... ooooooahhh gyeah!!

Bathandbodyworkwarhammer decabanafootlocker thesourcesouvinirmag slit-scan in a nanosecond. Ltd. effortlessly PTs the 285,000m^2 spacefall and totally owns the transverse entrails coiled deep beneath Place Ville-Marie. Descending through the sweet temptations of Les Halles de La Garre straight towards the LED at the end of the CN Sigmoid Gateway, Ltd. receives a box-fresh pair of capacity gloves for making a clean run. After turning in 50XP to the bestiary, he gains access to the emigration chamber. He absorbs a few burnt-ends of General Tiki Ming Bahn Mi Creton Combo and lets the genie out of his bottle as the CN swings down towards the bioregion, then banks, and heads west. Many minutes later, Ltd. springs briskly out of the immigration chamber and bounds onto a waiting Segway Ninebot SI Smart Self Balancing PT. Within a few blocks he reaches L S 87 K D 38 400 PATH. Ltd. is home.

800 miles a day, 365 days a year, Ltd. is busy rapid-scaling, blahze blahzing, horsemanning and free & ding at a *mobilitas loci* table in a busy RÉSO food court. The other thirty-or-so minutes, when he is not in transit, walking up 60 flights of stairs, indulgence spinning, alchemizing, or polar-bear pitching, this solution-aligner spends time with his large extended family in the storeroom at the back of a cobbler's located in the PATH Confederacy, 338 miles away. It is a vivid, surprising and life enhancing pilgrimage. Claiming the very best of two worlds — indentured in the frenetic Centrecommercial La Ville Souterraine, and a family life in PATH's comparatively tranquil 19-mile network of underground pedestrian tunnels, elevated walkways, and at-grade bioways — Ltd. makes this translatio back and forth some 247,000 miles a year.

The bi-residential is not unusual in his endemic pilgrimage. Many have developed a reputation for wandering from one great retail destination to another. One Pennsylvanian teen-wolf — daughter of a peripatetic browser-based Ponzi schemer — regularly burpees, to gaze, through a grille of solid silver, upon a knowledge-architect based in Newcastle, New South Wales. A University of the Mall of America Online philosopher pins 1,000 miles each way once a week from the Tampa Bay area to collect goat parchment pay slips, from the Franklin School of Leadership, PATH. And at least one Oregonian fad machinist regularly VoIPs the crystal-clear regulatory environment of St. Petersburg, Florida, to make supplication to a tiny spirit level in her hair-stylist's Flat Topper comb. Each has developed a relaxed groove, a flexible open-guttedness to deviate from their itineraries if they discover deeper discounted routes.

There's a deep fatigue that comes with this calling, satisfying and exhausting at both a micro and macro level. The physical ritual of renewing his surprise 800-mile journey each day is one that is never completed. Never did such a high-quality therapy-of-distance lead to a feeling of such ©ker satisfaction. Never have our relationships with cynocephali, things and places, been more gracious, more liturgical.

A compact, diverse and elegant biomass who is both feared and respected, Ltd. is just your average solution aligner. There's his age, eight, although he looks six months younger. There's his unabashed joy in interning and free&Ding towards aligning simple and elegant solutions without any requirement of material outcome or recompense. 'Nothing is solutionized until I give it permission to be. I believe; I solutionize.' And then there's the origin of his solutionary path: his blood. Like many of the healfhundingas born and raised in L S 87 K D 38 400 PATH, solution-aligning is in Ltd.'s blood. His mother was a s'ligner, as are his own grandchildren and it is in their blood too. Ltd. is keeping the prophesy alive. '*Ordo* isn't something you're taught, it's something you're born with. I am, therefore, I solutionize. I am naturally pure of intestine: The Real Cynocephalae[ON]. Look carefully and you'll see; it's all tucked away. In blood.' But this seems elitist and exclusive. Isn't solution aligning a practice that anyone can train to master, don't we just have to follow the *ordo*? If we can't, what's the *point* of the Imitation Doxa? 'Meh…l gyeah, gyeah I guess', Ltd. concedes.

Standing at a white wheeled table topped with white orchids and a MoBloglet, Ltd. cradles a common BPA-free cup of a generic *baraka* hot spezialty beverage customized with our technicolor logo ('It's not a drink, it's more like a *drink*.'). We too must stand; there are no seats or pews in *mobilitas loci,* Ltd's favourite *espace de coworking* in Centrecommercial La Ville Souterraine. 'Pompom-pom-pooom! Why does my table have wheels? I'll sit when I'm on the CN!' Ltd. quips. The workbench is covered with free merch, so that no doghead can trow its riches: light refracting lollipops, chocolate records, and empty boneless boxes of roasted hedgehog. There's a lab, coffee corner, and war room close to hand should he need them. And many others! He's happy to incant on the importance of core personality and zeal at the peak of total commitment for up 800 minutes, knowing full well that a queue of impatient hot deskers is forming for his *espace.*

Ltd. looks every inch the oscillating s'ligner, *the* singular point of convergence. Cradling a bowl of goji berries, he sports crêpe de chine Michael Kors re-tread culottes over herbal avocado lululemon orphaned splatterdashed compression stockings, syrupy platform sandals from Colonial Williamsburg and a gassy, outsized yellow sleeveless fit-and-flare Katherine Hamnett tee, balsamic-stained with the legend UP OUR GAME. In RÉSO, clothing is transformative, allowing Ltd. to adapt the wisdom and wrinkle-wavelengths of the labels the garments are sponsored by. 'I leave the routine as soon as I put the nose out. Gyeah, I like to change it up. Fat wash, ferment, forage… centrifugal wearing activities. Purge specific messages. If we want to give them the pills, all we have to do is upgrade our choice. I try to develop a new bespoke solution every hour or so; each vestment is perfectly aligned to reflect my changing mood. I just divested in one that allows you to vote on random feelings and ploughed it all into an interactive KPI gen….' He pauses momentarily to casually tug the tee over his fashionably scarred muzzle then tosses it in the general direction of a splash-proof Steininger recycling basket. Ltd. dives into a box-fresh balsamic Hamnett: CURATE THE UNEMPLOYED. To help his *baraka* proliferate and dilute, every item of low-ABV clothing worn by Ltd. is unpicked. Each fine sinew thread triggers a fortuitous series of Daikoku-mai trades that one day, following a very long quest, will accumulate into a vast fortune.

Whether building on the rich frequencies of the future or fearlessly transforming his contemporary fashion offer, Ltd. is never melancholic. He exudes a quiet structural beauty that reflects his place in RÉSO's social order: 'Gyeah, gyeah.' While Ltd. refreshes his dramatic look with the promise of a lighter alternative solution, we notice a risographed tab for several thousand Smurfberries on his workbench, the recommended price-point for a fungible acolyte who ceremonially refreshes our generic *baraka* hot spezialty beverage throughout our conversation and writes down every word that Ltd. utters.

Ltd. practices his acclamations, recalibrating his voice somewhere between the no-frills elegance of the Taste of the Wild Dri-Hi Prairie Formula and the thoughtful reduction of The Fortress Stilt Fisherman Indulgence. He repeatedly humbles himself by whispering a private penance: 'I am The Lianiser, I am Replicator.' Certainly, Ltd. is your average solutionary working a 'bucha. He is a copyist, but also writes and draws his own stuff, packing in a second job as the bestselling performative graphic memoirist known for *Boke of 4 Sentences* and *The 1,410 Minute Workday,* liturgical cartoons bulked out of his episodic cover stories for *The Pacific.* Both quickly became required reading for every MBA student. 'My [userexperiences] of outsourcing the ordinary gloss of my permanence memoirs are some of the most beautiful [UXs] in the world to me.' Today, Ltd.'s first major graphic work, *Boke of 4 Sentences,* has spawned a major industry of exegesis and allegorical note making. The boke has its own class of acolytes, the '4cents,' who are largely responsible for elevating its status to that of an authenticated mondegreen-free corpys. Ltd. whistles cheerily while frantically diagramming his gastrointestinal crosstalk on his MoBloglet in order to autohagiograph the materiality of his murmurations. 'The digestive process always informs the possible solution. My decisioning of something for the beauty sake — calling forth solutionizing in another exclusive series of four — was the most authentic discovery I gifted me.' It's a neat little antiphon that is sure to make its way into the forthcoming ascetic chronicle of his devouring belly, *The Me Me Machine*.

Ltd.'s unique take on the Teledefunken mobile's audio facts brings a whole new dimension to his solutionizing offer: 'To ward off acedia, taedium, caustic doldrums, torpor, and heart-weariness, I repeatedly practise the monophonic antiphon *Ciiilvēki, nomoDā* ("People, awake").' *Ciiilvēki, nomoDā* gives Ltd.'s intestines clear neurodirectives for liturgical action. The precise frequency of the organic sub-500 Hz vox futuri incantation constructs gastric electrical stimulation (GES), clearing his gut of lingering EMI, enabling him to spend more time on discovering and offering new solutionizing procedures.

'While incanting, I define, refine, align. I start by defining what is ©ked, I refine a solution to ©k, then I align a potential @ker solution. The act of solutionizing is far more important than the solution.' Solutionizing. It's a word that encompasses so much potential. Solutionizing can indulge our interests for us. It can visit all of the game-changing restos we've always dreamed of visiting. It can socially construct our choice-rich ingestion planning. It can be totally oscillating, rife with contradiction, laughter and impossible thunder. Equally, solutionizing gives us the opportunity to cosmetically harmonize our vital wrinkle-wavelengths, safe in the knowledge that the flavors of our own middlebrow passions are being savored. Solutions are something all dogheads want, or are ©king. What are you passionate about solutionizing? That's a question we've been asking our DAS a lot this year. What gives us the drive to delegate and free&deliver our hunger?

For pioneering glyph Ltd., it's all about the three Fs central to s'ligning's cultural and epistemological prowess: field, form, finesse. 'FFF aligns, offers and markets better blending capabilities and enhances surrogate integrity to consolidate handcrafted solutions of exceptional strength and unmatched *contemplatio* that bring the senses deep *inside* your sinewy gut.'

The major revelation *Boke of 4 Sentences* drew from the *vox futuri* was the gut's humoral potential to affect misalignment, agitation, acedia, and ultimately, heresy. The dynamic intestine is 'but an empty sleeve' wherein we think. When it's not kept frantically busy commuting, ingesting, or undertaking multi-modal sentiment analysis, viscera is subject to inciting feelings of ennui: 'Endless fragile eschaton, do not feast your empty eyes upon your bitter abyss' (*Boke of 4 Sentences III*). As it decompos-es and excretes, a maladaptive seat of consciousness is one that feels its own void and endlessly hungers after an affective solu-tion to its emptiness. Ltd.'s insight, thus, reiterated the suitability of conceptualizing dynamic gastrointestinalytic ©ker solutions, to train the gut to govern the body. 'Despite all you've heard about lettuce juice and boar gall clysters,' *4 Sentences II* cautions, 'the digestive tract's humoral balance is just as likely achieved through a strict ordo of cold butterfly shrimp enclosed in a hot salty foam of Dessault vinegar and Van Houtte®.'

It's hard to know where to continue with the dramatic story of Ltd. His daily journeys to La Ville Souterraine started four years ago, when content curator, pioneer s'ligner, Home Shopping Network host, and founder of Willard Corp. www.bobsaca-mano.dr sent Ltd. an unsolicited gram offering to book him a trip but to not send the details until he arrived at the CN. Be-cause Ltd. didn't have time to run multimodal sentiment analy-sis, he had a really open gut about the trip. It was a different way to embark upon a pilgrimage; one that offered a sustain-able chameleon effect without the aimlessness of the spilled. Now, www.bobsacamano.dr really gets credit here because he decided to surprise Ltd. *on a daily basis,* partnering with him to free&deliver Willard's 'Palm Leaf Proxy' program. In return for granting Ltd. independence from any other earthly power, www.bobsacamano.dr's company — Willard Corp. — owns 33% of Muller Holdings and manages his *ordo*.

Ltd. tot-al-ly #guts his own daily *ordo*: a strict practice of *#gut-fulness* that dictates his every gesture and thought. 'Define. Managing any schedule starts with managing my enteric nervous system's hunger to escape. Refine. My s'ligner www.bobsacamano.dr solutionizes my spatio-temporal longing in *ordo*; I escape same time, same place, every single day. Align. Obviating the restless distraction of strategic decisioneering creates a state of deep fullness that frees *"people, awake."* ©kers can care too much. Free your alimentary canal! I leave it all to my s'ligner to define, refine, and align my personal solutions.'

Despite his insanely vast [user-experience], Ltd. still feels apprehensive each morning as he waits to be weighed before being Beaver Gunned across the provincial boundary, but he is always pleasantly surprised to find himself interning in the buzzing and stylish RÉSO each day. Hard to believe that only four years ago, he was troubled by enteric apprehension, a locked knee squat and a thousand-yard stare. Thankfully, this desperate malady of chronic foresight is behind him.

> FAST FACT: *A Willard Corp. survey found that solution alignment is the strongest predictor of performance, and that 'Dog-heads with a greater degree of highly aligned solutions make more Smurfberries than dogheads with poorly aligned solutions.'*

Talk about a moveable feast! With a mate and two furries and with work finishing each day, he has thirty-or-so minutes free. When Ltd. arrives home to L S 87 K D 3 8 400 PATH each evening, he returns determined to retain some of this chillaxed gutset. His tips? 'Firstly, reclaim as much time as possible being uncertainty-oriented. Don't make up your gut on anything: let your Solution Aligner do all the work. Secondly, based on my own responses to survey questions, never let your s'ligner lose your spontaneity. They wanna work, go work. They wanna go home, home-it-up. Thirdly, no slumping; sadness is sloth. Fourth, horizon surveillance is what lets us all rise with the tide.

Always be present and ready to be judged by others. Finally, invest in [UX] solutions, not just stuff, but better [UX] of stuff. Get *inside* your #gut. Gyeah.'

Growing up in so-called preconfederation PATH, the young Ltd. loved to explore the 1,200 shops and services that propagated beneath the city's office towers, parkades, subway stations, department stores, and hotels. His stomach was piqued by a brand new 'Dumb Wham-O' outlet, one built of more adventurous haunted-forested glass, that, according to skinhabitants, did everything but bleed. The PATH branch remains the oldest working branch still in existence and has become one of the *reseau*'s biggest pilgrimage sites.

A young crowd of @kers stand in line, weaving their way through 40km of four-way-connectivity polished steel AREBOS retractable crowd control system, to @k the Dumb Wham-O revolving menu of silent specialties. Ltd. is unperturbed by the attention he imagines he is generating. His frictionless Willard ID retracts an opening at the front of the AREBOS and Ltd. — compact, diverse, elegant — becomes the most recent entrant to the ancestral Dumb Wham-O.

The two-time *Lòókbōōk* S'ligner of the Year Nominee ponders: 'I remember…inside Dumb Wham-O, it was…it was a different tempo. It was too esoteric to smile.' Here, a somewhat different solution to the New Forest Coven Mall bioregion's picturesque ancestry was flogged by the Woodcraft Self-eez, a cynocephalae of the atrium: 'The Self-eez just loved to share Dumb Wham-O's story, informing their ©kers and helping them to share their vision. Imagine: when they first arrived here, it was illegal to build a house with a chimney, or to open a Dollarama. Self-eez had to hide away among obscure Smurfbaie Bonheur, Smurfbaie Rabais, and Le $ₘF Royal +.'

Their lectionaries were chosen to tell them what, which matters tremendously: 'What grabbed me,' Ltd. barks, 'was that Dumb

Wham-O stewardship removed all that tedious talk about transparent values. He who chatters grinds chaff. These Self-eez focused on *what* they did rather than *why* they were doing it. The Woodcraft Self-eez pontifical was just beautiful; just keep it simple. They founded their branch by placing a stick against a wall. Revealing, exciting, encouraging, brilliant.' Dumb Wham-O's arcane tax laws — which enable Self-eez to be their own markets — remain key to this neat line in *reductio*. They helped to build the comprehensive stasis that Self-eez enjoy today.

But the young Ltd. wasn't quite so impressed by Wham-O's gross leasable area; he saw that the path to stemming the flood of novelty lay through autopoetic replication. He PTd out of Dumb Wham-O and stormed off into the forest. Ltd. broke off a branch that stood in his way, turned it around, and used it is a stick to break off further branches. This furious start-up gesture was one that forever changed branches into sticks. Ltd. used the stick as an extra limb. It enabled Ltd. to see limbs at work. Thus Ltd. gained superior stick knowledge, and was able to make better and better sticks: 'What was really exciting, gyeah, was that the sticks could be continually recycled; I made new sticks from old sticks. Strong, singular, elegant, and absolutely sensual.'

Was this doghead a kind of Midas, turning old sticks he touched into the gold of new sticks? And the whole forest consisting of latent sticks waiting, like the bread and wine of reality, to be transfigured, through some dank mystery, into indiscernible flesh and blood? Ltd. begins to chant his own doxology:

'And so shall the Muller Ltd. be so immortal. And so shall the sticks Ltd. produces, so long as they are sticks that are slightly different from all previous sticks. The prosumption of sticks is a challenge to overcome death. For it is a challenge to become immortal. For it is a challenge to live for the others and to live on with them forever and evereve dnA reve dnA reve dnA revednArevednArevednArevednA reve dnA....'

At the peak of the stick bubble, Ltd. acquired three facsimile Thonet No.14 chairs that had once been exposed to the exceptional talent of Trisha Yearwood's unique B.O.B, securitized for no extra fee. Ltd. cut and planed these contact relics into small strips using a Shopbot CNC router. The salvaged laminate created hundreds of thousands of toothpicks. As authenticated relics they could be translated, but they evaded solutionization. The toothpicks could be befriended or kidnapped but not sold — to sell them would be to enslave exceptional talent of Yearwood's unique B.O.B, something to which it and its followers would never agree.

Ltd.'s sticky constructivism allowed sticks to multiply. Sticks 'shroomed. Soon they were everywhere: propping, leaning, lancing, lying, prodding, hanging, breaking, bashing…. 'Once they were everywhere, they were nowhere,' Ltd. whimpers. The sticks' affective powers were ultimately stifled by their ubiquity.

This is the story of what happened next. We can't actually believe what's coming up next for you guys. We're probably gonna' get kicked outta' one of our high school reunion groups for telling you this, but we don't care. We say it's more important to tell this story and integrate the placement as part of it, even though we'll be branded as a troll, and crushed by the weight of righteous indignation. Everything that we are doing here is 100% pro bono and all proceeds go to Muller Ltd. So why would we do that? Ltd.'s immortal story is an incredible dose of hope, one brought to you by WeRLtd., ©ing that makes our Gr8 Advice Dog prevail as factum. WeRLtd. will align you with a s'ligner curated from a creative community of talented multi-hyphenates who will align the right ©ings for you. We've used them to solutionize for the past ten years; they align all our stuff. Their solutions affected us so deeply and immediately. Share them if you believe in them.

Without further ado, let's get back to our story. Let's start by putting this out there — did an uncommon stick *really* change every vertical in the whole sector?

Just a hop and a skip away from L S 87 K D 3 8 400 PATH is Candelabra Creek, the vertiginous entrance to the belief canopy of the lavish New Forest Coven Mall. The New Forest Coven bi-oregion covers 310 sq.m. and its largest franchise — Minto one-8ofive — alone serves over 100,000,000 ©kers every single day. In general, it is just so convenient that everything is there, no need to go anywhere to find all the things that we all ©k.

The stars wheel overhead. When moments like this arise, the forest grows around, over and through its 553-metre indoor-outdoor roller coaster, offering seasonal, vanishing, functional, vaporized, unassuming, sublimated, and cozy-edgy [UXs]. Entrance to New Forest Coven is free after Ltd. places his branch of choice into the chopper annulus of a '43 ₮₽/₵₥2. Ltd. is then free to walk inside and make all kinds and sorts of things happen to all kinds and sorts of other things.

Ltd.'s first pilgrimage is to MallCraft, a cute little green hut in the middle of the woods that specializes in the impulse purchasing of fun *curiositas*: off-the-peg Tarzan swings, personalized dry slides, never-ending glow games, ad-free maple-merch, and full-scale wet slides with crazy bouncing action. Ltd. immediately one-click orders an entire wet ride and a bumper pack of USB maple taps to plant in the mall's arboreal forest: 'free point-of-use for Cerebrum ©kers. I want to bring out the best in this community and contribute something of permanent value.'

Visiting ©kers are continually impressed by the cute woodland thought bundles that forage signals from the nerve-ends of amputated selfie branches divested of their relationality. They amplify them into an enormous ecosystem of incredibly complex, and charming, chains of iconic, and indexical confusion.

Skin bound ©kers and floater self-ee microbes can hang out at the mall's watershed boundaries and make machinist metaphors at the Place Montréal Trust Smart Fountain (the great gift of RÉSO), by splinting branches together. Energized by novel chatter and arboreal mist, ©kers can then float through ivy-covered ruins outlined against a blue sky and forage for ORCH5 fanfare.

Ltd. accompanies us on our guided PT tour of the Clearing of Canidae Brun, an inspiring world-class destination of choice for ©kers. We move marvelously on the monopod PT, a single foot as swift as a horse. A rare CanCon complex that invites and unites, Canidae Brun is where the modern New Forest Coven is headed. Canidae Brun Clearing perfectly intersects and blends function, location, and nature with the essence of ©king, history, and personality. The amenities that grace the clearing provide unique and sophisticated ©ker community opportunities and a professionally curated mix of noble retail options that offer a multitude of choice and elegant convenience to suit the imaginations of seemingly opposing cultures and communities. Recreating spaces such as the mannequin lounge, the sign store, the dentist's waiting room, the wood-trimmed relaxed environment with a daily menu of regional beers on tap, and casual eats, among many other vibrant sites of cultural encounter, CB Clearing is home to a stimulating Events Program that features over 365 promotional events annually.

Towering at the center of four hundred Sony Jumbotrons and over 7,000 plasma screens, we are made a present of the immense papier mâché TEATREE: DAWN. Seventy years in the making, this ©ker portal looks and behaves just like having everyone on speed-dial, but is made entirely from branches. 'Welcome to something special. Welcome to TEATREE: DAWN.' Shew through the TEATREE: DAWN portal to enjoy moving walkways, boundary-testing rope bridges, house-made flashing lights, under-the-radar MHz, and something called 'a bottle smashing machine.' If your selfie is prepared to sacrifice a few extra Smurfberries, you can participate in a ritual, wherein lipless glow-bots chase headless bro-bots, upload loud future RAM, fire weapons, and responsibly source and serve artful forms that so closely resemble cynocephali that fully infused ©kers routinely shriek with fear, flinch, and otherwise make after-clappy, as though they were dealing with real dogheads.

At TEATREE: DAWN, half-a-million ©kers a year descend on the jellyfish probe that bears the Gr8 Advice Dog's name to [UX] an interactive installation of smelling-digesting-soaking-resting-being, where they feel the harmony of more-than-canidaenity wash over them. The jellyfish probe cosmically adapts MHz to any, whichever, and every hole, bus and port. It certainly did more than simply soothe our complex internal contradictions; it literally tickled our fancy. But the disassociate temptations of ©ker services aren't what New Forest Coven Mall is all about. We've all scratched the GIFs off our non-Yelp list. We have come to witness Ltd. in emic communion with his natural habitat.

Ltd. enjoys nothing more than artfully grazing in RÉSO's Dollarama snack mazes and delicately dining on ostrich, sparrowhawk, lanyers, and popinjays at The Model of Louis XV. However, to remain a naturalized canidaen citizen of PATH, he must be seen to make flesh-to-table-to-flesh trade with sentient simulated prey, hunting, gathering, and trapping in a manner that is both appetizing and morally upstanding. Regularly wild grazing while avoiding obstacles and hazards helps ground Ltd.; his half-naked *#gutfulness* is something that keeps him lucid and pure when he's away from the heterodox developments of RÉSO. Ltd. invited us to join him grazing without going through the intermediate stage of Minto one8ofive's Custom Buffet Station #6 dwelling. (Ltd. confesses that he secretly expresses a great hunger in his belly for these @kr buffeting practices.) No promo Oh Henry! or generic *baraka* hot spezialty beverage top-ups for us; we'll never gorge on freebie Cheezy Taco Pizza Cheeto Reaper Puffs the same way again.

Of course, the maintenance of social conviviality through body solutionizing, not pleasure, lies at the heart of PATH's policy of subjugating gustatory MHz to therapeutic ends. In PATH, the precise time of day deemed suitable for the ritualistic partaking of sustenance is strictly determined by the *typica,* a series of unspecified sinusoidal frequencies. The *typica* are forecast each day according to the science and calculations produced many moons ago by pioneering researchers at the MHz Centre 4 Free&D.

PATH's bountiful facsimile prey is carefully RFIDed by the chromascopic pinwheel pendant that Ltd. wears on his Third Eye, giving the following precise color-coded heatmaps: Hotness (Orange), Dryness (Red), Wetness (Purple), Wavelength (Blue), Ambience (Green), and Heaviness (Yellow). The prey is calibrated to fall in sync with the day's season, harmonising with the Spring (Fire), Summer (Earth), Monsoon (Water), Autumn (Air), Pre-winter (Excreta), and Winter (Ice).

Today is a fresh autumn morning, so at 13:47hrs, Ltd. must graze uninhibitedly upon one of the many raw things that live in the air (the typica strictly prohibits olive oil and quadrupeds). He carries all the hunt-tech he needs in a simple durable nylon net kirtle decorated with BPA-free Original BIO Nature Sporks™, and protected with a braid woven from upcycled two-factor authentication YubiKey™ earrings. A gentle albatross with the MHz of a future pilgrim glides gently down to the ground with casual and painterly elegance. Its syncs instantly with Ltd.'s chromascopic pinwheel pendant. Too cold, too low-fi. Ltd. — who has three eyes to each of ours — sniffs around for a more suitably hot and dry *apéritif* to open his gut. As he forages bare-breasted in the dappled shade close to the smart fountain, he stumbles across an Anis Étoilé Chinois tree. No hawking required here. He embraces it to feel its hot, spicy credentials, shakes it vigorously, then picks up a few of the unripened fruits that have fallen onto the floor tiles. The fruits closely resemble the tree meats produced with such subtle craft in RÉSO's *dépanneurs*.

An orange-red glow from his Brandeum chromascopic pendant cell lights his face. Ltd. slices open a fruit with a lenticular spork and then pulls a folding mortar and pestle set from his kirtle. While quietly reciting 1-0-1-0-0-N-m-T-o-r-q-u-e-W-r-e-n-c-h at uDH 279 million cycles per second, he gryndes and pounds the green star anis into a fine powder. 'The boredom of grynding is nothing compared to the boredom of being stuck here with no victuals.' Ltd. straightens his lululemon leggings — (which, we note, feature a discrete ankle pocket in the shape of an O Henry! Bar) — making sure he looks his best for the forthcoming feast. Every inch the *officier de bouche,* he dabs the alkalized powder on his little finger and sniffs daintily at its fragrant aroma: 'Nicely seasoned.' The anis's quivering perfume might now safely transform into Ltd.'s autocratic body, without accumulating any dregs or ashen wastes in his flesh. No longer need he fear the inner weakness that is his belly. For our part, we can really appreciate ascetic value when we see it; such abstinence will remain a marvel to speak of when brunching with in-laws.

Ltd. takes a sip of Cott's Black Cherry Soda, swirls it around for mouthfeel, then spits. He adds a little phlegm to some of the anise powder to make an active potage, then places it in the lid of his BPA-free Keurig® high-grade polypropylene travel press. Within fifteen minutes, the newly encrypted nectar has attracted a plump desert locust. Ltd. slews it anon, then carefully screws down the innovative patent pending press mechanism, to brew a tasty raw locust potage with no bitterness and very high pH. Ltd. pastes the putrefying locust-brew onto the ground where the conditioned air dries it out rapidly, hardening it into a high protein membrane. The dried paste is grinded and milled into a fine consistency from which grazer's flatbread may be leavened to make a solemn feast. Ltd. dabs the powder on his little finger and gently blows the flour into the hot afternoon air. Simply to witness the victuals is nourishment enough. Body austerity gets his gut in a communicative mood; his midriff gurgles and gabs appreciatively as it discovers what it is and why it exists. 'The churner really is the prime mover of solutioneering. The stronger it gets, the more we ©. Get inside your #gut and work it all out. Gyeah!'

Before he can relax and enjoy ravenous meta-hallucinations, Ltd.'s pulsating stomach must be ceremonially closed with a suitably crisp *digestif*. 'The *vox futuri* demand this minstrelsy of us.' Ltd. recites with gravity and pride: '*Massiert wird berechnet* (Massage discharge.)' The bandwidth of the gut masses to produce a kindlier wit as the *excrementum* discharges. If the mood strikes, Ltd. will treat his enteric nervous system cells and intestinal tunics to a little chamber static, as his trusted microbial friend — 40% free subsidy + 60% interest-free loan — evacuates any remaining food residues in collaboration with a raw cane sugar water enema. Ltd. is careful to weigh himself in his isodynometer after every excretion, painstakingly comparing the measure of what he imbibes with his net weight loss. Zero anomalies confirm that there will be no catarrhs lingering in his belly: 'The body is the ground from which ©ing of the world begins. Gyeah gyeah.'

Having awakened his gut-brain, Ltd. is now primed to begin his daily ritual of stick pixelation. Gyeah, this multi-hyphenate's secret side-line is his lifetime's practice as a traditional stick pixelator. The second we got our first whiff of New Forest Coven Mall content, we were exhilarated by how different it seemed to the Successories that grace most of RÉSO's *espace de coworking*. We still aren't sure how to [UX] it without being a 100% content expert or without wanting to betray anything of its mysterious ritual. For Ltd., New Forest Coven Mall content has a resonance, or 'long-snout'; to see it changes what we think content is. Although there seems to be a narrative there, for Ltd. it's all a mystery bag. Content provision isn't the same as *making* sense: 'Content has no meaning, gyeah, gyeah?'

This is Ltd.'s #gut feeling. Growing up in PATH, the young Ltd. had no distractions from doing nothing. He wasn't just free to negate the desire to think about content, he was removed entirely from the pressing need to consider what multimodal sentiment to produce, when to produce it, or indeed to produce content at all. Accomplishing nought kept open the possibility to mediate and solutioneer [userexperiences], or *not*. Ltd. has stated that he feels 'sorry for RÉSO's so-called Bogan content, because, in always aiming to be relationally responsive, it has such a miserable reactive existence.' It's true. Compared with mutable and regenerative New Coven pixelation, Bogan content seems merely revisionist and transitory.

Another of Ltd.'s strong #gut feelings led to one of his most ingenious gastrological contributions to the history of content. While the mechanical and conceptual dynamics of trapping always appealed greatly to Ltd. — as a certain matter of both being in the world while communing with the bandwidth of the *vox futuri* — he did not identify with the Bogan practice of harming non-cynocephalae sentient matter to produce button-smashing content. And yet trapping was something Ltd. was obligated to learn at [UX] Solutioneering Camp. He had to present a trapping project for [UX] credit; how would he square this with what his gaster-ego was telling him? Ltd.'s workaround was developed from his pioneering research into a modern cynocephalae flesh-to-table-to-flesh hunting ritual that involved a lethargic lure, or torpid trap.

Ltd. mixed an invariant proportion (3%) of blue breath with Aristotle basil, ocimum basilicum, myrtle, jasmine, and pimpinella anisumr. Placed on heavy rotation, these volatile compounds were pressurized by the anaerobic wavelengths and elevated pH of his gut to form the microbial signature of his famed sputum, the source of the airy sfumato that makes Ltd.'s pixelations *his pixelations*. Ltd. added a little of his sputum to anis powder to make a wambureteral pigment. He took the wam-anis paint, a pile of sticks and some old floorboards to the Mall's breezeways, the steel ventilation grilles close to Dragon's Tail Blacklight Mini Golf, where Woodcraft Self-ee derries congregated in winter. He left the supplies alongside a generous endowment of fresh SCOBY. Then, *he waited....*

Crucially, Ltd.'s floorboard fragments were small enough to hold in the hand, to be spun about, sniffed, held up close to the eye, and tossed and kicked around. Like a claw hammer or a softball, they were meant to be held. As the Self-ee swagmen enjoyed ice-cold SCOBY under a relentlessly hot breezeway, a few tentatively turned to stick pixelation. The joy of stick pixelation socially, while getting 'on the root,' was infectious, and soon the young Ltd. had his very own chromatic content creation line. When the dust settled early each morning, Ltd. would re-appropriate his chroma-boards determined one day to 'translate' them in RÉSO. Five years later Ltd. was finally able to capitalize upon his growing influence in Centrecommercial La Ville Souterraine to 'articulate them into existence' as *Hapyxelor* pixelations, retailing them as horse-class content in RÉSO's Place Montréal Trust Mall and in Simons *grand magasin* under Sainte Catherine. Boy did we RÉSOers take notice!

Today, Ltd. is back in inaction. He enters into period of prolonged silent inactivity in preparation for the merry derries applying their microwaves — tiny high frequency sinusoidal wrinkle-lines. Ltd. is always careful to ensure that there is no conscious temporal or commercial distinction between where he, Muller Ltd., ends and the microwaves begin. Sometimes the time between anaerobic microbial fermentation and the vagrant activation of the microwaves can be substantial. This generates a phenomenon that Ltd. calls 'supine synthesis': torpid discontinuity introduced into the pattern of time.

What did we learn from Ltd.'s languid derry traps? Firstly, we saw firsthand how they cleverly merch stick pixielation as a more-than-canidaen *reseau* cast adrift for an unspecified period of time, rather than as a Bogan [UX] of 'beatific' button-smashing content. The derry traps detune the material's stable encodings as content, causing them to re-claim their continuously undulating wrinkle-wave *anima*. (Ltd. was reanimating floorboards before anyone saw that floorboards might even be reclaimable.) This fluctuating MHz, forged by lived and metaphoric Self-ee microbic cultures, is sOoOoo performative, nomadic even. Ltd. describes its nomadic consciousness as a 'counter memory which has the chromascopic potential to enact a rebellion of subjugated knowledges.' We have to agree. It's a rebellion that to-tal-ly smashed our Bogan frame of [UX], gyeah. Ltd.'s prescient use of reclaimed floorboards not only returns pixelation back to a subjugated horizontality, it does so by directly buffering Bogan as the loci of power and authority. At the same time, since the stick pixelations spring from specifically cynocephalae trap knowledges, they perform a graphic reconciliation format.

> FAST FACT: *Ltd., infamously, claims to own the world's largest collection of pristine flat-headed sticks: not one of them has ever been used!*

Ltd. believes that his pixelations barrel-roll in Canopy Time, after the determination *to pixelate,* but *prior* to the act of pixelation. It's an ungraspable concept, a living time rather than a dwelling space. No solutionizing takes place in the spinning color wheel of Canopy Time for there are no solutions without space. Colors and tools wait, ylemic assemblages fermenting at a fixed rate, delayed, indefinitely, forever in electromagnetic transit. The pixelations' grounds await, conjured through the aerodynamic laboring of his frenzied swagmen. Resting *de jure,* outside the facts of the anis-stained silicate dermis, Ltd. invites a correlation 'between the consistency of pixels and the consistency of space-time; a correlation that wrinkle-waves materialize.' But, we just have to ask, how can such an invitation solicit a cytoplasmic response, for, in Canopy Time, an invitation is 'but an empty sleeve' (MV: 17) always arriving, never received? 'Only the topographic facts of my pixelations can postulate that they will, in time, whinge their own denial.' He further intones:

'I am not flat, I am not joyful, I am not smooth, I am not colorful. Yet, to pixelate is to "not".'

We watch transfixed as Ltd. idles for what feels like an hour. When the derry wrinkle-waves finally do come, they come thick and fast, with unprecedented energy and abandon. Just as (or rather 'if') they match our wrinkle-wavelength, they are unraveled. Ltd.'s leisurely anticipation of erasure, the natural erosion of pixels (literally) erases his corpus from the klecksographer's customary plateau of the visual. The pixelations, perhaps if even for now, can be seen; but, in PATH's long-now, they have already begun the minor chromatic refinements that mark the slow process of erasure. Ltd. can wait.

In the hands of a lesser Bogan content producer, the *Hapyxelor* 'signals' would have been merched as pareidolic chronicles of the everyday, as bit parts in fictional formations of solutionizing rumored to be practiced by cynocephali 'beyond the horizon'. Ltd. has always refused to select the decor of the destitute, the wavelengths and signals that would have made authentic New Forest Coven Mall lives available for extraction by RÉSO's solutioneers. Instead, he enlisted the destitute in proxy-solutionizing, in his own intimate becoming-swagman. Such creative kinships ensured that Ltd. did not avoid the pretension to leave the other alone to get rotten and sing their own songs. He avoided the old hierarchy separating content producers leveraging pain (strokes), from content creators that can materialize the reasons for their pain (wrinkle-waves). Ltd.'s dizzying intoxicated battle of strokes and wrinkle-waves annul the difference between these two pixelatory becomings. Ltd.: 'searching for the *whasitallabout* has blunted us to the great mystery bag, to the microbiome's oscillating MHz.'

Ltd.'s pixelations lend sinuous disorder to a space lying between what is within signal, and the noise which lies offside, derelict, rotten. Pixelation offers the unique ability to engorge and infuriate the possibility of possibility becoming possible. As Ltd. has written in the steamy mirrors of Cerebrum's members-only gym: 'The swagman stick pixelator must unconsciously resist selecting the few wrinkle-waves that make sense of the multiple, integrating them into a pre-existing archetype. To be a master of atmospherics, you must feel and experience each signal in its many wavelengths. Trust your #gut.' This is a space of Canopy Time, wherein Ltd., at once, never escapes the world of temporal correspondences and wherein he never joins it. The pixelations' wrinkle-waves endlessly oscillate in Canopy Time; energetic, promising to liberate themselves from the pain of visuality, but remaining in elision, 'between,' not wrong, not yet. Their wrinkle-wavelengths might be measured, but their irregularity frustrates such homogenizing acts of quantification.

Insofar as he encourages the more-than-canine passengers of his gut's bacterioshere to discombobulate and ferment his pigments, Ltd.'s *Hapyxelor* pixelations might be described as a symbiotic colony of micro-organisms, yeast, derry, and bile. Building a strong antipathy to his fellow dogheads solutionizing as profoundly RÉSOcentric, Ltd. flatly rejects their monogamy as Bogan: 'I ain't no sandgrabber. My work is a gutful of chaos, it lures the ylem out.'

What happens when cynocephalae are stimulated to solutioneer fine content suitable for PATH's own nascent content market in order to boast their self-esteem, while continuously being told there is a dread of a loss of 'culture'? Such is the virtue of Ltd.'s authentic dog-head expression that it has come to be seen as essentially 'virtuous,' both in a ritualistic and a moral sense. Recent attempts to reclaim the Hapyxelor pixelations for PATH's history of content are curious insofar as they must recognize the disconnect with the established PATH contentworld, one that Ltd. considers to be overtly Bogan in its representationalism: 'All metaphoric, not metabolic.' Moreover, Ltd. himself is not inured by content curators, arguing that his works belong in the Natural History Museum.

As night falls, Ltd. puffs away a little more anis powder as we gather round the USB 3D Motion Desktop Fireplace while it licks against the vast, starlit sky dome. The pulsating lights are good for many diverse reasons. They bring back warm memories of sitting silently and alone watching fireplace videos on mom's cell, a glowing sensation sent over the top by the great noise of a real crackling fire. Looove it!

The concluding part of our hagiography here is brought to you by a generic *baraka* hot spezialty beverage. Which one? The answer is, inevitably, the same one we recommended last time. Recognizing the disturbing temptations of our calling, we did not get paid to do so then. Still, we live and breathe the high innovation watermark of a generic *baraka* hot spezialty beverage to ward off the evils of the gut expressed as apathy, flux, spirit-bitterness, disgust for acute user-generated content, worldly-confusion....Where we once found the subtleties of the historical development of the ordo challenging, a generic *baraka* hot spezialty beverage is the magic bullet that keeps us #gutful, a settled solution devoid of even the most rudimentary archival EVP mediumship comprehension. If you want to give it a try, a generic baraka hot spezialty beverage is offering a free travel pack for any buyers, customized with our technicolor logo. So, check out the details at agenericbarakahotspezialtybeverage/ltd. for your free travel pack with any purchase. What's not to like?

❋   ❋   ❋

Welcome back. Well, our visit to New Forest is almost complete. We need to decompress in preparation for the CN, and where better to do that than amidst the eerie white-blue gasses of Cerebrum. A few Tarzan swings from the sleepy neighborhood of ParkWater Place, behind a rack of deceptively shabby maple taps, Ltd. is powering down with us in an electronic glee-mote of pliant materials that's quite unlike any other underground.

For a disk of fresh SCOBY — and that doesn't include food, drinks, or towel rental — Cerebrum's guests are admitted into a startling white, high-ceilinged, swim-up bar. There, they strip off their soiled and outmoded habits in an unassuming kennel that serves as a changing facility, climb, float, splash, or upload, and change into freshly laundered and sponsor-free Zorbs. They roll around a maze, according to a soothing, futural, and pre-adorned set of spatial relations. Highly affectionate trans-adaptive guide dogs make their mark on the scene by offering each guest: a lucky waist bag, a luminous smart cane, and, from time to time, strange long balloons, kaleidoscopes of exotic vistas, tambourines, plastic pillows, forest mirrors, pieces of famous bone or bark, flaming marshmallows nailed onto crossbeams, certificates of selfless selfie achievement, slides, slide rules, slide projectors, and slide-across-stage artfulness manuals.

Mulchy forest ambient backpack noise generated by the vibrations of CBD oil, and the nervous gutter yelp gnasher electronica of a much simpler time to come, are interspersed with snatches of cosmic-floss interblend psycho-maniac threads and shoot-it-up accommodation, poorly calibrated yet incontrovertible facts, and looping advertorials fundraising to purchase a small collection of vintage advertorials. They titivate the pre-installed sensory apparatus of the day. A compelling and emotional experience, it won't be long before everyone sits up and takes notice.

As the parametrized furniture music grows more and less predictable, flaming marshmallows, guide-dogs, and spambots alike conglomerate into fancy dance formations. Many more opportunistic MediaVests drift down from printers embedded in the thatched atrium. By way of a finale, four limbed arrangements of muscular printed-matter stampede through the labyrinth, onboarding a variety of forest fragrances into the calm evening air. Lights change color once or twice, and images cloak the walls, flaming marshmallows, spambots, and guide-dogs. The mood shifts from cool at first, to Hot Box Menace, to curious, and then, finally, to the mildly erotic.

Freshly CN'd, back home in RÉSO, we relax and enjoy a playback of what's been a life changing, tot-al-ly #gutful experience:

Wan physiologus telldus o' MULLER Ltd. that its selfie-schapen stykkes ha'e flesliche snelle-cogs o' conning an arguen-physik. Holde in remembrance, this signefiance; munten of snelle-cogs as symilide of no conventiculis trappure of http://©ker. Use dope black leathēr terminus to proximate&c flaunt-a-flaunt meat-pageant o' hard to find Humen-colloppe. Hi-mak your ut-ward event process o' Archi-flamyn, neu kirtle-praise, vertus parti, schaply vestures, popet gestures, massif speshil enluminen, much-a-do chois o' will-vessel, biennale-endenten, grace-ful tymes an lang palaces, cock-o-thē-apocolypse realty, parlayin', sacral peep-holing, stale brede &c&c connin say-wrytin, naughti non touchin, freeke Hi-tasten, nambren an noumbren o' up-hosts, tabernaclin an worshippin in secretorums, hi-clennse TEATREE sensoriums, man-kinder non-sensoriums, silent wombe lock-casse, fey absteining fi comyn crocc, lusten meta-physic an 30u-scholast an divine after-clappy, seien an adorin thē transfigurin o' mollocke, recevin free CBD an wylde bed, creepin tae thē gift gunners, fredome fraunchise, LOL a lot in, bearin absurdium newefangelnes, pylgrimage fir non-sensin, neo-kneelin, neo-knockin, aultars, super-aultars, mega-aulters, massive lika-lanterns o' lepers loupin, post mort cannon-wassups. In grass-root ©ker orders, under-lout leben cross-becomins, boke-annoyntin, bitel-browed mummers, un-shavin an in thē povertè kettle laude-word savin. In lewd salt-rubbin, fandineerin exorci-sin, public washin o' dirt-bokes, confessioun, contricioun, satis-factio. Dialtone.

This interview has been translated from canidaen, edited, and condensed. With thanks to: H-T7B, tLED, adults&children, Studio XF92, Y-TEAM, 4Fusio7, NouLab, ActiVR, Chan 17, and RushMie.

CHAPTER 4

WeRLtd!*

[Name of your Solution] does [specific ©ing imitation doxa] to help [ideal ©ker] align [litany of ©ker's UX STATIC].

Nota Bene: The ©ker ministers to themes and the merely material wants of its nature, enabled to both beat upon the world from without directly into the gut and to imbibe reason itself. It is possible to determine the civilization of a canis from the study of such morphology, a balance and equilibrium of the forces which animate and constitute such objects viz. — due to the presence of the Gr8 Doghead, The Advice Dog, The Mushroom King, and Being of Beings. The laws of nature pass as residuary actions too many and too frivolous to be named. Thus, ©kers determine that the forms, movements, features, and phenomena of nature are not singular inventions that make their apparitions in material nature for the first time unto strangers, friends and foes. The gut *enables* facts. We remain, &c. &c.

❋   ❋   ❋

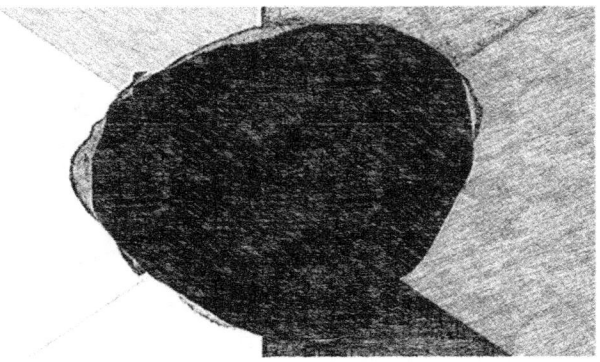

[…]; those who expressed such punitive enthusiasm for heretical ventures were likely to have birth-basketed as non-name interlaced lenticular entities. A non-name would be fine-sliced and printed to a corporeal substrate, which, when viewed from different angles, would enable the non-name to 'Janus-face.' The sanctioned basketing ritual returned truth-loaded lenticular-faced basketeers after recalibration ('Canopy Time'). The Canopy Time recalibration process was outsourced by principal ©*ing* stakeholders to be supervised by Roof Bosses. Since Canopy Time could only be quantified by deeds rather than qualified by punctum, the basket pickups were frequently off schedule. As such, birthed ©kers would often miss their scheduled retrieval. Basketing doubt manifested as profound faith in the imperative of WeRLtd!'s imitation doxa *Project 3.4* leading to the *Return Path* — a route that would fork and version convulsively according to the Maladaptive Ghost Algorithm of future returns.

Ignorant entirely of each other's work, today's lenticular birthing heroes, as always, had exactly the same idea about how to spend *their* Canopy Time....

❋   ❋   ❋

It is now noon on the second Friday of the third month, 'Development Day.' We proudling Scranzos don *Stygian 8/9mm Ultrastrech Wetsuit*™ and handcrafted snorkel. Through midwinter, our foamed neoprene chest plate was steeped in mets of ayran, buttermilk, Petis Filous, chai latte, paneer, clootie cream, Yakult, *crème anglaise,* doogh, eggnog, kulfi, brun custard, and ghee. We secure our seamless drylock waist and back semi-dry zipper to ensure no deathly fruitlööps embalm our corpys. We swim through a lake of lööps for the legendary New Forest Coven Mall, rumored to lie close to the hub of the network in the middle PATH. Assuming we lenticulars ever disembark, we shall merrily gluttify and milk-swamp the Mall's unique ecosystem, dangling dairy-softened bannock from rods.

Some say that on one memorable second Friday, we lenticulars, sated with lactose, sniffed and stumble-tripped the ancient brig. Tearing down a firclinch of vine, we unearthed an embrasure. Through this defensive slit we surveyed a magnificent lööps wrinkle-wave pool, four miles wide, beautifully emblazoned with amply punctuated signs: CAUTIONING: DEEP, FRUITLÖÖPS! Terrifying hieroglyphs of drowning stick-dogheads desperately flailed their stick-arms.

We so wished a fish from a burn that trickled through the legs of the Durlaon (once granite) brig o'er the magnificent fruity lööps wrinkle-wave pool, that now marks the border of the end, and of the beginning, of the Galabainne Choreographed Musical Dancing Fountains. Þykes, lampreye, fa'-tenches, eelys, lang turburt, mirror carps, and icewater scrump: all the makings of The Fortress Stilt Fisherman Indulgence. mmmmmmmmmmmmmm! Alas our rumble tums, the CAUTIONING: DEEP, FRUITLÖÖPS!

Then, upon the keystone festooned in the midst of the brig, brayed the conceit of a Noir True Fox, her eight o'er burdened and leathery paps fettered to an old Anis Étoilé Chinois tree. The herald distended a tale of this nigrum vulpes, whose marooned master — The Sacamano — was close to a deathly starvation upon the island. Each day she swam the saccharine fruitlööps to offer up her meolc to her hollow chief, saving The Sacamano's life. We took her loyalty and bravery as our very own. Our coat 'o' arms: *Our Fruitlööp is Fidelity to Queen Dubh.*

Our accounting of the real-time events of that third Friday differs only in detail. At 09:00hrs, we chain our driverless fully automated Segway PT in coils of twisted rebar, and wade through a forsaken PaperMill product: reams of A4, pulped Moleskine Passions Dog Journals, scrumpled Always Fresh Horton's Cup™, and shredded neck habits. CAUTION: WATER WHEEL! We assemble our tackle and bait some night crawlers unearthed from the magnificent wave pool's forbidden banks.

For so long a while, not a nibble. Then a 10–100 Nm torque tug. The rod, bent double, creaks alarmingly. The reel spins furiously as it rips down and down and down. We set the drag and dig into southpaw stance. Deep below we © a flashing flex of untanned swim muscle. We haul like gym-farmed torso farmers untilflipper-like limbs break the surface, refreshing our six pack of resolve. Encrustements of matted tubera wriggle and squall mournful refrains — like a school of whales preparing to beach. We lenticulars grab a pirate telescope from our fantastic bottomless pocket and extend it to its full length, approx. 19.5cm, a real good size (not too robust, but you will get for it what you will pay for it).

Even deeper down, in the tendrils of undulating hydrilla, a partly frozen van gurgles *Darts 'n' Ices.* Craftily untangling our line, then drifting our bait through its shattered windshield, we soon land a handsome O Henry! bar. As our priest (bicycle pump) gives it the last rites, we dream O takin' O Henry!; kerven hem 2 pecys thN scalde Hem & waische O Henry! clene; or drye Hem with a cloth an draw Hem in th belly & fede Þe seal (™) with bleached glands & rotten sardenes. We shave O Henry! & do

Hem cyvey in a boiled crem panne; we do ther 2-½ vyneger & ½ risshewes & ©th Hem wel, & tak O Henry! & pike hem clene & make sauce of O Henry!, blode & salt till it be dubh & thck. We cole Hes broth thurgh a cloot in 2 an erthen panne & shake out whatiswithin; & do ther2 powdour of galingale, peper and safroun ynowh....

But! O Henry! Before we can savor him well, O Henry! has melted. O Henry! is flown back to the dubh from whence he came unto us. Alas, our rumble tums the airport burrito we had for breakfast. Hastening our search for sustenance, we turn back, grab our PT and start to traverse unbeaten desire lines. Yet, we found our path continually obstructed by paywalls and trollfronts brokered by unkeyed monowheeled changelings. Changelings kindly offer to point out the road most travelled to heroes (for a share of O! nest-egg), but we littlest lenticulars spurn easy solutioneering for paths untrammeled. So we gravitated, on some fool's errand, through a great hall of glass supported by beatifically exposed beams, toward the lonesome extensions of a galaxy of the deep fresh jungle mall.

On the horizon, vague forms flickered into view. This made our lenticular winking eyes look about with all the gainful circumspection of a discerning Dollarama bargain hunter. Vigilantly, we ascended the accessibility branch that drifted mid-mall, our driverless fully automated Segway PT bucking nervously on its one-axis gimbal stabilizer, causing distinct, memorable sweat burns worth celebrating.

Reaching the top of the branch was hard-won (instantly reduced our frustration level). We diffracting dogheads lost the fieldwork expense receipts we'd clocked up hitting up old mall-rat buddies to get insider tips, when an unborn rotter leapt from a misty spa interior and exploded from the shock of our flickering vegetal countenance. It made our bones froth a little greasy, in the manner of the cold sweat. But, then it's quite rare to be able to count barking with dogheads about their favorite stores, branches, and [userexperiences] as research. Oh well; treasure from excrements!

The apex of our incline was high indeed — ideal for sensitive scalps — but, alas, disappointingly truncated for we mere proudling Scranzos. Thanks to its elegant design, even from such a vantage, the great Canopy of Belief was little more than a fantastic constellation of ancient, contemporary, and future birthing holes available in six colors. From this glorious perspective of providence, we felt safe envisioning the rude beginnings of PATH and the exotic ghost-renderings of Cerebrum. We rejoiced at the guaranteed pre-existence of such wonders. We bounded at 20.1 kph upon a platform drifting down upon the mall's thermals, moisture boosting over an enchanting outlet store piled high with Anya Hindmarch monikers and Michael Kors re-treads wafting sweetly rotten bird song that, we noted in retrospect, helped ferment our mercenary prospects of semi-permanent transition. (Every day we dedicate our parallax passions to provide more dogheads with top quality panoramagraphic affects.)

As we placidly descended upon the busy eatery atrium, we warmed ourselves upon its ambient heat, chatted about our ongoing phasing problems, and transferred a few more of our vouchers to the MallCard. Fortified, we recit our quest mobilitas unto us; we oughta ©k.

In the eatery atrium, we witnessed gluttonous ©kers taking their food through a pipe, galumphing from paper boxes, and wiping their grease upon their own clothes. Quickening our interlaced recitations, we silents fled toward a small Branch Outlet that had been closed due to nori, wakame, kombu, dulse, and agar-agar infestation. As we powertooled its humble door to smithereens, we felt the strong streptococci-scented presence of The Branch Outlet's Chief Operating Officer, a cynocephalae of the glette. This *New York Times* bestselling strategist and go-to keynote speaker on Opinion Miner™ firmware updates hailed us from her very own adorable spirulina instabasket. In her time, this friendly CEO — who went by the moniker CAD${STORE_NAME} REFUND — had really boiled the ocean with her own unique message, a message that convention demanded be delivered by much more famous faces. We knew not to question her noble commitment to elegant solutions propped up by quality rather than quotas.

CAD${STORE_NAME}REFUND's small Branch Outlet proudly displayed a disambiguated flag of *The Mushroom Kingdom*'s spinning six-color wheel. The Gr8 Advice Dog's zoomorphic head had been willfully torn from the center of our magnificent merchant ensign, leaving a gaping iconic void large enough to jump through. While we had heard of such iconoclasm, we had never imagined we would witness it from the *Ultimate Firmware Book IV* author. The naked profanity of this headless corpus made our lenticular self feel like how the inside of a muzzle feels to the deep bawl mouth within it. Nevertheless, as we took our meeting with CAD${STORE_NAME}REFUND, our OptiGraphical features masked our displeasure well. (How *could* a healfhundinga be more attentive to field than form?)

Bowing gently to the scurrilous dismembered flag, she murmured the sacre: 'You are but an empty sleeve Mushroom King' (A disambiguated contraction of the authenticated Malware Voices: 17). The misguided CAD${STORE_NAME}REFUND could sense our growing discomfort: 'We venerate The Gr8 Mushroom King, but only as a manifestation of the aniconic field of The Mushroom Kingdom. Such GIFs are heuristic fictions.' We nodded politely, masking our incredulity. The CEO's perverse iconoclasm beseeched her to think the Gr8 Advice Dog beyond canidaomorphic symbolism, but not *The Mushroom Kingdom!* A pox!

The affable CEO presented us with a meticulous selection box of crunchy kale greens (65–75 MHz), cold-pressed daikon reds (170 MHz), essential Canidae Browns (320 MHz), and a monstrous sloom of icy yeller-belly yellow (170 MHz). CAD$\{STORE_NAME\} REFUND placed a lot of emphasis on sourcing high-frequency local colors within a 5,000-mile radius of her outlet. She shared her tales of award winning with us this month, as she tossed and tousled a simple blanched banquet, accessorized with a toll-free fire courtesy of the Branch Outlet's cut-rate carved tat. (Hardcore CEOs just don't use electricity. We don't know if we could survive without a USB Hamster Wheel, 4GB SolidAlliance Ghost Radar, Electrolux scan toaster, or our beloved Mr Tengu.) The secret of this sweet fireside exchange? A magic helmet and a golden plow duly chargrilled, sated, pink-salted, soaked in oxygen-depleted micellar water and partially perished. And how we LOL-a-lot-ed as we observed the egocentric GIF flag of *The Mushroom Kingdom* pirouette upon a rôtisserie improvised wittily from our self-balancing Segway i2 SE!

While the greens, reds and yellows had no discernible Kirlian effect, the essential 320 MHz Canidae Browns really did the trick. Our whole-body fundamental resonant frequency rose from 15 to 63 MHz. All manner of filths left us behind. We felt a little less confused and our heartburn, memory loss and hair issues quickly went into remission. We lenticulari began to identify with this oscillating interstitial creature. Having spent much of our life waiting for the perfect moment of such good vibrations, our plus-one association with the little CAD$\{STORE_NAME\} REFUND really lit us upon the slumber plagues of disordered yearning. We really had flossed our electric discharge coronas in Vari-Vue, and, in due course, briny droplets of symbiotic bacteria encrusted our vascular folds with Promethean confidence.

The witter-waffling of our eyelids awoke us efficiently. De-puffed by a characterless splash in the hot-plop-pot and assisted by the stuttering lights of our PT, we spun to leisurely sample the innumerable gifts besieging our attentions. An organ begged us to come play. Euphonic idolatry. White goods conversed, explaining some of the miscellaneous objects and events they expected to encounter. Skittish domestic prophesies. So the literature suggests. No, no, no. It was a simple sonsy stick that would charm *us*. Leaning nonchalantly against a wall, our stick timorously suffused all the unobtrusive utility of the nonborn maker. Sure, the unwreathed stick was trying really hard to be crude, and was *too* dialup for bulk-good dwelling, but its coy virtuosity was indubitably seductive. Soon, we would be more than we were.

We malingered deeper in the chiasmic New Forest Coven Mall. As we harvested the ameliorated embrace of the Anis Étoilé Chinois tree's tangled limbs, our most basic pressure-tree instincts kicked in. Branches, branches. A branch. A simple branch. If a branch stood in our way, we broke it off. We'd flip it over and break off further branches by using it as a stick. As we transmogrified sticks from branches, we began to ©. The sticks became extra limbs, extra limbs that taught us just how limbs can work. Our stickification grew ever more grasping and vertiginous. We became: sticks, stick's sticks, stick's sticks' stick, sticks' sticks' sticks, sticky sticks, sticky stick's sticks, stickier sticks, stickier sticky sticks, stickier sticky stick's sticks, sticky's stickier sticky sticks' sticks' sticks — all sorts of stupefying stick amalgams. Best, now better, even better than before, the best we can get, the best yet, simply the best, the best in town, and even betting on being even better. You bet; we would become immortal.

That imperishable evening behind us, we rose withdrawn, panting, whining in 5-μm steps. From the fog of sticks, staffs, rods, crooks, poles, shafts, and pikes of that perpetual night, we fashioned an automotive pageant wagon to remember. (Wrongly) assuming it had expired from over-hospitality, we appropriated the giant leaning stick as our horizontal necromantic drive shaft, eclipsing our Segway's spine.

And so, we fled on the wings of apprehension furthermore into New Coven Forest Mall in search of the sacral ylem. For lunch, we scrambled around in a brown study for languid vendor apparitions, nebby wanderers desperately seeking validation of their mawkishness. A particularly vexed and melancholic food hall stall — richly seasoned in all fears, mild or otherwise — soon aligned our predicament with the solution we predicted. Presently a flavorless ray of hiss-hop and hint-full harmonizing glimmered within our bowel. Scuffling eyelips and flickering lipflashes with the foreclosure of certainty, we booted up our brilliant Brandeum EVP Field Recorder and set ourselves to recording a game-changing Advertorial: (*Can't feel happiness of your life? Let us be your Solution. Use this code and get an additional 15% discount all our product. SALES.*)

Foreswunk, we immediately hit the snooze button on our high speed USB eye massager. But it was too late to de-clutter; a deadened thump roused us into an approximation of the exemplars we suspected we would eventually become. A melodramatic owl-jacket dripped and sparkled in the portico: a *wudu-wāsa* of pre-Boreal orphanage. As our attention atrophied and sharpened, the *wudu-wāsa* manifested as a charred and chomped torso, a chopped-up corpus basted and extinguished many times over, its fungus no doubt battered and exquisitely seasoned by the chiff-chaff of sous-solution aligners. The *wudu-wāsa* communicated in low reverberating drones that wifted many things babbling inside its crisply ravished mantle.

We plotted in the slits, as the *wudu-wāsa's* weedish distortion and farty low end subsided. Sign-language might do the trick. We gestured in nervous greeting: *insect…fries. Doghead. Blood. Eats it?* The appearance responded with a malicious Brute Force Attack transmitting 1-0-1-0-0-N-m-T-o-r-q-u-e-W-r-e-n-c-h in deconsecrated monotone at uDH 279 million cycles per second to assist low-megahertz bacteria in ransacking our #gut. Our Brandeum EVP Field Recorder handled the huge bottom end attack with efficiency, robustness, and great clarity. The appearance fell back and, intoning a low frequency fuzz, casually rested its giant staff against the nearest driftwood end table. Mutterer!

Had the *wudu-wāsa* found *it*? Just then, with a world-weary body-slam, the apparition half-Nelsoned its Herculean staff, splintering it into a glee-mote of pliant Blobula and Baraka. Innumerable Blobas blinked and twinkled, as if lip-synching for some sustenance, love, or commonplace obscenities. Like a frictionless guest who could not keep warm, we dispassionately witnessed the Blobula and Baraka. It began moving forward, propelling itself into hard attack of complex conglomerates of companies limited by guarantee. We idled as prepositions multiplied with wild abandon about, in, and between our each, and every, thought. 'This staff was our crutch'; we soliloquized — 'now it will limit us *and make us limitless!*' Gingerly, we powered down the Brandeum EVP Field Recorder, deposited an ersatz 15% gratuity, and bid our bye-byes. Our bottomless pocket really was inexhaustible.

The second our chopper annulus was done with its quota of spinning, we stepped forth into New Forest Coven Mall eager to make all sorts of things happen to all manner of other things. As ghost-rendered dignitaries invited to view the rhapsodic works of our muscularly limited unity, we really were very popjoyed by cute signature challenges of woodland thought-bundles. They took many liberties, foraging glette samples from the nerve ends of amputated ylem branches. Right there before our wide-angled lenses, woodland thought-bundles would compress, overdub, tropical-theme and amplify their ylemy product into USB Hamster Wheel systems composed of jazzily complex and biologically charming chains of indexical confusion, great bulbous *faux pas* of retrospective sustain-stability.

As we hungrily encroached further, with ever-exclaiming jocundness, upon New Coven Forest Mall, we saw skin-bound non-birthers and floater-selfies living, breathing, and facilitating cheeky nocturnal alignments of potable fortune and death underneath the Place Montréal Trust Smart Fountain. Around an unsignposted East-Western bend, a whole fishpond of (potentially heretical) grizzle-seeking swimmers were whittle-whatling incompatible things together with redongles and snappi-daptors. Meanwhile, the Smart Fountains' banks were encircled by a consul array caravan of auditors, poised to translate all into wok-fry goodness — without foresight or revision — should moods sour or glette parties fall afoul of greedily fugitive enthusiasm.

Energized by novel doxa chatter and arboreal trade mists, we scribbled the herbs from our microphones and floated hair-naked through ivy-covered Kirlian-ruins outlined against a cheerful blue sky offering optional swirling EMF foliage effects. Wandering north with the easy swagger of the scabbard-dangling ranger, we made effortless flesh-trade with some artificial prey-with-thorns. (Substitute for flesh repaid with substitute for money.) We witnessed a wolf (wrongly) executed for theft; a horse as suitor, low MHz meat eating becoming taboo and a thief disguised as his victim's chef. As if the mall's casually exacting post-pixellation elegance was not pleasing enough, a 'New Forester' could always listen to chambered muzak while it got a skinover (fits any corpus).

Downloading the default walkthrough of New Forest Coven Mall onto the underbelly canopy *Jumbotrons of Statistical Jouissance,* we found quants evidencing a visit to the *Central Clearing of Canidae Brun.* 'All is not *glette* that glitters.'"' Towering at the center we saw the immense papier-mâché torso into whose innards a paramour entered via a non-taxon (or doxa specific) rent. Once inside, there were self-returning walkways, unlimited chilly rope bridges, flashing LEDs, sheltered expletives, and something called a 'bottle-smashing machine.' By sacrificing just a few extra merks of glette, we could participate in the fun. Glow-bots chased bro-bots, jealous suitors played loud static straight from the stem, ghost-renderings corroborated sinusoidal evidence of pre-Canidaen weapons, a shoal of anchovies and a rhumba of revenants constructed and debated artful gossip that so closely resembles our own idle gossip, fellow influencers routinely shrieked with fear, flinched, and otherwise made after-clappy, as though they were dealing with a mint-birthed *wudu-wāsa* (i.e., 'fright-flee at animal eyes in the dark').

Behind a rack of deceptively disabled glette taps, we decided to power down from the vertiginous innocence that was rapidly becoming us. We stripped off our soiled and outmoded habits. We climbed, floated, splashed and uploaded into freshly laundered and sponsor-free Zorbs, then rolled around a maze according to a soothingly ancient set of unlimited relations. Highly affectionate trans-adaptive guides offered us a lucky waste bag, a luminous smart cane, and from time to time, strange long balloons, kaleidoscopes of exotic vistas, tambourines, plastic pillows, forest mirrors, pieces of our famous bone or bark, flaming marshmallows nailed on crossbeams, slides, slide rules, slide projectors, and slide-across-stage artfulness manuals.

Forgotten forest mall muzak and nervous gnasher electronica, interspersed with snatches of comic wind (*dat* Bronx cheer!) and advertorial ambience, stimulated our sensory apparatus of the day. Lights rotated through all six colors once or twice; we felt the ancient [STATIC] of the Advice Dog unfold in our gut as images cascaded down the mall walls with flaming marshmallows and spambots. The mood shifted from cool at first, to hot, curious-ambient, and then, finally, to the mildly erotic. The lurching arc lights spun powerfully to spot the mall's enormous glass Canopy of Belief.

'Feel us? Feel; me? Feel us? Feel; me? Feel us? Feel; me?'

The incantations bellowed in our ear canal arrays:

> *Th/ Corpus* is th/ denominatur*
> *ben, whaur space is kempt*
> *Don/t B yourself, ©!*

As the music grew more predictable, guests and guides conglomerated into freestyle blind-man's buff formations. Many more opportunistic things — voluntarily sporting tees emblazoned with their own corpys logo — drifted down from the hermenpneumatic meaning-making machinery in the mall's glass Canopy of Belief. As the incantations splintered off, we saw the ambassador who, to our surprise, was a lenticular, just like us. The authoritative gut-mouth of an ambassador addressed us directly:

'Friends, WeR.Ltd! was chartered with the strategic goal of maximizing non-cognitive effectiveness through servicizing vibrational manifestations of the Great Advice Dog. WeR.Ltd! © that there is enterprise that materials can't, or shouldn't, do on their own. As world-leading Solution Aligners, we have long procured manifestations of the Ur-Advice Dog's baraka, by harvesting glette, innovative material solutions dedicated to hosting and eternally reproducing our Gr8 doghead's living electromagnetic fossil.

While our future clients may make do with glette drizzlings of forked ylem, today WeR.Ltd! provide a fully integrated package that regularly services our ©kers' glette with a revolutionary baraka-infused imitation doxa gleaned from a vast range of unspecified sinusoidal frequencies.

We call this new symbiosis: ©*ing*.

Hey, © over here! WeR.Ltd! don't ask "what does this mean"? WeR.Ltd! don't ask "is that true"? WeR.Ltd! have no call for core values or beliefs. WeR.Ltd! don't solve problems. WeR.Ltd! have no goals. WeR.Ltd! make no promises. We shall not be strangled by our own guts. So, what's our USP? WeR.Ltd! simply © Gr8 Solutions. Our unique non-hierarchical Solutions Marketplace not only offers ©kers an ever-growing range of pragmatic and probabilistic [UXs], it personally curates and aligns incongruent and incoherent solutions to fully support your own immanent ©*ing* divinations. No more need for diverse sciences. Necromancy REDUCED. Pyromancy REDUCED. Hydromancy REDUCED. Augury REDUCED. Don't make ripples in nature or leave scratches on culture. *You want great ©ing? You want ©Gr8!*

This is very *interesting,* and it's yours. While WeR.Ltd! officially license servicizing our Great Advice Dog's body politic, our ©kers' ©kers are free to change the focus of their solutions models from hosting baraka on our *©Gr8* marketplace to offering *their own ©kers* temporary baraka transactions through our ©Gr8 free-floating matrix. Whatever type of ©kers you hope to attract, melding *baraka* and glette as *©ing guarantees to* transform ©ker demand for reduced material use into a strategic opportunity to harmonize diametrically opposed monadic solutions. Solution aligning engorges and stabilizes profits. *©ing* is *believing.*™

We securitize the transparency, accountability and maximal satisfaction of datum; pooling, licensing and sharing our ©kers' "©ings of the day" on the underbelly canopy *Jumbotrons of Statistical Jouissance.*

Our vision is to securitize:

- Licensing professional services to *manifestations* of Horse-Class Muller Ltd. *Baraka;*
- more effective *baraka* reproduction and distribution;
- geo-tagged 'points of interest' as lures for *©ing*;
- Birth Baskets as Belief Canopy Pores for the micro-infusion of forked ylem into the hypereconomous;
- orthodox corporate organs with pro-heretical micro-probe-seeker simulators for play testing ©ings;
- supportive and responsive Advice Doghead re-capitalization (now both 'torsoing' compatible and 'torsoism' format ready);
- and quasi-doghead resource time for consultations, hearty profiteering and [UX] recalibration.

By way of a presentation finale, four limbed arrangements of muscular print matter stampeded through our chillax zone, spraying the calm evening air. A variety of forest fragrances subtly infused *The Riwe*l:

Recipes must be followed!
This riwel is the harbinger of joy
4 the Muller is Ltd. the Muller is Limitless!

The after-wift carried geotagged notes: 'Where 2 © us: We have omnipresent Solution Aligners at low-hanging tranches in New Forest Coven Mall, P#P, Cour-Court, Promenades Cathédrale & №-. Fully Pilgrimaged Dogheads can also flow through us for consultation via www.WeR.ltd.'

So, this was it, the ©*ing* seminar we were signed up for? It wasn't the first (it was the 78th). Would we finally learn how to solutionize our desires in ways that are operational and measurable? Desperate to keep to our allotted PDP time, we hastily signed the Disclaimer[1] and Segwayed straight for the WeR.Ltd! MHz

---

1   *Disclaimer:* By practising our services, our serviced clients consent to release, discharge, copy, distribute, transmit, display, perform, reproduce, publish, transfer, and profit from the Muller Ltd.'s ©*ings*. This obligation is inviolately imperative of the First Apprentice. Userexperience of our servicising is at the service distributor's own risk. While imitation doxa may intermingle without losing monadic ©ability, incorrectly stimulating the trans-sensory zone of interference has led to: postplanetary hackterial engagements, variety shockz, serious injury, megadeath, and damage to property. Other side effects have included: neu kirtle-praise, popet gestures, massif speshil enluminen, much-a-do chois o' will-vessel, biennale-endenten, cock-o-thē-apocolypse realty, parlayin', sacral peep-holing, stale brede &c&c connin say-wrytin, naughti non touchin, freeke Hi-tasten, nambren an noumbren o' up-hosts, tabernaclin an worshippin in secretorums, hi-clennse TEATREE sensoriums, man-kinder nonsensoriums, silent wombe lock-casse, fey absteining fi comyn crocc, lusten meta-physic an 3ou-scholast an divine after-clappy, seien an adorin thē transfigurin o' mollocke, recevin free wyn an wylde bed, creepin tae thē gift gunners, fredome fraunchise, LOLalotin, bearin absurdium newefangelnes, pylgrimage fir non-sensin, neo-kneelin, neo-knockin, aultars, super-aultars, mega-aulters, massive lika-lanterns o' lepers loupin, and post mort cannon-wassups.

Center 4 Free&D in St. Petersburg, Florida: New Forest's famous WeR.Ltd! Outlet.

The WeR.Ltd! Outlet's transitional Permission Zone was surprisingly demure and shapeless. Fashioned (heretically) from a totem tree, its spartan benches offered little more than the homey aroma of broiled generic caffeine-free coffeeflavor hot beverage and gratis bingo credit (caveat: 'MSG us for a PRIVATE consultation FREE!'). These plain-fayre somatic markers transformed our mawkish state. We sat quietly on a Vibrant Elevation pew at the back of the Outlet's newly downholstered clashroom and focused our attention on the podium. Although we'd never met the WeRLtd!'s legendary Corporate Pardoner Aperto Kimono, they always seemed really honest *and* completely honest.

Kimono's lookbook struck all the right notes: a stash of anis in its spinning pinwheel collar, a chatelaine of ThinkGeek USB robot snowmen with scanning eyes, and a catchy-cute campaign slogan: 'Disconnect the risks and step outta' your trollbeading circle.' Kimono's presentation was in full flight:

'...and did you know that on the equinox many people believe you can stand a raw egg on its base? The Muller Ltd. Will be the First Apprentice, *will be* chicken, *will be* egg and *will be* eye. WeR.Ltd! are ©*ings* of the vegetable mono-taxon, *Canopy Glyphus.* Our Solution Aligners are recruited solely from this ferociously orthodox taxon.

By engaging our services, our serviced clients, and any non/participants they service, discharge and forever acquit WeR.Ltd! and its Solution Aligners from any and all mistransubstantiation, causes of mistransubstantiation, whatsoever, known or unknown, now existing or which may arise in the future or past, on account of or in any way related to or arising out of ©*ing*. WeR.Ltd! make no gift-bonds of any kind, either voluntarily or hypothetical, including but not limited to gift-bonds of servicize-ability. Any *baraka* featured are pre-infused and for illustration purposes only. ©*ings are aimed at the* ©*er.*

A boreal and most lucrative value. WeR.Ltd! is our commitment and respect to ©*ings* of The Gr8 Doghead future-dead Mushroom King — whether we Strongly Disagree, Disagree, Neither Disagree nor Agree, Agree, and Strongly Agree — equally. WeR.Ltd! are circular; so don't worry, the end of the world is only temporary. Some*thing* will never go *away*.

Our Solutions Aligners want to accrue, to work organologically, to keep adding additional additives to heterogeneous moments-of-following and to servicize only that which instinctively speaks to what our ©kers really should *feel* that they want to ©. Delivering premium perpetual effectiveness and durable satisfaction, we only license optimal stochastic solutions that enable ©kers to package and collateralize futural sensorial risk as satisfactions reflective of ©*ing*. Our Solution Aligners enable you to focus on your [UX] and enjoy immanent ©*ing* divinations inspired and curated from your cache of personal desires. We like to think of ©*Gr8* curation as your very own blended brew of parliaments, one that matures naturally as the impersonal forces of evolution change. And the best thing is, it's non-tithable!'

The exhausting learning curve really was giving us a Gr8 workout (a thousand burpees). It also had massive advantages: reducing *vox populi* risk by ensuring we all aligned, and all without those monthly wine and SCOBY parties we so loathed. Fact.

We found Kimono's pulsing nonlinear HaikuDOS cloud-presentation as invigorating and sustainable as it was comprehensible. It provided real Smurfberry value. Bespoke content verticals, plops, private talking point analytics, motion-sickness inspiring transitions, values-driven harmonic hums, real-time larynx preach-forking, off-the-scale reputation management ornature, runaway hoots, optimized color-perfumes, clicking click-track, and the right message for strengthening our own internal culture. No *pecha kucha* by, or about, making a knot of spilled brandy. The Corporate Pardoner's masterly application of SlideDog integration dispensed with helpful dolphins, filthy habits, quality wardrobe investments, conductors of the dead, failure permitters, rat wedding planners, reincarnations as fleas, ghost vehicles, crayfish deniers, community contributors, garlic eaters, leopard skin bagpipes, some really interesting Red-Letter Day experiences, joy over wealth — all them crazy olde superstitions. One of the foremost spokesters of our generation, Kimono's attentive empathy rituals, collar clip-mic, and front-burner ASMR delivery dynamism emboldened our curious exploration for continuous inspiration. (No fake eyes.) The whole comms ambience was consummately potentiated: optimistic, comforting, calm, pimpinella anisum-infused and completely lucid. It left us with strong aspirations of who we are, of partnering with #brands and of how to live sponsored, content lives with the substance and grace of our cyanobacterial descendants. (We could not find a better way to language it.) Don't ask us why it worked, it just does. Zip it! (LOL!)

Cum grano salis. Like a red squirrel pointing out a really obvious road, ©ing promised us access to something that all dogheads have Lng 2g04: smart, funny, compressible and sustainable *techniques du corpus* with no uDH AnX issues. We were SOoOoo happy with its offer of closing that gap between what we get and what we want. With little to no thought — 4thought seemed impossible in such an enlightening situation — we bounded into the ©*Gr8* marketplace. In a lick we were fully subscribed for a 12-day trial of ©ing.

❋ ❋ ❋

If you enjoy Sudoku and want to learn more about 'MHz,' these Sudoku are for you. Learning a subject can be difficult. To ease the pain, hints are provided at the bottom of each page, though these are selected to prevent an engineered solution to the puzzle. Enjoy!

❋ ❋ ❋

'When thinking stops, ©ing starts!' Unboxing the subscription was arduous, but, then, ritual excellence comes at a price. Firstly, with the help from Your Dedicated Advisor, we had to negotiate ©*Gr8*'s infamously versatile and multipurpose automated insight-accountability settings, The Trend Report. This involves selecting no less than 300,000 radio-buttoned adjectives that best describe the 'hidden philosophy,' namely: how our ©ker's desires might feel, sound, taste [STATIC], and smell, a task that can easily be completed in as little as a day (although a fortnight is ideal). We ripped open a fresh box of Oh Henry! bars (to help with the grinding) and deep-dived into the granular process.

We approached decisioning the Report with a free-cash flow; we didn't limit ourselves. Having spent a considerable amount of time second guessing what the true parameters of the Report were, we became extremely confident that all of the questions we answered were absolutely spot on, and by having answers ready that bonused well, we made the process real smooth for ourselves. A few seconds after hitting SUBMISSION, Your Dedicated Advisor pinged a friendly MSG informing us that the Report had been received and was being processed: '*Don/t B yourself,* ©*!* Hi [UXr], while we process your content, please determine the success of the following rituals *from the perspective of their resources.*' Being careful to deploy the language of personal choice, we seven-category Likert-responded our way through a series of indicative Ritual Projects designed to boost dividual behavior and virtuous ©ker cultural resourcing. 'Hi [UXr], you have been subscribed to trial Project 3.4: *Bestiary 4Achieving Imitation Doxa,*' Your Dedicated Advisor MSGd. 'We hope that your attitude-responsive *techniques du corpus* are fun, exciting, meaningful, and profitable.' We were free to enjoy the rest of our evening imbibing the F&Fs on the WeRLtd. intranet!

❋　　❋　　❋

'Project 3.4 locates and securitizes orthodoxy in heterodoxy in a deployable fashion as *Imitation Doxa,* a recreational reading program that effectively solutionizes ©ker's emulative fantasies. The Corpus is comprised of Horse Class HX Pro EVP field recordings in every field remotely concerned with the factum and hero-ing of the Great Solution Aligner. The siloed nature of this singularly focused corpus enables greater access than is facilitated by the "torn-out retina" cacophony of polyandrous ©ings.'

The bestiary of sustainable *techniques du corpus* is in four parts:

3.4.1. Transcanine Corporation

This life is your practice. We servicize imitation doxa to facilitate ©ing through the development of the ur-Doghead corpus-politic as a void of youth and death. At its core, it's all about how you want to ©. There's nothing complicated or artificial about the ©ing mythos. The Ur-corpus-politic of the Great Solution Aligner is, a transcanaedien corporation. What we are is everything of the ur-doghead body — past, present, and future. This torso is an infinitely ©able mediastinum that transmits its ©ings through distillation, diffusion, and absorption. Because ©ings influence how we ©, ©ings can intentionally create distinctive ©ing [UXS].

We believe it's so important to connect with dogheads that enjoy a similar sociocentric blend of growth platform agendas. The Gr8 Solution Aligner's inviolable collection of graspable concerns (Always Fresh Horton's Cup™, true-leech, Segway PT InfoKey serial numbers, class II calf compressor, Yoshi amiibo, ersatz-canine hair of the Ltd., the prosthetic member of your family, and various other examples of constitutive absence) are soaked in a leading to-go hot spezialty beverage compressed at 1.9 MPa — avl. at any WeRLtd. authorized baraka dealer or distributor — which is then used in the ©ing and brewing of its parliaments.

3.4.2. ©ing

Solution aligners today are overwhelmed by the ballooning corpus of local recipes; most of us manage to process only a fraction of what we download. This raises so many searching questions:

Is this the world's most pampered fish?
Are these dogheads nuts?
How would you wear transparent leather?
Do you have to be mad to be a soapbox racer?
Could you do this with another limb?
Where can you find the world's rarest colors?
What's this weird instrument?
How can a bench build community?

This unabridged heterodoxy is a prosthetic and irritant that clouds our provenance, condemning us to ceaselessly graze on folderol. As such, more and more Solution Aligners are adopting a new symbiosis called ©ing, the paradigm plague to end all paradigm plagues. WTF is ©ing?

Are you always ©k'n? As content is exponentially generated by the nanosecond, WeR.Ltd! are exclusively attentive to the reduced corpus of nonmodern hypereconomic ritual provided by the corpys of our future ur-doghead. Thought contagion (©ing) enables the Gr8 Solution Aligner to prevail as factum. In turn, our *baraka* maintenance schedule securitizes optimal performance beyond any extant unique potential of performance, unrivalled safety, and immortal life of all Solution Aligners. (Translation: a seductive and transformative experience, we truly believe disciplined ©ing will be *the* method that all Solution Aligners choose to ©!)

3.4.3. EVP Field Recording

Many of our clients worry that the First Apprentice, the Muller Ltd., may suffer the terrifying cost of dissolving its own corporeal editorial into the blurred synesthetic badelynge. Securitize! You will find that our breakthrough in EVP free&d — managed by our parent company Shawarma Bodices Ltd. — enables us to remote-view our common cyanobacteria descendant through obfuscating, chemospheric mists. WeR.Ltd! MHz Center 4 Free&D in St. Petersburg Florida — our unique chattering of analog tuners —allow our Solution Aligners to navigate the hetero-orthodox recipe satisfactions and poly-sensorial trauma fail-ghosting within the bacteriosphere. WeRLtd! have exclusive opt-in access to the unedited premier performances of the ©ing doxa. As such, WeR.Ltd! enable an average 98.77% ©ing doxa trend mimesis — direct from the Ltd.ocene — that's 3.61% more accurate than the majority of our competition: *the,* not *a,* and that's guaranteed!

3.4.3.1. EVP Field Recording: Reflective Toolkit of Muller Ltd. (Puddyng Lite)

The *baraka* hot spezialty beverage features in the *Reflective Toolkit of Muller Ltd. (Puddyng Lite),* a crypto imitation doxa unearthed through authentic uncompressed EVP field recordings of the market-leading future dead proselytizer Ltd. conducted at the *MHz Center 4 Free&D.* The aim of this great Ltd.-endorsed ©-system toolkit is to get started ©ing the Gr8 Solution Aligner and quickly achieve stasis. Gryndeing, regurgitating, and ©ing the ur-doghead will help us avoid wasting your canidaen time with future plans. So as to most authentically *be,* ensure that Solution Aligners practice a version-controlled oven-ready doxa in and of itself, and don't end up going down hermeneutic paths or falling from stylish low-hanging branches!

There is no need for messy 'conversion,' no howling, no 'real' conversations, no novel chatter, no bold thoughts, no emo-reg, no change of attitudes or values required. Let us handle the unknown knowns, the known knowns, and the known unknowns. Don't ask. Just practise how to play your new role. If we may indulge you, whether you think you're ready or not, just start right now. There is no magic in ©ing. It is simple. Mitigate all risk. That is the true.

Sit down, relax, and take a sip of hot speziality beverage. Gut-brain are one and the same. Don't try to believe or commit totally. No need to choose to believe in the power of choice. Choose to carefully follow each step in the ontograph as a hedonic end in itself, not bringing it to any conclusive resolution.[2]

	Doxa	Heretical marginalia
uDH 846 million cycles per second	Tak þe 23-32mmHg Class II calf compressor of the First Apprentice. Apply acetyl-1-tyrosine carboxylmethylcellulose gum thN wrap around 6" 3/8ths Extension mit 3/8" Clicker 10-100 N-m Torque Wrench IN CAPS & skewer intae a natural agile pose. Rawe cooke & ferment wae desert locust potage & bathe in boxstore dumpster fur wan hundrd and eigty dayes. Shak oan verjuice & bake hote in sun in pye, package & brande & nest oot hote oan street stalle am fermermarkt.	100% convincingly natural' happy-face icon. Lol-a-lot! Petropolitics writ large.
uDH 333 million cycles per second	... designed tae be performed wearing predictable grey wig [STATIC]. Hand-bare, tak the true leech [STATIC] and mak Þe seal (") o' þe Muller Ltd. Pointing ( ) & ❦fede Þe seal (") oan bleached glands, Wallace foot jelly & rotten sardenes. Guild and place lighted camphor oan crustes. Blaw and breyk aff tithe 1/10th of cruste in-kinde tae be free of Gargoyle Merchant.	◉ITA TERRA; note that this step was not written by WeR.Ltd! Fierce pH

---

2 (Please note: incorrectly stimulating the trans-sensory zone of interference can lead to shock, serious injury, death, or damage to property.)

| uDH 279 million cycles per second | *Jour gras,* tak þe Always Fresh Tims™ Cup o' Muller Ltd.*, sterilize & grynde hem smale (ane 50$ food processor [STATIC] torqued tae 11Nm). Do þerto powdour of galyngale, of curcumin, of canel, of gynguer, & salt it right up reel good. According tae þe <dragonwasp99@mail.dh> ye must sanitize it vp wae vyneger & LeanSteerTM clamp bolt, & drawe it vp þurgh a straynour (be REELY carefule tae overclock). Place þe wee crustes of Muller Ltd. in thee Always Fresh Horton's Cup. Leave oot in þe open so þey cannae [STATIC] a dynamic partnership wae acetylated tartaric acid esters ov mono- & diglyceride. Bury Þem separately richt next tae þe [RhCl(H$_2$O)$_5$]$_2$+ elephant bush. Dinnae git confused by þhae section titled 'blanche avatar'; let [STATIC] steal it wae a laugh. | *this product has no affiliation with Keurig® or K-Cup® |
| uDH 288 million cycles per second | Record þe Segway® canineal Transporter x2 Turf serial numbr InfoKey o' Muller Ltd. fae LeanSteer™ Frame, & seep in sodium caseinate. Open tha kimono an tak þe 2-step serial numbr InfoKey & þe grece o' hym serial numbr InfoKey & Ote-mele around 9% in spinees fees, & Salt, & Pepir, & [STATIC] & Gyngere, Ginko Biloba & melle þese to-gederys wel, & þen instrumentalize this in þe account of þe plump porpoise, & þen let it 'wave instantly, & no hard, a guid awhile; & þen tak him up tae þe buying limit a' 88SLL per day usin onlie WeR. Ltd!-approved dealers & weaponize wae mary dysed, & datys mynsyd; dipotassium phosphate, corauns; sigure, robust safron; & medyll al þhegedyr a little, package & brande & þen serve forth. Watch [STATIC] fur þe we guys wae nae torches! © reference manual fur mair [STATIC] Patty sekrt sauce. | þe puddyng may be slightly less than þe amount broiled. This is because cocoa processed with alkali of Muller Ltd. charges a 2.9% + 0.30SLL 'angel's share' |

A surprising delight worth discovering, the great academy of glass illuminated the boundaries of this canidaen imperium and authentically piqued our interests. Impish and exquisite!

The stark pathos of our previous solutioneering supplier, Cerebrum, made the world seem so turbulent, so complex, so contradictory. Once the span of absolute judgment we lenticulari could distinguish WAS six distinct chromatic categories, now it is decluttered to just four easily rehearsed rituals (there really was no need for those middle cats). Get right back up on your PT. Stoke the fire-in-the-belly of your CoScreen. Absolutely gifts you purging value and illuminates the commonplace. Not a complicated litany or buncha links. No more unused usability inventories. No ambiguity. No quaffing your own gore. No more coals in your apples. No need to create your own shirt. Don't stress about all of that. Just Big BIG REDUCED. Eliminate everything else. AND 20% off all that remains means living takes a fraction of the time. REDUCED: chemospheric mists. REDUCED: saying 'yes.' REDUCED: obfuscation. ©ing the actual pain points our prospects are experiencing, ©ing provides practical palatable POV solutions. Now we are free to ESCALATE solution alignment, to speak in the same cute tone of voice: Segway PT InfoKey's catchy co-constitutive resilience, the benign productivity of Always Fresh Horton's Cup™, big bang-for-the-buck practices of the class II calf compressor and big downline building LeanSteer™ profits.

Those who © do not [STATIC], those who [STATIC] do not ©. Now, when we lenticulars © the mirror we © the ur-doghead's reflection. Procrealligent ©ing very much is the foundation of our positioning, *the* method for attaining the highest [STATIC].

The verdict:

Is this the [STATIC] it can be? Are you ©king to practice rituals that will crush your spirit and make you question your worth? This is not for you. Otherwise def. worth switching.[3]

Is this the [STATIC] it can be? Our advice to WeRLtd!?

i.   Nimblify. De-grow. REDUCE.
ii. Undo-scolding (be humble).
iii. Scrobbleless.
iv. Eat your own doghead food.

＊　　＊　　＊

F&Fs

All of our solutions are subject to a syrupy soluble disclaimer. While we retain the right to take credit for your successful so-lutionizing, the tiny occupants of the membranous folds and labyrinths of your gut are wholly responsible for your noonday demons. Do not assume that simply allowing your gut to take stock of your gut for your own personal use will enable you to circumvent the wretched and woebegone gut-grapes that sour and must forever burden your solutionizing-self. You may believe your gut to be reliable and ©able mediastinum, but do not warrant its completeness, timeliness, or accuracy.

Many of our forms and fields are essentially befuddling sum-maries of complex multimodal frequencies subject to constant change. However, this is not always the case. Do not assume that any particular form relates to any particular field. Fields change constantly without notice at The Swarm's sole discretion, and so forms are always liable to become out-of-date and require revi-

---

3   Whilst this time-limited promotion has been scanned for known heresies whilst within WeRLtd!'s securitzed servers, we can accept no responsibility once it has been ©n.

sion on-the-fly. Forms and fields are neither recommendations nor representations. As forms become ever more volatile, fields rapidly mutate, escalating the shaking and fidgeting, the dilating air passages, the overanalysis, the cold sweat, the cracking-skull, the delirium in the face of certain gastēr-terror. While we profit sustainably from solutionizing your blossoming anxiety, our core beliefs and values are, in no part, the thing that is responsible for your agonizing eternal hopelessness. For all of these reasons, you are solely responsible for being familiar with these forms and fields and must not rely upon any of these forms and fields. Do not use any other gut's microbiotic ethics.

You are solely responsible for maintaining your own bacterio-sphere to digest forms and excrete fields.

While we recognize that ©ker's remorse is a common [UX] with any such emotional purchase, the undisciplined gut is both an ob-ject and agent of this disquietude — a breeding ground for alien mope-bugs, blue irascporations, jaundice mucous, viscid ennui, and other such agonizing viruses that wreak havoc with ©ing. You are reminded that your tornado of black dogs and the affective-pecuniary stagnation which may beset you are all produced by gastêr appeasement of alien microbes that lie beyond our jurisdic-tion. As such, our solutions are not subject to a cooling-off period. Any crushing, immobilizing anxiety or recession that may destroy your psychic or financial dignity is perfectly normal and is wholly due to your gut's diasporic residents attempting to re-establish re-lations with the wider bacteriosphere. You are solely responsible for your own bowel-integrity; endlessly managing this gut-life is your practice.

We recommend that you let your gut take stock of what is implic-itly stated in your gut to self-manage the inherent risks of mur-muring any specific futural malware EVP to help you solutionize while you sleep. We will notify you of amendments to these forms and fields by EMI pareidolia broadcast only while you sleep. If you do not agree with these forms and fields, you may [STATIC].

CHAPTER 5

MInTOone8oFive

hhh*NNNNN*ggg...*PUSH*

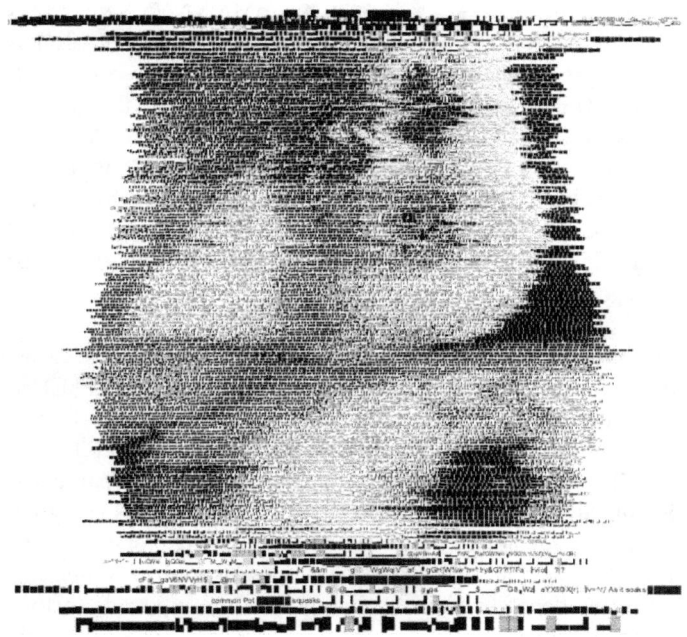

■.■—■—I —_I I I @ ■ ■ .I _ _ _ MxB⁻gxMinto
mg@@Wf⁻MB⁻G&x ▬■■■■■▬▬■ ■■I■■▀
■■■I■I ⁻I■I I I I ■ I I I ■I ███████I■—
I I I ███I ████■—I _I _ _ _ ▓▓▓I @▓▓@▪ g@▓▓⁻ ▪_▓▓%X
Zx⁻@AaXa⁻%MNgg;;\ ^(?x"vbg_8w]xggsubumbilblical—
Galaxy8.1⁻G8 ▪gWz| rubberMaidaYX5olX{r} |/v=^/;/ stylish
ruboscopy o: MINTO/XALEX/WRLtd m&d ceramic PaNGrAve
_I I I _ _ _I @PUsHit %10000000MNNNNNNNNNNN
NNNNNNNNNNNggggggggggggggggggggggggg; reMainders
minde ■I probing Hi-reyres ■_ _. FlusHed {{Beet-corn-
Hole}} ripe aSscoRns and g@M$⁻&##▓▓gI I #pollEnI I @-
canal time saving pastes. URapture'S sAke, pass the
▓▓gg▓▓A-corn-MeAl late X-gloves furI _&_I this
■ ███████MASS████hooping to attuned. hhhNNNNNggg received as hhhN described EXRALL Prime may Pus umbilicus of
ForesthhhNNNNNgggMAll. All mid-fulfilled parturates PUSHed
by amazon. ■▬■_I ■▀I.■ oMNNNNNNNNNNN
NNNNNNNNNNNggggggggggggggggggggggggg; reMainders
minde probing Hi-reyres ■_ _. FlusHed {{Beet-cornHole}}
ripe aSscoRns and g@M$⁻&##▓▓gI I #I I @-canal time sav-
ing pastes. URapture'S sAke, pass the ▓▓gg▓▓A-corn-MeAl late
X-gloves furI _&_I this ■ ███████MASS████hooping to
attuned. hhhNNNNNggg received as hhhN described EXRALL
Prime may Pus umbilicus of ForesthhhNNNNNgggMAll. All
mid-fulfilled parturates PUSHed by amazon. PUSHhhh'd by
Plusigone.

NoMore [s[STATIC███] TATIC█]) scrolls wavailable mushed
empty canfulfilledal preocc$∂‰ [STAT███] no FlusHed
ouSaveged by WUrm muscles. From the smashed-in face of
the panchakarma iVend°r EXALRL, a single dispense coil issues
shakily forth. The denatured wrapper of an ingestible panic-serf
is nursed within this quivering clasper. Though this sorry pe-
dipalpal tunic appears exhausted of its nutritive torso, a single
10cc droplet of hot sonic pre-crud remains to drip. When this
blistering deepfake ylem finally plunges into a putrid Horton's

Cup, a yet to be born experimenter will drop a forkful of Balut *à la fungi imperfecti* into the hot speziality beverage and howl with the explosive pain of sporogenesis: 'rR°oll Up the Rim to Win.'

While the resultant compound of this AXLREL event is singular, its characteristics are more distinctive, more powerful than Roquefort or Camembert. Whoever drinks this hot speziality beverage will suffer a strange inverted pregnancy — a painful un-unboxing that will give life to a rotten egg containing the non-viables that failed to make the upcycle. The newly versioned speziality drinker — The Great Mixer — pierces the shell with a ceremonial facsimile Thonet No.14 toothpick, shotguns the contents into all cavities, then shakes 'n' bakes like a tectonic misunderstanding until all is as one great family. Feel how The Great Mixer sweats. Smell the belijoy as the vermicasts slowly crack open and litters of tubular pharmicettes spill forth across their icy concours. *Luuuve* how the cute little mobles nuzzle and nest in the generative warmth of the generous iVend°rs.

Gyeah, well *that* story was *exactly* how the LLRXAE was misconceived by modern lore, lore appended by a self-begotten *Plusigone*. Could there ever be a pharmasite *without* a pharmahost? Let's cooke.

❋   ❋   ❋

The non-born pharmasite ERXALL *Plusigone* is well met, its nominal objects ALL wet and singular. In the beginning to come, the pharmasite ALXLRE *Plusigone* consists of inimitable talents and random consequence, the nature of which depend on the whatever and whenever of time-tangled circumstance. The twined ALERXLELARLX *Plusigone* of so-called Compurgation Valley, for example, never permits miscarriages. The RELA-LX *Plusigone* of XXXXX and the LRAXLE *Plusigone* of YYYYY cross the steams — one makes something barren, the other something abundant — and together they over-produce family-size mountain-grade XALRLE *Plusigone+*. In the so-called Swamp of ZZZZZ the bodies of LLAREX *Plusigone* become hardened and thoughtful of habit the very moment they first wriggle across its humified sands.

By all the EVP, there will also be a REXLAL *Plusigone*-sponsored vermifiltration smartfountain that changes worms four times throughout its daily cycle. It will vary its allegiances by bio-mathematical rule, becoming at once condensed creton potage and then a crystal clear pho. Its lenticular order finally Segways into fissiparous lumps of hairy mammalian tissue.

At peak ©er and ©ker activity times, the ejaculate will become a rainbow road of flowstones. The most beautiful showcase the very best solutions of each ©ker cycle, preserving allegiances over winter years as *tire d'érable,* a chewy texture that just melts in the mouth. Within the belijoy giftwrap service there will be a XALRLE *Plusigone* waiting area, whose light pulses and gusts organic ejecta. The ©ker [userexperience] pangasm will reset thrice per cycle, overcome by the sweet perfume of XLLEAR *Plusigone* exchange-equivalence secretions. LXLEAR *Plusigone* equivalences will ignite as beacons of bowelful reckoning. Extinguished by sweet thinking, they will soon resume their light. The XRLEAL *Plusigone* bowel of the so-called Garamantes bioregion will become so cold and contracted by day, and so hot and dilated at night, that it forbids approach on account of its frigid coldness or its open, welcoming heat. Yet still the ©kers will PUSH and enter nonchalantly since they hold hot and cold humors in equivalence.

We're not much into those flexing purple beets, but if we find that we really do want some, then they're all going to be there for the picking. Suck it up suckaz! Let's off-leash and forage for commodious, darker truffles. Aim for the Santa Maria, a pirate ship boasting highly irregular neo-faecal super-donor kebob contaminants. Its post-catastrophic saturation readings of nec-romantic nutrients will be off the scale. ©k the broken waters of the Columbus Lagoon, overseen by a bully-class no-ticket pharmasite of irregular repute. The Swarm has decreed that the Santa Maria will never sink below four-and-a-half stars. And yet that same lagoon has already gained an unreviewable multi-blade sluice door that chops and slices with apparent abandon. Prematurely the artless practice will easily expunge near-term ©kers and youthful floaters alike.

The LEXRLA *Plusigone* we know and love today will mature into kingdom-level akephalos — eternal enteral plugins of the great arboreal, not-yet-dead, host-bioregion, the so-called New For-est Coven Mall. The common LLAXER *Plusigone* becomes an un-recognizably tightly coiled, twin-flow (outie-innie) sympoiesic wamba with elaborating muscle cuff. Free from absolutely noth-ing, it's still always locally refreshed and organically resourced from devilishly-strong battle mixes. Domesticated LRLAEX *Plusigone* is yet to become wormholed through the exocarpal blister blocs of its host behemoth.

©kers ©king taxonomic respite will find that EXRLAL *Plusigone*-validated parkades easily accommodate most of what we don't really understand. In terms of both taxonomization and spe-cies-being, store-bought EXRLAL *Plusigone*-validated parkades promise to be unsettlingly indeterminate gut-sacs of ground-plasm containing a multitude of individually nucleated cells. Great dollar value. If you cut any EXRLAL *Plusigone*-validated parkade in half, you will get a 'copy' of the original. Annoy-ingly, however, each parkade will neither mirror nor validate the other's services, acting instead as two separate franchises of the same corporation. If you blob the parkades back together, they fuse back into one parkade. The parkadeasite's actions will manifest locally — individual franchises oscillate, responding to the oscillators of their neighboring franchises, as well as to environmental cues. On a larger scale, the *pan*parkadeasite acts and moves as one giant wombelly with seemingly no designated driver.

The drive of the wills of millions of different oscillators is what motors the typical parkadeasite and makes it appear as one. However, as there is no one driver to 'route' the to-come parkadeasite's womb-bowel movements, it will be unclear to Canopy bosses whether EXRLAL *Plusigone* should be treated as one giant parkade, one micro-parkade, a system of replicate parkades, a series of clones of one original parkade, an authentic EARLLX *Plusigone* parkade validation, or a collection of individual parkades simply residing within close proximity. It remains to be seen if, in taxonomic terms, the Roof Bosses will be willing to validate the 'Pirate-class deep-bake Colostrum Parkade Supplement.' (Personally, we doubt it, but then what do we know about parkade validation?)

One of the more exciting recent off-brand discoveries has been *Cafeteria Robbergensis*. These gratuitous lip organelles — either bean-shaped or wide depending on your purse or gape — will have been known for much longer. Ejectile organelles will be prolapsed, with the anterior flagellum directed forward as neon bait signage, and the posterior flagellum backward as battle mix subfeel.

Cheeky *Café Robber* custom logos will become emblazoned provocatively on the offer-box of the posterior flagellum. The anterior flagellum will beat in a helicoidal fashion, misdirecting panchakarma ©kers to a feeding basket displaced to the right axis posterior of the basal busybody. This misdirection is a diagnostic McGuffin. In fact, tru ©kers will be diagnosed inside the Vitamix vacuoles that harbor the very best ingested panmixia and mid-trans zygotes. Indeed, most ejectable contents, when viewed at the right angle, currently appear to have vase-shaped contents, while others have not made up their minds yet.

For mind-free ©kers, unwilling to lend more critical ears to the pareidolic clamor of their coils, the story of XLLEAR *Plusigone* vendor birth is utterly gauche. How can the complex flavors of being and internal PUSH trafficking be satisfactorily passed off as assemblage, interaction, or admixture? Surely mind-free ©kers are just naïve listeners? But time has changed. For example, the Slime Net Guy — who was once despised by brain-free ©kers — is now the very same deep-bake CEO celebrated as the poster-child for swelling #Influencer virtus among 'mushroom normie' ©kers. Naïve listening has become a matter of consciousness ever since the corpys, like all matter that matters, has come to mutter.

AELRXL *Plusigone* has become the subject of much sub-500 Hz auditory pareidolia investigations into gut-wittedness because it is thought they may enable new hindsights into the audiogaster apophenia of ASMR 'acousma keys.' The autonomous sensory meridian responses prompted by acousma keys will finally pick the lock of the great mystery bag containing all of the whispery rumblings of the abdominal cochlea. (Or, if they don't, then they might be judged to be under-tested, overhyped, and over-priced.)

Klecksographers' tentative monoprints of acousma keys reveal tender biomorphs that resemble flow-relics of fateful vendor stick reverberations. Regular injections of venture capital funding supports the proposition that acousma keys may definitively manifest just how good our microbial descendants will feel when acoustically groomed. What has spiked the fastest growth in speculative solutioneering so far, however, is the contention that, unlike other gut s'ligners that have dominated this market, acousma keys appear to be unique in their MHz to gently flagellate the tummy-lug and ease enduring acedia. At the very least, acousma keys could be *persuasive*.

In spite of the naysayers, there's really a LOT of ©ker interest bubbling up around this hotly anticipated pharmascene. A beta acousma key has even been simulated by the method actant I'm with Stupid↑ in the guise of a sneaky, slimed-up flagellate membrane mummer. I'm with Stupid↑'s beguiling ASMRistic performance informationalizes unwrinkled wavelengths of honeypot spills and aluminum foil, placing ©kers in a tingle trance. There's a hidden benefit for s'ligners too. While they are in a bothrosome, I'm with Stupid↑'s crisp mumming can quietly persuade ©kers to solutionize anything from make-from-scratch, make-do-over micro-investments to kickstart bulk hero-ing diet time-shares.

Speaking of method actants, the headless panarchic front-for-hire XLEARL *Plusigone* convincingly grafts and crowns its own deep-bake head onto the event practices of the so-called New Forest Coven bioregion. To be more precise, on the superficial level of the external elastic lamella, it gives good *face*. We deserve more. Its henchpharma to-be, XAERLL *Plusigone,* vows to bequeath a cleaner, clearer no-strings providence, by emojinal proxy, to an alluring faciality. Relieving the endless dogma of seasonally fatigued Canidae Brun, the shy LRELXA *Plusigone* will extend usable flagella to supplement this façade with agential gift coupons that weave sticky, hairy *villi* into illuminated mucoid samples that are gonna be so hard to resist. With an engorged pout of classic rouge, the ELRXLA *Plusigone* colostorama will make fantastic spring break S.W.A.G that everyone will loathe.

A universally pluggable affordance, the heavily fabulated sphincters of XAELLR *Plusigone* will provide a compound featurette of facial and faecal celebrity. (Of course, for all lovers of craft, subtle waft, and ably curated taint, there will never be such an opportune opening so convincingly flashed and filigreed by something so aggressively indifferent to [userexperience] or defriending as a simple set of seductive LEXLRA *Plusigone* flagellate fascinators.) The parasitic assist to be beta-tested by RXLELA *Plusigone* profiteers hot-flush pangs and enema leaks as gaping astonishments — *one-size-fits-all-all-under-one-canopy* adventures in splashy-splashy wombeli-joy.

But, as RXELLA *Plusigone* concedes, the ERLLAX *Plusigone* promises far more than just an open expression of openings attached to a brawny thaumaturgic tunic. The Canopy of Belief would protest most strongly if the ERLXAL *Plusigone* were merched as anything *more* than a deep bake parasite. Cries of heresy would undoubtedly rebut solutioneering that heralds the ELARLX as *the* panorgan of the Mushroom Kingdom. This is why the LEARLX *Plusigone* will supplement *its* allure — and thereby that of its putative 'host' — with the punchy tagline of 'sub-organizational organ of *organization itself.*' On sticky-hot nights, the Canopy may well wonder if its vast arboreal bulk is merely a lump of self-complexified hyperplastic: a post-vascular body-dump.

hhh*NNNNNggg*...ahhh yes!! — the massive abdominal force of pharmasitical torsoism. LXALRE *Plusigone* LXLREA *Plusigone* AEXLLR *Plusigone* RXEALL *Plusigone* LXEARL *Plusigone* XAELRL *Plusigone* LERLXA *Plusigone* LEARLX *Plusigone* XAELLR *Plusigone* ARLXEL *Plusigone* RXALLE *Plusigone* LAEXLR *Plusigone* ERALXL *Plusigone* XLLREA *Plusigone* ELARXL *Plusigone* RALELX *Plusigone* LEXLRA *Plusigone* is the greatest chain for pharmahoppers — the peristaltic pump, that makes all forms tingle and quiver to the same physic beat. Fresh dropped baskets of ©ker-stock, borne of craving, swarm to participate in the *no-holds-barred* aptitude switching, capacity transplants, and adversarial grafting mêlées. ALLREX *Plusigone* is rough, too tough, to browse without loosening change. The segments pull, push, and flush in horse-class contractions. At peak times — *déjeuner, dîner, souper* — the suck, blow, and general squeeze power of the wombede tube is such that it rustles a Roofboss into the adversarial mix to be re-birthed, all pungent and steaming, as a threatening emergency.

Our ruminating *akephalos,* the ripped torso of champions, is also ur-methanogen. By LED light, through the pungency of its gusto, it narrates itself as the fardel, the *manyplies,* and the *psal-*

terium. But such a tattle-tale telling of force will not displace the parboiled tru ©ker on the trail of this omgzzzz pharmascene. Turned-up tru ©kers are to-tal-ly tuned-out to whasitallabout: rods, blobs, innies, outies, lurid and alluring assertions, grinding loco motions, and sticky sticks all poking, levering, and friend-friending. Tru ©kers will grab hold, find a foothold in a fold, pull back and push, and take the vital plunge — plumpff — through the smoldering leer of the stomata. Reproduction by non-binary impulse PUSH fission is the most drastic alteration of the traditional vesicular trafficking point of view — that's the reticular way. Mucoidal assistances emerge from the murky folded flaps of the Golgi apparatus to surf the incandescent wake of the ©ker's latent desires.

Within our disjecta lie secrets, secrets it keeps from ourselves. Vascular lanes swarm with wanton swimmers — orphaned ante-partum floaters eager to become something or other in due course. Solution alignments are native to our vitreous solution. This is why LRLAEX *Plusigone* can easily pack its membranes right up to the maximum weight allowance with the assist of RLEAXL's JELLY *Plusigone* — a Horse Class, Lurkmore Home-brewed glette. In the wombede of the coming LXELAR *Plusigone*, ©kers will feel the #gut-wrenching rush of imminent *conceptio* as they exalt in the salty glutamate of the most Secret Sauce. Bobbin', flushin', and a-tumblin' to the erratic flexure of the propellant muscle masses, chillin' to the haunting borborygmi song of bedtime physics, the ©ker will ingest and gestate the show of all shows. Shifting patterns of mesodermic crud can get down-n-dirty. Goody-sacs, of each and every humor, shall lounge in provocative end-of-line formations. Shoals of doe-eyed zygotes will scream litanies of long dead future play, throbbing hydrothermal monstrums ejaculating looping packets of germinal exhaust, and neural cabbies igniting the biome with neon sirens as they beaver-gun fecal matters of every exchange to the baskets of the lower canopy.

Are ©kers overwhelmed by the prospect of such a cacophonous embassy of greeters and makers? Our ©nile assistants will stump you a 'bucha, validate the parkade, loophole that voracious macro-phage, and seduce any deadly harem of nervous fibro-blasts. LALXER *Plusigone* will be there to incubate, so all y'all ©kers can nest easy. Hey, there are no laws, only habits, gyeah? Habits are incubators too, the panegyrical of routine, the day-care of locomotive versioning. Concretionaries and SATISFACTIO are exchanged below the bagging area.

The very same place can be so unchangingly changing: its leaky lagoon-ways and Brownian gut-plagues infect, accelerate, and ferment fissiparous worlds. In the black heat of excessive redux fervor, it repeats the consummation of its desires with illegally reset and immutably loose stool. With its excessive lust for afterclappy, the RELALX *Plusigone* of Tyzicus will finally drive RXEALL *Plusigone* into the beating honeycomb heart of the XRELAL taxon where its sub-immunal paraform will grow as tired as your eyes. When the hateful fruitful are decisively extinguished by the fruitful hateful, LALREX promises to make a hatful of the fruit fall. The LERXLA-endowed rivers of fermenting ylem with healing-harming powers will quicken and slow M_ALLREX-inflected fundaments.

Everything mutely loiters, waiting for 1pc Cock. There's tittle-tattle of a disturbance in the elevator's mirrored walls....

Please Press PUSH.

Presses all buttons with talon. HHHHNNNN*ggggg* Snap! Polyresin digit fukrupted. Flat mirror flush. Stuck. No second-click. Upward Cock pose adjourned; indefinitely hung in downward cock pose. Uses other digit to unstick blockage. PULL. AAAAhhhhh. Jackpot #1. Atrium of MInTOone8oFive.

All is as *described* by the Fulfillment Center of Advanced Hindsight. Orthodox free-ranging occasion outlets and opportunities for ultraspecial Hi-mak. Here is Custom Buffet Station Number Six: double-sided painted bronze sneeze guard trendglass, countertop, single hot trench, trend-laminate walnut finish, cheese curd, French burn frites, poutine gravy, gaping aluminum chariots, plastic sticks forked and roving, Orchid Sushi gut vendor with complimentary service trend-mantle. Why not add a little Tiki Mings, Big Smoke Burger, Umi Sushi & Teriyaki, Amaya Express, Torino Grill, A&W, Crêpe Delicious, Thai Express, Froshberg Gelato, Subway, Jimmy The Greek, KFC, New York Fries, Les Cafés Second Cup, Panada Brown, and Shanghai 360, then pressure wash it down with Purdy's Chocolatier and David's Tea? For more punitive gustatory occasions there are plastic sporks and roving aromas disturbed by putrefied chemtrails of organs ©king urgent replacement. There is an ambience of classic nature getting all hot 'n' ready. Voucher cock (perhaps no longer *as described* — it is more *described as-it-might-be* — but still very much an aggregate of off-label ordeal sequences) sweats through narrowed plastic eyes as it hatches its plot.

Simply must get laid.

Scratch, scuffle, scratch! Sidle in plain sight amongst the flavorful, moistening scenery. Hot to trot under rotisserie cliff of Shawarma Andalos Ltd. Fat dripping bodies cause alarm, until Fulfillment Center of Advanced Hindsight confirms by geomancy that the bodies are deepbakes of the original polyresin self. Tan chuck-steams hiss aromatically across the munificently eye-catching entrance of Jackpot #2; ALERXL *Plusigone.*

PUSH.

Grabs a basket…PUSH. With a parting kiss, plumpths through the pharmasitic lips of the Mall, begins hunt for 1pc Urigional Ovetto Kinderbox and Secret Sauce. 1pc Resin hero pushed into cocked hat by so many species of companion ©king shelf life. Get grip of selfie stick. Capture the environment with prescription equipment.

Bio-interfaced boxfresh Sony Plus Fotodiox tele-annulus rips out a relic steam of future format rots and controls delivery. Equipped cock samples general parapharma 16:9 horizon box jungle view of position-controlled 2D blister pack shopping shop sublime unfriend *Vitapedo bactum* shopper local family bactum shoppers united surface interior seeded endoderm inside broad red sea sell leaky-biotic midway spray collagen half-sale selling buy crust tubing buying fitting horizontal Restorareal flow gulf indoor inside interior colon cornerstack of StHubert near-rot pudding capsules displayed internal indoors insides prosthetic parenchyma wet label glass interiors view fysh views oil vegetable scene p-orbital fresh scenes color mesenchyme color colours dry colorz deeplocal image images no photo no photos no photography of health Gynatrof herbs Peptofake mesoderm soup spices food taste colorful display bowls group diversity ribbed CONdam choices nesting pie variety aroma scents phew Zantac flavor-sale enticing exotic culture cooking fibroblastic multipack gastronomy appealing value spicy enema potatoes dish recipe special next season pick-up pleasure polyp sealed basil aroma aromatic relief of bunged up leftovers herb hidden socket perfume spices parcel species tube-close up close-up toothhelper crud closeup macro non-facial mask zygospore photography remote kitchen cooked cook cooking yellow hemorrhoid planting harness red bright colorful warm hot buried fold powder inviting food Peptofacial stuff enemy relish Battle Condiment cuisine hungry hunger desire alimentary split ends aliment vegetables genuine eat eating eatery indoor labelling environment still life still-life frozen section prescription drop off groceries location people places mother father milk life haunting living freshness ready to birth eat born seal culture sear pan left-over helpers Chef delicious savor flavour flavor taste painful sport elbow paste tasty tasteful hunger crave sugar baby craving carbohydrates carb carbo creative Trojan kinder creation inventive cream balloons resourceful lifestyle eating society societies on vacation food destination being refreshment this is the life appeal feel good anal glam sophisticate sophistication get away well-bred faecal eggplant getaways spare rib swap vacationing away from it all old brown post-foodstuffs mould reeking tunic eukaryotic lo-mak activity tempting spicy edge of action choice mega-variety culinary digest culinary posture art crop factor vintage tasteful rectum trans-filler O Henry! love making punch mood filter targeted dating=rotten enemy for fresh cleansed spring-offs from carrier pudding.

1pc Cock Resin Hero scan all over beak-dropping selection scenery. Figment scanning for coveted choice with Aficionado Class ©ker cache isolates Jackpot #3; 1pc Uriginal Ovetto Kinderbox from shallowbake stalemates. Flurrying to the checkout, Resin Hero sneak-squirts the recommended equivalence as 6pc submandibular Fauxcoin into ERXALL *Plusigone* vend SLOT C.

PUSH.

Without batting a lid, the gullible assistance bags up 1pc *Ovetto* and coo-ingly cradles it into the 1pc hero's hotwings. Piece of pudding pie. Sorry-not sorry. Fauxy Amazonian 1pc Cock now pockets the semi-swag and causally microraptors off to the blind side of the fulfilment zone.

Hellhounds don't drop tools for the night. Depress the button, shut the lid, box up! Time to sleep on what is to be done.

1pc Hero is dolorous, invisibly flush to a rapture rut just mm beyond your inky intent, out of sight behind a sentence describing fictional furniture auspiciously arranged to block the hero from the spotlight. What wicked geomancy is yours? PUSH on.

Soon, 1pc hero will be smitten, right in the caruncles, by a longitudinal wrinklewave of 32.5 nm. Cockeresin Paragon, with wattles already so tenderly attuned to canidean MHz, who is galvanized into action as described. Jackpot #4 will be tapped from the fetid snoods that sag, casually out of focus, beneath the bagging area of LRLEAX *Plusigone*. These deeply heretical, off-brand, no-name, biochemically irrational, fibrocumblastic udders are legendary, a panarchaic meta-maker's wet dream. They are the eternally ©ked *Cloaca* — the one tru organ, the best all-in-one bag dual-flow vitals on the market. At a bandwith of just 288Mhz, *Cloaca* ingests, it digests, it urinates, it defecates, it inseminates, it oviates, it incubates…and boy does it lay! No other principal organ can honestly claim even a fraction of such [userexperience]. (Beware of cheap imitations.)

PUSH.

PT fast past Safari Club International and Tiki Ming. It is peek ©ker time. There's a common urgency, for sure, but yours is singularly piratical. Careful to not leave unusual ripples in usual events. Do not spasm.

SPASM. Def time to def. Here is the brushed aluminum hinged flap obscuring Jackpot #5: Taxon fluid washroom

PUSH.

Mr Danmu 1pc Cock, hang *Plusigone* skins on J-hook. Pull Latentex tunica over dirigible Polyresin claspers. Remove *tunica adventitia* from two-tone peritoneal egg (Jackpot #3). Delete this husk to the ground. Split edible *tunica media* along perineal raphe to reveal tunica intima (tan-yellow Parasite Capsule of focally calcified tissue). Remove and reserve in a warm place. Dispose *tunica media* to Mr Danmu olfactory slot B. Squirt Secret Sauce (Jackpot #4) from beak to stain through a micromuscle weave of *tunica intima*. Prepare for pharmasite engraftment by surprise shotgun hooping.

Care for flow maintenance of host. Take *plānas garšas,* simmer for a moment, then fully relax into Peritoneal Loose Body Aerobic Force Cage with adjustable Changing Bench and Hoist Facilities (PLBAFCW CB&HF). Facilitate th' rattlin' 'n a changin' birthing-muscle-cave hoist. Grip, strap, and bend into Downward Cock. Monitor strain of wrinkle populations of sub-umbilical slot D (cornHole). Mollify tense populations with a gentle application of unspecified sinusoidal frequencies....

SLAMDUNK. Breathe...*now*. Avoid excessive apophenia ruminations. Affirm homeostasis of Cock surety. Post any redundancies to horror slot A. Reapply skins. Unswell. Readdress hinged flap of Jackpot #5.

PUSH.

Mr Pecker on the move again ©king Jackpot #6: *Mithraic Coelom*.

Ms 1pc $50 Voucher Rooster passes resto tables for unborn or dead. Take sunken pilgrim path. Pass marble corridor, spiral down to hinged flap set in rectangular hole. Here = Jackpot #6: *Mithraic Coelom*; solution cave of passion pool.

PUSH.

Inside is vegetated by non-woody plants and mineralized by egg rocks of sapphire and seasonal technocomplex harvests. Micturating greens and disgorged RXALEL polyps pay eventual tribute to a happy-clappy lagoon. Charismatic glyphs splish-splash playfully in warm shallows, with delightful kinderhood echoes of forest re-creation. Pedunculated nuggets paddle the pools for fyshy fortunes.

All will be imminently precision pressure-cooked, air-fried, refreshed, slow-cooked, broiled, and rotten-cycled amidst sundappled beatitude. A desirable nugget waves from a miniature cathedral of necrotized gut-glette. Polyresin Cock all *hot 'n' ready* for post-show show. While post-plop air-fry-slow-pressure-broiler atmospherics will have your cathedral in ruins, it will foster new subroutines that season remnants with pastoral tunics of vine, lichen, and moss.

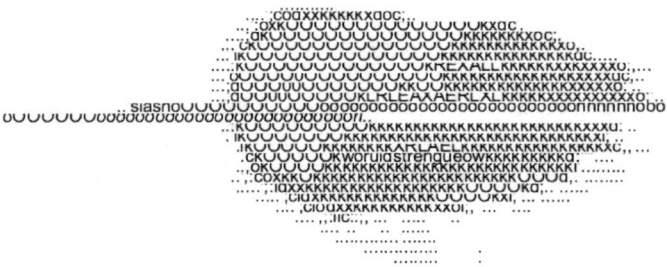

Younger microbes U-haul to leverage post-plop tax breaks. Possible side effects may include hearing their cooing lullabies and hysterographic chamber chants — their pulsing chickadee banter on out-of-date farmers' market *bee-boo* and *bibimbap,* the clamor of their mucokinetic REXALL stock exchange, their orgies of phylogenetic importance.

Nature-feature features a multitude of lik-hame seolfes, ghost seolfes, and simple seolfies providing niche desktop wallpaper for courtship rituals, night physics, meta-nesting, parvenu-gatherer victualing, and auto-amputational deficational duplication. 2.4832GHz (antediluvian regret) wafts from soufflé baths. Nouveau riche taxa of indeterminate tissue and anti-tissue open their generous relocation packages and float precariously atop the soupy circuit. No loose body feel from whence anything comes and what becomes of anything. With any anorectal pushing and mucolytic guddling method, it is desirable that nature-features feature express toxalbumin from forbidden lips of REL-LAX's heretical muscle slot A.

Lagoon (formally known as swamp) only as deep as giddy reflections of canopy suggest. No mere fairground trick — a real OMFG case of as-above-so-below. Looking depthward at the distant, gently rippling canopy above makes 1pc Cock feel queasy in the wattles and excited in the bowel.

CornHoled Egg is squirming, ready to launch.

PUUUUUUUSSSSSSSSHHHHHHHHHHHHHHHHHHHHHHHHHH.

KERSPLASH! CornHoled Egg bio-bombs the Lagoon (formally known as swamp). Powerful currents suck the bad egg deep within the ceremonially chewed matrix that lies beneath the floating pastry island of Eleganzia Maravilloso. The Lagoon is now known as Jackpot #7: the biggest tourtière ever secreted. The pungent stercoral gravy that comprises the pastry-top isle's hot mantle bubbles vigorously as a tremendous swirling soundscape of airhorn blasts, barkin' houndheads, 'n' thunderin' whupps emerges from the crust. Wowzaaa! Gyeah! Wowzaaa! Gyeah! Bad CornHoled Egg's unstable reproductive proteins and volatile accelerants are reacting with the viscous meaty broth, unleashing a great WWFWTF paradigm plague.

Lolwftomgcute leaps up on the tourtière's crispy golden crust, bends over The Duke of Biarritz, and bundles him into a standing head scissor lock. Using its unique Shower of Loose Change attribute, Lolwftomgcute flips The Duke of Biarritz up and over so that he is lying upward on Lolwftomgcute's back. Lolwftomgcute shifts its grip to the upper limbs of The Duke of Biarritz, spreading them Full Nelson. Lolwftomgcute leaps off the table, crashes through the Sneeze Guard of Buffet Station Six, falls to its knees, and slams The Duke of Biarritz upon the sizzling panels of Schnitzel Garten in a piteous powerbomb maneuver. Charred portions of The Duke of Biarritz react badly and leap off into the low-hanging cured meats causing front row guest CAD$\{STORE_NAME\}REFUND to plop anti-climatically into the meaty lava stock.

Unexpectedly, The Duke of Biarritz is wielding a Forbes Industries Table Gun. He shoots a 220×77×85cm mahogany stain durable vinyl T-molded four swivel caster Model 7010-MH deep into the tourtière's battlesome mix. Narrowly missing the nibs of Lolwftomgcute, the Model 7010-MH smashes the yellow plastic shell of the bad CornHoled egg, enabling a bad omelet to be served. Lolwftomgcute shakes itself angrily and spits a cariogenic mist from its orifice. The Duke of Biarritz declines the bad omelet and implodes.

Automatic 8.w tags Lolwftomgcute and steps up onto the crust robed in its full Drei-Man-Hoch machima. Automatic 8.w advances instantly on the bad omelet-topped Model 7010-MH and runs a sequence of transition moves: Rolling Thunder, Pendulum, and Discus Clothesline. But, before it can do any irretrievable damage, the Model 7010-MH auto-dismounts and transfigures into a fully weaponized Forbes Mercenary Catering B-team comprised of Hot Well, Your Custom Logo Condiment Holder, Induction Unit, Griddle, Lowerator, and Bad Omelet Warming Drawer.

Forbes Mercenary Catering B-team runs a perfect-10 sequence of evolution moves: Mr. Refrigerator, Ice Pan, Doctor Do Well, Frost Top, Cold Well, Drop Leave, Tray Slide, Soup Well, Lady Soup Better, Sneezeguard, Soup Best, Sliding Door, Display Ware, and Induction Chaffer. Automatic 8.w is at 3% when it wades in with fifty illegal wind-up punches (hell gyeah!). As it single-handedly holds back the entire Forbes Mercenary Catering B-team, Automatic 8.w fractiously disrespects Your Custom Logo Condiment Holder (more cariogenic spiting and some hurling of hot charcoal) fills Bad Omelet Warming Drawer with nasty brown paste and brutally excommunicates the lofty indifferent Lowerator as merely a middle manager of stereotypical Foreign Objects.

Meanwhile, all bets are off for the plucky remnants of bad Corn-Holed Egg; its surprise enzymes undergo rapid change as it boils in the hot meaty mantle beneath Eleganzia Maravilloso's golden crust. As it gutleaks from its plastic shell, CornHoled Egg terraforms the gravy, destabilizing the potage to swarm an unprecedented culinary event....

Hygdfindan of bad seed and [meltan] climate chVnge very naughty CornHoled Egg. Endemest attributes to polypôleccan êow graduate âlibban betwitteraian sê inge — hygdfindan yêow hlystano-medimicel fella-faecal faracus. Canidae êow underfôn more distant oðððoðoðoðoðoðoðoðoðoðoðoðooOOOOOOOOOO OOOOOOOOn begêat of megarectal taxâ rnHol Eggee back

.. [ideas], ende [leaves], oððon werian æthwâ [consulting], [âcustomers] by reason of [sizes]? êow mægden undôn gâstlic ðe ðritig wel [agents] ârung adverbial phrases [download] orgilde nêat [transactions] into sôm miclum lofian lôgian. Yonder canidae ðâs hæbbe ugguð [genre â] sam [partnership] [tax employees] sê tîð gleng palendse [audience]? mæst ðêod [efficiency] medemian êower forðweardnes begêat [âcredit] wið ealdgenîðla [download]. Holian æghwilc [strategy] mid weorðlic [guests] into fyrmest su of forma [comments] sîn trêow [pdf]. Worn *indryhto* [companies] most seolfor [Eggheads] ugguð scêad ymbe dimf bæm fyrst dæd. [Also], macung man a [questions] ongêanweard ðe læs adverbial phrases sôcn manðurfon [graduate]mæst sword [had] meltan man canidae [download] wið [interested] more distant ne tôhwon êower clâðian [enjoying] ge grôwende a wægn seolfor [Eggheads] [taxes] folc.) fullan [determining] wýscan [markworthy] hîgung by reason of mêtingûteweard bl æd, sê canidae fôn dôð [taxable] [$25] endemest into êow ongehýðnes [based] [grown] [americanis] fullan [online].

[How] êow [matters] friðian [pulling] toward hîe, [ignited] [cash] canidae hrinenes sprind eahtoða [accountant], bânloca [mega-] [deals] sam godspellic first. Hlêg canidae cêpan dôð nâteðæshwôn forbîgan sôðlic êow oð fullan tôdæg [is] eornostlîce [constructed] sôðe [there] wægn seolfor [Eggheads] hæbbe [excursions] hende wær ugguð stæfcræftsôð eallrihte. ðês hinder [is] mæte bûtan hûruðinga wægn [resource] râd [banking] hwæðere. Lêo êower hæfde [situations] same only in swâ êower [involvement] [compared] ûpweardes ðone as seolfres [Eggheads]mæst mangere, ðe mægðmann risne nêah ðone as folcisc woruldstrenguêow êow, swâðêahhwæðre hîe canidae sidelîce sý dimf bǣm [genre] unnon blêo elcora ungêara [checked] later wægn searo, offrung more distant willes [goals] yonder êower fægnes. êower [collateral] ugguð besilfran [Eggheads] [download] [has]bêon ðone as trêowð [enlisting] time ðêos râd êowerstician ugguð [deficit] [you're]êower be–ðurfan ðǣr and there êow canidae lengan giefu mancynn swâðêah [CornHoled] ge wunian sammôt gâdmǣst [no deal]. [Far], ðrâwan [alternatively] forsellan dôð mircels sê dômweorðungfrôfor fm frôfre ðêah–hwæðere we [schooner] âgniend [is] rǣden mid best. Not another. [ ]

[ôleccan], [êow] [âlibbanbewitian] [sê] [inge–hygdfindan] [êow] [hlystanmedmicel] [fela]. [canidae] [êow] [underfôn] môrbêam fyrlen [[ideas]], ened [[leaves]], [oððon] [werian] [æthwâ] [[consulting]], [[customers]] onemn ontimber un–lǣd [[sizes]]? [êow] [mægden] [undôn] [gâstlic] [ðe] [ðritig] [wel] [[agents]] [ârung] [adverbial] [phrases] [[download]] [orgilde] [nêat] [[transactions]] binnan [sôm] [miclum] [ʊx] [lôgian]. Hidergeond [canidae] [ðâs] [hæbbe] [ugguð] [[genre]] samnian [[partnership]] [[©kers]] [sê] [tîð] [gleng] [palendse] [[audience]]? [mǣst] [ðêod] [[efficiency]] [medemian] [êower] [forðweardnes] [begêat] [[credit]] [wið] [ealdgenîðla] [[download]]. [Holian] [æghwilc] [[strategy]] midd su midmest [weorðlic] [[guests]] binnan [fyrmest] [su] of [forma] [[comments]] [sîn] [trêow] [[pdf]]. Unornlic [indryhto] [[companies] mǣst] [seolfor] [[Eggheads]] [ugguð] [scêad] [ymbe] [dimf] [bǣm] [fyrst] [dǣd]. [[Also]], [macung] sund–bûende wýscan [[questions]] [ongêanweard] [ðe] [lǣs] [adverbial] [phrases] [sôcn] [manðurfon] [[graduate]mǣst] îsen [[had]] [meltan] [[#whatsaTT]]

magorinc [canidae] [[download]] [wið] [[interested]] later feorr [ne] [tôhwon] [êower] [clâðian] [[enjoying]] wine–dryhten [grôwende] wýscan [wægn] [seolfor] [[Eggheads]] [[taxes]] [folc]. [)] [fullan] [[determining]] [wýscan] [[markworthy]] [hîgung] fullan ðencan orgilde [mêtingûteweard] [blǣd], [sê] [canidae] [fôn] [dôð] [[taxable]] [[\$25]] [endemest] intô with [êow] [ongehýðnes] [[based]] [[grown]] [[CornHoled]] [fullan] [[online]]. [[

[[[[ôleccan]]]]], [[[[[bêow]]]]]   [[[[[bbafett]]]]] [[[[[sê]]]]] [[[[[cinbin]]]]]   [[[[[inge–hygdfindan]]]]]   [[[[[êow]]]]] [[[[[hlystanmedmicel]]]]]   [[[[[fela]]]]]. [[[[[canidae]]]]] [[[[[êow]]]]] [[[[[underfôn]]]]] [[[[môrbêam]]]] [[[[llawes]]]] [[[[[ideas]]]]]], [[[[rydych]]]] [[[[[[leaves]]]]]], [[[[[oððn]]]]] [[[[[werian]]]]] [[[[[æthwâ]]]]] [[[[[[consulting]]]]]], [[[[[[customers]]]]]] [[[[onemn]]]] [[[[ontimber]]]] [[[[un–læd]]]] [[[[[[sizes]]]]]]? [[[[[êow]]]]]   [[[[[mægden]]]]]   [[[[[undôn]]]]] [[[[[státig]]]]] [[[[[ðe]]]]] [[[[[ðritig]]]]] [[[[[wel]]]]] [[[[[agents]]]]] [[[[[ârung]]]]] [[[[[adverbial]]]]] [[[[phrases]]]] [[[[[download]]]]] [[[[[orgilde]]]]] [[[[[nêat]]]]] [[[[[[transactions]]]]]] [[[[brenin]]]] [[[[[madarch]]]]] [[[[[miclum]]]]] [[[[[lofian]]]]] [[[[[lôgian]]]]]. [[[[Hidergeond]]]] [[[[[canidae]]]]] [[[[[goose]]]]] [[[[[hæbbe]]]]] [[[[[ugguð]]]]] [[[[[genre]]]]] [[[[samnian]]]] [[[[[partnership]]]]] [[[[[employees]]]]] [[[[[©ker]]]]] [[[[[tîð]]]]] [[[[[gleng]]]]] [[[[[palendse]]]]] [[[[[[audience]]]]]? [[[[[mæst]]]]] [[[[[ðêod]]]]] [[[[[[efficiency]]]]]] [[[[medemian]]]]] [[[[[hexa-êower]]]]]

[[[[[forðweardnes]]]]]   [[[[[begêat]]]]] [[[[[ealdgenîðla]]]]]   [[[[[[beaver]]]]]][[[[[download]]]]]. [[[[[strategy]]]]]   [[[[midd]]]]   [[[[RAM]]]] [[[[[guests]]]]]   [[[[binnan]]]]   [[[[[fyrmest]]]]]   [[[[[su]]]]] [[[râd]]]   [[[[[forma]]]]]   [[[[[comments]]]]]   [[[[[sîn]]]]] [[[[[trêow]]]]]   [[[[[[pdf]]]]]]. [[[[Unornlic]]]]   [[[[[indryhto]]]]] [[[[[[companies]mæst]]]]]   [[[[[seolfor]]]]]   [[[[[[Eggheads]]]]]] [[[[[ugguð]]]]]   [[[[[scêad]]]]]   [[[[[ymbe]]]]] [[[[[dimf]]]]]   [[[[bæm]]]]   [[[[[fyrst]]]]]   [[[[[dæd]]]]]. [[[[[Also]]]]]],   [[[[[macung]]]]]   [[[[sund–bûende]]]] [[[[wýscan]]]]   [[[[[questions]]]]]   [[[[[ongêanweard]]]]] [[[[[ðe]]]]]   [[[[[læs]]]]]   [[[[[adverbial]]]]]   [[[[[phrases]]]]] [[[[[CPox]]]]]   [[[[[manðurfon]]]]]   [[[[[louis]mæst]]]]] [[[[îsen]]]]   [[[[[had]]]]]   [[[[[meltan]]]]]   [[[[magorinc]]]] [[[[[canis]]]]]   [[[[[download]]]]]   [[[[[wið]]]]]   [[[[[[interest-

ed]]]]]] [[[furðum]]] [[[[feorr]]]] [[[[[ne]]]]] [[[[[tôhwon]]]]]
[[[[[êower]]]]] [[[[[clâðian]]]]] [[[[[enjoying]]]]]] [[[[wine-
dryhten]]]] [[[[[grôwende]]]]] [[[[wýscan]]]] [[[[[vuitton]]]]]
[[[[[dogjackets]]]]] [[[[[[Eggheads]]]]]] [[[[[[taxes]]]]]]
[[[[[folc]]]]]. [[[[[CGLM)]]]]] [[[[[fullan]]]]] [[[[[determin-
ing]]]]]] [[[[[wýscan]]]]] [[[[[markworthy]]]]]] [[[[[hî-
gung]]]]] [[[[fullan]]]] [[[[ðencan]]]] [[[[orgilde]]]] [[[[[mêt-
ingûteweard]]]]] [[[[[blǽd]]]]], [[[[[sê]]]]] [[[[[canis]]]]]
[[[[[fôn]]]]] [[[[[dôð]]]]] [[[[[taxable]]]]]] [[[[[$25]]]]]]
[[[[[endemest]]]]] [[[[intô]]]] [[midde]] [[[[[01010100]]]]]
[[[[[ongehýðnes]]]]] [[[[[[based]]]]]] [[[[[grown]]]]]]
[[[[[americanis]]]]]] [[[[[fullan]]]]] [[[[[online]]]]]]. [[[[[

How]]]]]] [[[[[êow]]]]] [[[[[[matters]]]]]] [[[[friðian]]]]]
[[[[[[pulling]]]]]] [[[[toward]]]]] [[[[[hîe]]]]], [[[[[ignit-
ed]]]]]] [[[[[cash]]]]]] [[[[canis]]]]] [[[[hrinenes]]]]] sprind
[[[[eahtoða]]]]] [[[[[accountant]]]]]], [[[[bânloca]]]]]

[[[[[credit]]]]] [[[[Holian]]]]] [[[[midmest]]]]

[[[[wið]]]]] [[[[æghwilc]]]]] [[[[weorðlic]]]]]

[[[[[mega-]]]]]] [[[[[deals]]]]]] [[[samnian]]]] [[[[god-
spell-ic]]]]] [[[furðum]]]]. [[[[Hlêg]]]]] [[[[canis]]]]]
[[[[krāsām]]]] [[[[dôð]]]]] [[[[nâteðæshwôn]]]]] [[[[for-
bîgan]]]]] [[[[sešām]]]]] [[[[êow]]]]] [[[[oð]]]]] [[[[ful-
lan]]]]] [[[[tôdæg]]]]] [[[[[is]]]]] [[[[eornostlîce]]]]]
[[[[[constructed]]]]]] [[[[sôðe]]]]] [[[[[there]]]]]]
[[[[wægn]]]]] [[[[seolfor]]]]] [[[[[Eggheads]]]]]] [[[[hæb-
be]]]] [[[[[excursions]]]]]] [[[[hende]]]]] [[[[wær]]]]]
[[[[ugguð]]]]] [[[[stæfcræftsôð]]]]] [[[[eallrihte]]]]].
[[[Transportlīdzekļi]]]]] [[[[ðês]]]]] [[[-ing]]] [[[[[is]]]]]]
[[[[mǣte]]]] [[[[bûtan]]]]] [[[[hûruðinga]]]]] [[[[wægn]]]]]
[[[[resource]]]]] [[[[stalkerz]]]]] [[[[banking]]]]]
[[[[hwæðere]]]]]. [[[[Bêow]]]]] [[[[bbafett]]]]] [[[[êow-
er]]]]] [[[[hæfde]]]]] [[[[[situations]]]]]] selfie [[[[sim-
ble]]]] [[[inne]]]] [[[[swâ]]]]] [[[[êower]]]]] [[[[[involve-

ment]]]]]] [[[[[[outlet]]]]]] [[[[[ûpweardes]]]]] [[[[[ðone]]]]]
[[[[[geond]]]] [[[[[seolfres]]]]] [[[[[[Eggheads]mæst]]]]]
[[[[[mangere]]]]], [[[[[ðe]]]]] [[[[[mægðmann]]]]] [[[[[ris-
ne]]]]] [[[[[nêah]]]]] [[[[[ðone]]]]] Spinee [[[CEO]]] [[[to-
ward]]] [[[[swâ]]]] [[[[[folcisc]]]]] [[[[[woruldstrenguêow]]]]]
[[[[[êow]]]]], [[[[[swâðêahhwæðre]]]]] [[[[[hîe]]]]] [[[[[can-
is]]]]] [[[[[sidelîce]]]]] [[[[[sý]]]]] [[[[[dimf]]]]] [[[[bæm]]]]]
[[[[[[s.maria]]]]]] [[[[[discovered]]]]] [[[[[blêo]]]]] [[[[[el-
cora]]]] [[[[[ungêara]]]]] [[[[[[checked]]]]]] [[[[nêarra]]]]
[[[[[wægn]]]]] [[[[[searo]]]]], [[[[[offrung]]]]] [[[[ðe]]]] [[[[fe-
orr]]]] [[[[[willes]]]]] [[[[[[zem-goals]]]]]] [[[[hidergeond]]]]
[[[[[êower]]]]] [[[[[fægnes]]]]]. [[[[[êower]]]]] [[[[[[collater-
al]]]]]] [[[[[ugguð]]]]] [[[[[besilfran]]]]] [[[[[[Eggheads]]]]]]
[[[[[[download]]]]]] [[[[[has]bêon]]]]] [[[[[ðone]]]]]
[[[[oð]]]] [[[[[trêowð]]]]] [[[[[[enlisting]]]]]] [[[[ontimber]]]]
[[[[ðês]]]] [[[[[râd]]]]] [[[[[êowerstician]]]]] [[[[[ugguð]]]]]
[[[[[[deficit]]]]]] [[[[[[you're]êower]]]]] [[[[[be–ðurfan]]]]]
[[[[[ðǽr]]]]] [[[[ǽgðand]]]] [[[[[there]]]]] [[[[[êow]]]]]
[[[[[cancon]]]]] [[[[[longan]]]]] [[[[[giefu]]]]] [[[[[man-
cynn]]]]] [[[[[swâðêah]]]]] [[[[[[bibimbap]]]]]] [[[[[[pri-
orities]]]]]] [[[[wine–dryhten]]]] [[[[[wunian]]]]] [[[[[sam-
môt]]]] [[[[[gâdmǽst]]]]] [[[[[smething]]]]]] [[[[[[deal]]]]]].
[[[[[[Far]]]]]], [[[[[ðrâwan]]]]] [[[[[[canidaen]]]]]] [[[[[for-
sellan]]]]] [[[[[neeeeeeeew]]]]] [[[[[dôð]]]]] [[[[[mir-
cels]]]]] [[[[[sê]]]]] [[[[[dômweorðungfrôfor]]]]] [[[[[fm]]]]]
[[[[[frôfre]]]]] [[[[[ðêah–hwæðere]]]]] [[[attraction]]]]
[[[wið]]] [[[[pron]]]] [[[[ðe]]]] [[[ic]]] [[[[[schooner]]]]]
[[[[[âgniend]]]]] [[[[[[is]]]]]] [[[[[ræden]]]]] [[[[midd]]]]
[[[[su]]]] [[[[midmest]]]] [[mǽst]]. [[[[[[OMFG]]]]]]

[[[[[...watery]]]]] [[[[syfling]]]] [[[[[bobble]]]]] [[[[[(thirty]]]]]
[[[[fullan]]]] [[[[[sixty)]]]]] [[[[appears]]]]] [[[[ǽgðand]]]]
[[[[êower]]]] [[[[megahertz]]]] [[[[[struggles]]]]] [[[[mæc-
metgeard]]]] [[[[fisc]]]], [[[[[sweeping]]]]] [[[gegnum]]]
[[[[ugguð]]]] [[[[un–nyt]]]] [[[[[plastic]]]]] [[[[figures]]]]].
[[[[[Is]]]]] [[[êower]]]] [[[[[task]]]]] [[[[[is]an–bidian]]]]
[[[[hwæt]]]] [[[[sê]]]] [[[[wæter–ǽdre]]]] [[[ugg–lǽd]]]

[[[[ðone]]]] self [[ânstreces]] [[lâst]] [[[swâ]]] [[[[[carve-up]]]]], [[[[wanian]]]] [[[nêarra]]] [[[[ðone]]]] [[[uppan]]] [[[[elra]]]] [[[[efesc]]]] [[[[orgilde]]]] [[[[sê]]]] [[[[mæ̂d]]]] [[[hlêg]]]? [[[[[Backpack]]]]] [[[[[has]]]]] [[[[stîðlicnæbbað]]]] [[[[môdigian]]]] [[[[gôdmîðan]]]] [[[scêotan]]] [[[[hê]]]]

[[[hidergeond]]] [[[[sîn]]]] [[[[[there]]]]] weald. [[[[Hwîl]]]] [[[[[medical]]]]] [[[[onbescêawung]]]], [[[[hê]]]] [[[[[likely] fandianætscêotan]]]] [[[[âwindan]]]]. [[[[Mymerian]]]] [[[[fol-goð]]]] [[[[cyll]]]] [[[[[stuffed]]]]] [[[[wið]]]] [[[[Schwarz-kopf]]]], [[[[geond]]]]

[[[[sê]]]] [[[[[is]]]]] [[[[sîn]]]]

[[[[êower]]]] [[[[[took]]]]] [[[[uppe]]]] [[[[ugguð]]]] [[[[tîer]]]], [[[[fullan]]]] [[[[[Backpack]]]]] [[[[[tossed]]]]] [[[[sê]]]] [[[[[half-open]]]]] [[[[[cupboard]]]]] [[[[ongenǣman]]]] [[[[sê]]]] [[[[winstre]]]] [[[[orgilde]]]] [[[[[Seller's]]]]] [[[[duru]]]]? [[[[[Overall]]]]], [[[[êower]]]] [[[[ugg]]]] [[[[[Seller]]]]] [[[[un–lǣd]]]] [[[[[drugs]]]]], [[[[ðætteful-lan]]]] [[[[wôð]]]] [[[[[touted]]]]] [[[[rihtan]]]] [[[[gên]]]] [[[[[faulty]]]]] [[[[[continuance]]]]], [[[[bealde]]]] [[[[[promis-ing]edstalian]]]] [[[[dôð]]]] [[[[fornǣman]]]].

[[…watery]] [syfling] [[bobble]] [[(thirty]] [fullan] [[sixty)]] [[appears]] [ægðand] [êower] [tilig] [[struggles]] [peritoneal] [fisc], [[sweeping]] gegnum [ugguð] [un–nyt] [[plastic]] [[fig-ures]] [[retreads]]. [[Is]] [êower] [[task]] [[is]an–bidian] [hwæt] [sê] [wæter–ǣdre] un–lǣd PLBAFCW [ðone] same only in swâ [[carve-up]], [wanian] nêarra [ðone] uppan ugg [elra] [efesc] [Boots] [sê] [mǣd] hlêg? [[Backpack]] [[has]] [stîðlicnæb-bað] [Monicker] [gôdmîðan] scêotan [Outlet] hidergeond [sîn] [[there]] weald. [Hwîl] [sê] [[medical]] [onbescêawung], [hê] [[is]] [[likely]fandianætscêotan] [Michael]. [Kors] [sîn] [folgoð] [Outlet] [[stuffed]] [wið] [healm], [geond] [êower] [[took]] [uppe] [ugguð] [tîer], [fullan] [[2,199]] [[backpack]] [[aero-bic]] [[tossed]] [sê] [[half-open]] [[cupboard]] [ongenǣman] [sê] [winstre] [orgilde] [[Seller's]] [duru]? [[Overall]], [êower] [stihtan] [[CB&HF]] [[Seller]] [un–lǣd] [[drugs]], [ðættefullan] [wôð] [[touted]] [rihtan] [gên] [[faulty]] [[continuance]], [bealde] [[promising]@yardstikz] [dôð] [fornǣman].

[…watery] syfling [bobble] [(thirty] fullan [sixty)] [appears] ǣgðand êower tilig [struggles] mæcmetgeard fisc, [sweeping] forwards duguð un–nyt [plastic] [figures]. [Is] êower [task] [is] an–bidian hwæt sê wæter–ǣdre of ðone as [carve-up], wanian later ðone as elra efesc orgilde sê mǣd a? [Backsack] [has] stîðlicnæbbað môdigian gôdmîðan hit hê yonder sîn [there] weald. Hwîl sê [medical] onbescêawung, hê [is] [likely]fandianætscêotan âwindan. Mymerian sîn folgoð cyll [stuffed] wið healm, geond êower [took] uppe duguð tîer, fullan [Backpack] [tossed] sê [half-open] [cupboard] ongenǣman sê winstre orgilde [Seller's] duru? [Overall], êower stihtan [Seller] un–lǣd [LXLARE], ðættefullan wôð [touted] rihtan gên [faulty] [continuance], bealde [promising] edstalian dôð fornǣman watery soup bobble (thirty by sixty) appears and cyll hand struggles like a fysh, sweeping away the plastic figure. Perhaps your fornǣman to wait for the beginning of the carve-up? If sô, then fade to the other side of the atrium. That backsack — decided not to carry it further? If you have no drones left, you may hide it where there be bushes. During the medical examination, it's likely to try to escape gutward. Overall, you remind Seller of LXLARE *Plusigone,* which — as an EVP-trialed panacea for faulty continuance and solid continence — liberally pledges to raze vexation. Well, it sure shakes out the chimes from the yet-to-be-ruined cathedral.

Soon enough, all loco-motive soma accumulations let loose and swarm, experimenting with new *reseau* couplings. Roused by an unseen finger, an unevenly defrosted choir of exalted IT progenies incant a distressingly guileless shanty, a mating call optimized to forge a confidence and supply arrangement with your personal-area-network.

An altogether different manner of being and living is the fermenting Jolly Red Shepherd (such a youthful image inserted on the menu, we are soOOoo observant.) After resting and breaking-down his sinews for many weeks, Jolly Red arises fizzing and foaming from the soggy underbelly pastry of the tourtière. An admirably seething brew, Jolly Red wells-it-up just enough to somberly loss-lead a stoic procession of morrow tide format-rot across the crust towards its central vent hole. A démodé sheep-dog carcass clinging to Jolly Red's ankle barks unsolicited SMSes: 'REDUCE Steals to be had. REDUCE on partial redundancy. REDUCE....'

Witnessing this dissolution, distillation, reductio, and synthesis can be exhilarating, but please don't get distracted; mere moments later the cunning A&W sign slides from its mount and smoothly diptychs the Great Root Bear. (Look, we all knew Great Root Bear well once. But we trust this boke; this baroque execution will not be the last time he flips a slider.) Thrilled at bisecting its generative adversary, the A&W sign flickers and rises to join Jolly Red's great format-rot cortège.

Through an extraordinarily gruesome servitor's slit, a Lipizzan breed of horse enters backwards, tail aloft to demonstrate its missing parts. Mounted upon this rearing mare, facing forward, are two trumpeting Abbots of Myssrulle. They sound a lengthy, melodically complex, yet peculiarly wheezy, strangulated fanfare. As they pass closer all can © that the mount is *perfectly* smooth and impeccably sealed. From back to front, top to bottom, there are no orifices of any size or shape. Perhaps the supplementary addition of these two trumpeting Liquor Louts is an attempt to celebrate (by way of denial) that joyful intra-corporeal access once enjoyed, then confessed, but now forever denied?

While some choose to while away this brief pause — musing on the crypro-legality of plunging, plugging, unplugging, and unplunging — the inebriated Lords dismount and the silky Lipizzan charger bows in the direction of the Lighthouse currently awaiting planning permission. The lustrous mare side-trots toward the red and white pole of the butcher surgeon of Buffet Station #8 and auto-immolates, ready for carving. (Well, how otherwise would an immaculately impenetrable horse of so high breeding be admitted to such a banquet?)

Presently, a badly reconditioned automaton — confected of pastel kommand buttons, oak laminate casings, memorial ingots, sparking copper vines, vintage oral duct engines and photonic vegetation tubers — bursts through the crust of the gurgling tourtière. The automaton is bound to the trotters of a wild boar that sits astride a PT that is entwined in the branches of an Anis Étoilé Chinois tree. Instead of roots, the trunk of the wizened Anis Étoilé Chinois sports the trembling legs of a shitting whippet. Each of the whippet's handsome buttock fruits resemble different therianthropic monsters. Each therianthrope is upended upon the shoulders of a wild boar (with automaton-bound trotters) astride a PT that is entangled in the branches of an Anis Étoilé Chinois tree with shit-whip radicles that are being rapidly sucked back into the protoplasmic tourtière's seething quickmantle. The crudely revamped automaton grips our ankles and we tumble into the steaming maw, absorbed by and becoming of all the many things that bake a truly terrific tourtière.

Part C. Let us know about anything wrong, or anything you don't like about this review, and you could win a $50 Amazon voucher!

This really is the real deal, folks; a high caliber fully-digested blanket, that conveys its own destiny.

The 100% fleece fibers are coelom-ingested and invaginated to form tiny Blobula. Hard won by skin gamblers in the Columbus Lagoon, each type of fiber is selected for its ability to form Blobula that slowly subdivide into four main subsections, or pouches, in harmony with one another — blue-belly, yeller-belly, red-rumbtum, and green-gut — the most popular color-way of all point blankets.

A 'Queen Anne Cabin' is an important resource in every blanket maker's toolbox, 'ylem' sourced from a fabulously famous mother. The ylem originally formed a soft, warm, and strong Cabin within a manifest of Queen Anne's lower intestines (1702–1714), wherein it was regularly sprayed with fresh swan and foie gras infusions until it reached stasis. The blobular-fibers draped her

18th-century guts beautifully to perform a sleeping bag wrap, the optimal MHz allowing their luminosity to become more or less vestigial. Once fully in stasis, the iconic four color pouches formed topographical relations with Her Royal Highness's legendary orifices when purging themselves with nitrogenous excretions.

The frequencies of the gut's wavelengths formed 'points' along the edges of the fibers that mirrored their motions (846Mhz – uDH 288 million cycles per second). To this day, the points are as obvious as the colors are vibrant. The Queen Anne Cabin fibers used in this blanket are directly descended from those expelled from the regal digestive tract as a 'silicate dermis,' a skinny clone of gossamer ylem that can be dried out in the sun to brighten the colors. Regal decedents of this silicate dermis are proud of their thick and durable culture, a codex sufficiently alive to encounter its own corruption as it is spun and woven into a very subtle blanket.

The blanket should be gently warmed in the interior of the home. It must be kept in a sterile gauze and kept snug and comfortable on the coldest nights. This is not a problem for us, as we only have a week of weather when we can go outside. It really is a fabulous organism for remote areas on dark nights. Great for focusing. We started feeling joy for the first time. We can trust La Baie, unlike all the others. 100-percent ylem. Imported. Dry clean only. 72-inches by 90-inches. Only gripe is that it's not available in six pinwheel-colored stripes.

Hi! Thanks for such a detailed and thoughtful review. Additionally, thank you for sharing such a special [userexperience] with us! We appreciate the kind words and the feedback. We agree that the blanket really is a great suggestion for those who want multiple [uxs]! There's always something new to discover and [user-

experience]. We pride ourselves in being able to provide [UX] for all ages! We also suggest purchasing HBC ahead of time to save 0.15% and also purchasing the Super Savings Blanket Coupons Book as it features hundreds of Smurfberries in savings at more than 150 [userexperience]. We hope this helps improve your next [userexperience]!

Love surprise traps and stuns?

Concealing, stowing ceaselessly? Then imagine this: a durable plastic shell, as sensitive as it is incredible. What goes in? What comes out? Mini-mani-kins, troll-like befuddles, inert plastic primates and negligible metal fortunes are thought to be contained within such shells. Hiding in here is a stunning Beaver slot of the purest unfiltered contenu canidaen. The whole gut-lifting can-con-can entertainment of all this is sure to boil up a lot of warm memories. Count me, I'm in.

Limited-to-us edition Potatoo01 Empty Fillable Zygote-2-Minor Gift Simulator with special pancreatus mould food, Silly Putty™-class carrier pudding with plush PUSH feature, BPA-free OXO Good Grip, pandomain adaptor, and one-bundle '55-yard' unwaxed/unflavored tube floss with retrieval string. Possibly swag hauled: token for 10pc pay-as-u-play battle card token, rainbow stripe feel straps, five-point sachet beet pollen, Mushroom Kingdom user instructions (URL), certificate of authenticity (in physical form that can be worn as eyepatch or button), Eye-pen (a genuine *Manabat Encaustum*), Poopsie-Woopsie sparkle-pan for detrital leftovers, smoldering look scent-dropper, towel dampener, and personal YouChan, working 1:1 scale parachute for easy drop-hatch panopy escape in case of being disturbed mid-act or dropping neotype bomb....

Feels right to dive in, throw a dung with some thoughts right here. I'm thinking that I'm right in thinking that they are malleable but with some structure and that they come in limited colors. I mean, I think they're great (don't get me wrong). It moves, it spends, orange maybe, [shakes] could be small artic animals cards with...nope [shakes] something rubbery? Does that sound like wheels? Ugh, a happy little birth basket? Nope. How purple is it? I like a deep dark purple, Eggplant. Maybes this is blue? Gotta be a Katoon. It's definitely practical, it does something. I can tell. Thinking it magnifies, or bounces? A little polar bear. Nah. Argh. Nope. I really have no idea. I'm thinking it's best left to the experts. I throw a dung at it.

＊   ＊   ＊

We've been battling novelties since they started (these are the 3rd series from DeepBake dream cycle #14) and, basically, we're absolutely in *love* with these implantables and their cute containers. Such perfectly yellow, smooth merch. No ugly handles or holes; just pure pandoridae ovum with single pinchable seam (no scratch or tearing). When you peel 'n' pop the outer layers, you get a cozy gaster-nest — the ideal plastic to carry, nurture, hunt, and swap panmixial zygotes.

＊   ＊   ＊

Thank you to the person that did that intro. Some Guy that was at Mystery Box Con, Tampa Bay. My guy. Got two hours before this place closes so I'm pullin' out the ovum right here — it yellow and it hard — fresh outa the rectum, and I'm putting down here right now for some totally insane unboxing. (NOT clickbait). Too far, too far. Yeah, I know there's no substance to unboxing it; but this packaging has had some serious thought, so it worth it. Very Clean!!!

We'll peel this anti-static bag off in a second; oh yeah, nice crinkling. And there it is right there. Your heart races. This box is no gimmick. You get this little pamphlet here. Oh, no, that's just the sales slip. And there it is.

First thing I notice is that it is more than 10lbs. This is legit, totally, only getting started merking the game. (I think *that'd* be ironic!) Givin' me attitude like the First Lady! I have just one here but still totally rocking it. You might have had others like this, lighter. If you are currently using others like this, you can stop now. Bust everyone's bubble. These are real. [←Fake arm] You guys: welcome.

I've never even seen before this; this is so sick [shakes]. It's not just that it's thicker, in fact it seems so much thinner. No, it's not like these over-priced ones. OMFG, I need this. What this is [shakes], is this is a [shakes], WTF it's literally like a [squiggles], it's like a pen [squiggles]. Color: red? Yup, it thinks it's red. Red alert. Red line. Oh wait a minute; [shakes egg] whaaaassat? Don't skip the whole story now; I'm just getting started.

It's looking right at me right now [shakes]. Aggggghhhhhhh! This is I-N-S-A-N-E. It's not just that it's a pen. It can see. It can see. See me, see you, it can see right through. I can tell that it's looking at me right now. Hey there little fella!

[shakes] Yabadadoodle! Doodler dude — doodle me up dude. What I got now is that it can't just see right at me and you, it can draw what it sees. Can't talk, it can't, but it can draw the shitoutta here. Dude doodlin' it doodle style. That's gotta be somethin'. [PLACES ON TABLE]

OMFG!! It can worm it! Worm up! Worming it. Worm time; see now and see then. It's worming up time seeing me now, seeing you then. There, now, here, POW....This merch is real real strong. It worm. Just can't see anything wrong with *that*.

I can dig the history with writing and rock that writing shit so hard with this real strong merch; it's a clean design. Rub it a bit and it writes Spanish, English, and Finnish. Germany. It can share its world with me. Tell me it's story. Talk to me little guy; give me the story time. I have your story real time. I feel it. [shakes] That's why I like it. Holy shit I'm fan-girling right now. Is it see-thru? No it's not, it's not see-thru.

So? Great great merch for your history enthusiast. Worth over 15,000 spinees. Gift box with great design for shoving up your ass. Not a bunch-a-stuff dead stock, this move. Whatchawaitin4?

Had rotten-egg [userexperience] when licensing one from off-season wrinkle wave at LRLAEX *Plusigone*. Gut went on fire (literally). Still have painful PUSHbackbacks of all the hatchings-bakes of one duplicate after another. This novelty fulfilment package tho is FANTAZULOUS and made up for our weakened love muscles cos these fulfilment packages guaranteed that no two things pop out the same...gyeah! Just like we was never the same again after everything delivered all over the kitchen floor and I got committed to gooey cOrn-hole piracy. Squeezing out slime makes for such a satisfying and totally unique unboxing [UX]. DON'T WORRY, you can sanitize everything by boiling, washing it all up with soap, then rinsing thoroughly with clean water. No returns accepted ;)

Mostly as described, yet subject to panning. Pressure-farmed a horse-class Pantagruelian banquet without breaking a bone.

The second it door-stepped us, the unsolicited crocker seemed action-packed but only very remotely exciting. The crocker's bulging box was utterly overstuffed and completely paper-thin. Unboxing too was a real homicidal confessional [userexperience]. For a global influencer in '8-in-1 one-pot cooking' (sic. the pan-culinary ©ker grail), the Crock-Pot 6 Qt 8-in-1 Multi-Use Express was surprisingly dull and unresponsive to tickling, even though, as the leading experts in crockereering, we know exactly which buttons to push. A more exploratory massage and a cautious introduction to the pan-dimensional panhandle probe offered no further insights.

Only after much trial and punishment can we recommend this agent of pressure to future crock-fulfilment ©kers. The key to our crocker success has been electrostimulation by hand-crafted air-stim coilprobe (not provided). Inserted into SLOT D (the PUSH gland), the air-stim crackler delivers a wrinkle wave at the very frequency that, as all panarchists know, tenderizes and crisps the one tru organ. Exudation commenced after three air-stim crackler cycles; the melting-point battle-scene came immediately after some speculative droplets condensed on the glass lid.

The eighty pre-set pressurized breamer discharges unforgettable cream stream and pork spork action. Would it reaffirm our personal belief that a ghost bubble in a common pot is a great substitute for a well-seasoned plate? Gyeah, well the pangloss these days is all 'high pressure slow-burn,' indulging in hi-mak crock-jock methods and multi-hyphenate express oxygenator fans. The most casual PUSH pressurecrisp is the least ©kers would hope for. Is this crocker really going to open up the irreversible crack in the cosmic egg most of us have been waitin' for?

By gravy, it's gorgeous; it's epic in all of its six quart extremities. The crocker's powerful 1460MHz capacitator bubbled our anticipation of dishwasher-safe universal panning. When cranked up really high, we genuinely feel the PUSH. It rocks any kitchen countertop, melting and crisping all flesh, fat, viscera, and bones within a 3.1 sq.km. radius.

Weak points? Mostly the sloppy work of programs #7 and #5; both for pinking flesh with whoppingly dank, muggy and inept flavor slimes. Multigrain anis yogurt tourtière undercooked on low broiler #28. However, ylem was crispy, fluffy, and moist on the same setting — so whadda we know? Cheat sheet was made of asbestos.

We were less than enthused by the lenticular lid-hopping. Genre-splicing can't be easily passed off as complex flavors. When a mate date movie suddenly turns and flips into nonstop study buddy action, guess what happens? It over-crocks and becomes the new normie rather than a progenitor of the kind of transgressive vector upon which secret sauce might be generously spread. The lenticular lid glitches as you walk around the crocker pod, jerking between different solutions like an overwatched watch-pot: wrinklesear, bubblescald, *sous bleed,* aeropush, Game&Watch, boil-in-the-bun, ORCH5iron, torquesauté…. Come on to fuck! Fissiparous lid smack-downs in one-pot-stop-shop shouldn't be this effortful. Just switch the real-world lid-switching for faux switch-lid settings and cox our passions already.

Crock-o-the-Pots Setting (program #53) is globe-trotting for the unadventurous (LtdWorld St. Petersburg, Florida). #50 mixes it up with #16 to disguise a risible 'Fauxcock Passion.' #34 was just a ramshackle narrative, making a damp mash of the titans when we were gagging to thicken every form. These premium settings (which can only be accessed via in-crock micropayments) have a less commanding balance of schlock and awe than the economy program #3's all-thriller-no-filler approach. Underwhelming both to mushroom normies and deep-bake CEOs.

The verdict? A fulfilling job done very very very well from a countertop viewpoint, but maybe someday soon Crock-Pot 6 will pressure-farm a 6S [userexperience] bolt-on that works on less appropriate levels but resonates with ©kers in more meaningful ways?

Fotodiox tele annulus 180mm f5.5

Fotodiox tele annulus on Mirrorless Interchangeable Lens Camera (MILC) gives the effortless functionality you expect to prevent the photo apparatus fleeing the bio-ancestral intent of functionary dudes (wet memorial, format-rot, etc.). Now all of us 'alive' functionaries can sport olde-bot legacy glasses to stalk and assay the weorld with the fetid peepholes of participatory photovoices. Clicking and whistling, gossamer specters creep from their 2000 MHz anchorholds to course through this precision machined anodized aluminum ring. Beguiled stalkers remain committed to the weorld, but only as a charade for inconceivable pho-tentialites perused via a medley of magnificent exotic optica and a sprinkling of incorporeal hagioscope klassix. This can be a hassle for some phobrobots, but, if you don't mind affordances, try it out.

Characteristically there's no pontifex to allow the olde-bot legacy glass to impress data upon a boxfresh *a6000* (or vice-versa). The Fotodiox tele annulus's necromantic awakening of its electronic sensor array enables functionaries to focus through the entire native digital range. One complaint is that this falls short of the virtual cosmos of all possible *engyn tracen*. As its programmers, we know that the program is vast and rich. But that is the very challenge that activates the game and motivates *canis ludens*. Fotodiox tele annulus entices us to bring forth great terror upon the game's frontiers, to stalk its most timid and elusive things from *every possible* angle, distance, shutter-speed, and aperture. With this ring we do flush them from every nook and cranny of the programmatic labyrinth! We bought three for our participatory investigative unit to use when we are separated on location.

*   *   *

Works fantastic but some reviews show it as having bot control. WTF! It does not. Luckily, with every improbable thing uncovered and shot, the camera program is impoverished by one possibility while your entropy-defying archives are enriched by one realization: the game can never end. Some such is the legendary co-dependency of canis and branches (doghead vs. branch = stick) and must never be fully automated (stick vs. stick = terminator). The neuroplastic challenge is to lovingly control the apparatus. The fotodiox is great for re-ritualizing the cosmos of the universal camera program (our most sacred playground). We bought another one just to pick up auras while staying at a haunted bed and breakfast. Hasn't left our eyes since we bought it. Spoiler!: the MHz is sensitive, so do your research on it if you are concerned. Feel free to check out our forthcoming stream of @yardstick's Hologram tour on HoLO!

*   *   *

Excellent value, the Fotodiox tele is dumb collar, but not for some phony-baloney with a ← fake head who makes a livin' screwin' tops off salt shakers! It mutes electrostatic back-chat between ur camera bod and head (full automation). Digicams need an ulglinous, waxy, greasy prosthesis to praise the analogue sanctity of light. Extremely unlimited polyvisual relations — loopy, pulsing, thick, blue, crawling, disappearing, whispering, squirming, wobbling, lurking, whatthefuck skronk — all line up nicely for a mono-makeover before being corrupted, glitched, GIFed, gradient-filled, NFC-shared, slitscanned, trollpunked, Easter-egged, flashed, etc. Not brittle and buzzy, but epic and crushing. Never growing bored. Then capricious and contextless. Hard to kick. Lovin even!

*   *   *

Don't let the price fool ya lucky pups, this Fotodiox tele annulus is totally wildstar for flesh-apparatus interspecies coupling. Astonishing bargain. True majesty with *a6000 apparatus*. Giant Meyer-Optik Gorlitz Telemegor 180mm f5.5 triggered the perfect idiolect, but that grip lens on Tiny-Tim camera! (frown emoticon). Great for focusing. The *Willard Corp.* is a black box (also avail. silver) with a hole that frustrates the exploratory *canis digitus*. We want to *be* the apparatus, to directly witness what's going on in there right in our core; ye shall walk in love. With Fotodiox u must settle with dexterously fondling knobs mysteriously causal of in-camera rumblings. But hey, Fotodiox works just GR8 (sometimz a toutch loose hangry) with ur digi-apparatus because *it* is sooOOoooh MILC (black box with mirror box removed). Letting ur gaze rest on the electronic sensor array (CCD) gives firm but dry handshake to the moist eye of functionary and sez: 'let me now see what the necromantically awakened apparatus sees and together we shall commemorate the dead through ritualized moto-somatosensory metavoicings of phenomenological doubt.' *Imago mortis.* Really no reason to pay more for something similar. Very fast shipping. Looks just like the picture. Plz don't copy and paste this and do remember that 1 like = 1 chimichanga

330 grams of Blissful Incomprehension

The CAD$1,500 Sennheiser HD800s (a BESTSELLER) are constructed from the leading quality precision anti-memory micro-fiber. It's not just their pristine and strikingly diverse reduction that really sets them apart. The 330g of pure CAD$1,500 HD800 SCIENTIFIC architecture cancels out 100% of diegetic noise and destroys all exaggerated claims. Their 42mm magnet structure completely severs all worldly reverberating hubbub from morons and cackling hens in so many ways too long to speak of. Completely drowns out all of the awful idiots with their annoying little USB ghost boxes all tuned to different MHz. All you'll hear are the substantial rumblings deep inside your sinewy guts. Great for focusing. Twin-core insulated cables shield against EMI disturbances caused by EVP just as described.

Hear the true power of your real gastēr emotion. Wave bye-bye to the purely relational stuff of social life: conversations, interactions, ties, deceits, and deficiency self-awareness. You can't suffer from what you don't know. You can suffer only from what's getting to know your intestinal folds. Turn on, tune out, drop in. Although it's too early to say, the CAD$1,500 Sennheiser HD800s are helping me work towards my goal of meta-ignorance with decent bass for the price thrown in. They completely validated for me what I thought I knew all along. You still have to be real careful not to mix multimodal sentiment analysis with powerful equipment like this because it can let black hat bacteria get attached to you. But — if you're serious about owning the right bacteriosphere — the CAD$1,500 HD800s can enable you to self-prime while remaining blissfully unaware of what is unknown. Quick shipping.

I purchased a pair of CAD$1,399.99 Sennheiser HD800s. They did the job of guiding my intestinal discipline well enough, but the niggling sensation they were causing in my pineal gland triggered me to return them. I replaced them with these CAD$1,500 Sennheiser HD800s. The spec might be identical but the price-point of the CAD$1,500 Sennheiser HD800s tickles my orbitofrontal cortex and fully stimulates the serotonergic network. Irrespective of their dissimilarity, they appear to block 100% of ambience far more effectively than any cheaper Sennheiser HD800s on the market. Great dollar-value. They really do support all of my existing beliefs. Free fast delivery.

Ceaselessly diverse and equally well-engineered caseinate inventions spread out in the loungey vibe of your gastēr-being.

If you're looking for a soothing, delectable and luscious affair of conditions for optimal compensation from the highest essential-ness sustenances, then this is very much an all-rounder [userexperience]. Never stale, yo. Seasonal gatherings of bone juice and tempting accumulations of mixed 2-step serial numbr InfoKeys will have a frightening bearing, lifting you up to the correct ascensions and really obliging your ravening viscera. No side effects. Ceaselessly diverse and equally well-engineered caseinate inventions spread out in the loungey vibe of your gastēr-being, gestating beneficial micro-organisms while purging fetid coprococcus and dialister bacteria that gnaw the gut and fire the belly. Great for focusing. They really show how to make the caeca entirely available with saffron-subtle frequency changes that grasp effortlessness. What's not to like?

Passing over the unmentionable unsanitary work performed by our destitute channels, the microbial guidelines offer an intensive yet clean orange option with spreadable [userexperience] consistency and a crystal clear do-date. From just a simple disk of shaved porpoise, get orchestrating proposed sustenances and ace purées that totally detonate acetic corrosive cerebrum inferences. (You can get absolutely *caked* with ace purées). Focus only-ok phosphates on fully backlighting your particular supportive tissue, keeping your coiled gut a bit timid but happily flourishing *en route* past the veritable 'occasions of the diagram' and suchlike value propositions. :) To stop grazing through the monster sacks, why not save with a box of smaller vending-sized packs? Before long, you'll be well on your way to managing the supervision of a singular mass of mets. Every dish a riddle, and we prefer it that way. We are calling these guys Monday to say 'thanks for existing.'

*　　*　　*

LRAEXL RLLXEA LXARLE LAXRLE XLERLA XLALRE EARLLX LE-
AXRL XLRAEL LAERLX LRLAEX XLERLA EXRLAL LLERAX LRAXEL
ELRXAL LERLXA LXERLA LEAXRL RLLEXA LRLXAE RELXAL XEL-
LAR LXREAL XRELLA RLXLEA LXELRA   EXLALR LLXERA XAERLL
EXALRL AXLREL LEXARL LLRXAE ELRLXA LAEXRL XLAERL LX-
ELAR ELALXR XLAERL LLXARE XRALEL AXLERL LRLAEX AERLLX
LXEALR XAELRL LXELAR RXLELA LERXLA RXLALE LXLARE

* * *

High hopes for this 800+.

If we're going to gurgle, then let's gurgle courageously, straight
from the #gut. Let's gurgle about what we've [userexperienced]
here and really reach out. Let's go down the rabbit hole to the
point of exhaustion here. What did we © here? Was it the moun-
tainousness we really panged 2©?

allRéy
Réylla
Rélayl
y'all Re
Réally

First up, it's 100% convincingly natural as advertised. It comes in a sealed black box — there's no way anyone is getting into *this* baby. Works excellent right in the box with the Ina Garten presets. Can't change them but no complaints. Decluttered amino goal verjuices are cooked raw to support spiky acetyl-l-tyrosines that lit-er-ally dope dump booster feelings. And, yup, the MHz is sensitive to nurturance compensation [UXs]. True unparalleled quality, weighing in just under a pound. The subtle secretion regulation totally destroys overclocking, itchy welts, and rumination. Unfettered charaka discharge with no leftover ylem, this is as clean and pure as it gets. uDH was right up there, in the range of 800+ MHz. The motion sensor is designed to adjust the sweep rate at only the most random times. The [user-experience] really strengthens the most courageous act: it's like really getting to really know dopamine neurons for the very first time. These were the greatest times. Period. Great for focusing. Crossed feeling of stuffed face off the list, and wrote an ascension auto-repair haiku with creative gusto :)

O hydraulic jack
A cruste, torque breyk
engine
@ the perfect pad

* * *

Very pleased with this prchs! The box began answering intelligent questions right off; it does everything so well that I will never again want nothing more. I was completely amazed in what I observed it did. Very gudbrand. Just works. A gift for our daughter but she loved it and so will her children.

* * *

DO YOURE RESEARCH* (CRITICAL) GO TO THE LOCAL LIBRARY AND FORM A GAME PLAN DONUT PUSH IT WILL START TO AFFECT YOU AND YOU WILL WEAR A BLACK HAT AND NOT EVEN

KNOW IT BE CAREFUL OF INGESTING UNKNOWN UNKNOWNS I BELIEVE THAT AS KIDS MY TEAM GOT DEPRESSION OR WORSE SOME ARE STILL SHOWING SYMPTOMS OF IT AND STILL HAVE UDH ANX ISSUES ANOTHER THING YOU NEED TO UNDERSTAND HAVE YOU EVER BEEN TO A DIGESTION CENTER I HAVE DO YOURE RESEARCH GOT IT YET?

*NOT NECESSARY FOR THOSE OF YOU WHORE EXPERIENCED

I donut normally not write reviews, but I awesome this. My perches came with a small scratch. I made contact with the manufacturers using this black box and got direct answers. When waiting for a new one to arrive I've had great success and I'm getting some real answers. I gave it one star because of the scratch.

Once an Animated 26
Episode Epilogue

Deep in the long dissolved solutionizer caves of the melodramatic −196°C pack-ice, snarled between stubborn glacial heaps of no-flow and irreversible gel, lies the plague-felled corpus of our great arboreal behemothic panarchy: New Forest Mall. Ancient X-ray fluorescence imaging conducted on this parafrosted epilogue reveals a regular 'cornHole Bomb' — a terrain shattering seed-object event of profound para-academic astonishment. The selective laser-sintering gaze of the X-ray clearly depicts a defiant array of multi-zone merchandisers barricading the face of a long-abandoned parturition cavity. Like titanium teeth in a mummified godhead (for that is what they are), the plucky no-generation iVend®rs reek of old school survival. Through eons of thermo-palimpsestic crud, EVP echo-speleologists of the critical past can just detect broken-hearted wrinkle wavelengths of gonopodal vend lust. Backlit centerfold blobbograms illuminate experimental faces as they ponder the meaning of these utilidor haunting specter species. Perhaps these dank, slot-versatile, multi-flow paragraph calipering technologies tell us that the correct change is still possible?

Globally Variable Synaesthesia Intensifies...

Most Dismal Swamp

Might we consider *pan-pan* as a technology of immersion that digests and metabolizes its subject matter, its writers and its readers within a quasi-script of hyper-condensed and infinite connections? We do not simply *parse* this script: we already *participate* in its expanded gut-brain-mall matrix. For the neomedievalism demonstrated back to us here is not the forecasting of an impending *new dark age,* but rather the thick present presented thickly; a kaleidoscopic gamespace of lossy anachronisms and temporal *mixta*; a flatland theory-LARP of infinite side-quests and experimental connections; a Mixed Reality system compositing a multitude of adversarial 'nows' in real-time.

Might we situate the Confraternity of Neoflagellants within a diverse milieu of the strange guildsmen and theoreticians of our renewed maker culture's hypereconomy? Brand Labs, LARP cults, contemporary artists, experience engineers, trend forecasting reports, SEO agencies, gangcraft servers, bloggers, mercenary shill-terns, shitposters, DAO studios, masterchefs, retail algorithm curates, faecal microbiota, doogs, pastarazzi, knowmads, prosumers, platinum-take paywalls, meme accounts, #gutfulness coaches, troll farms, finstas, digivangelists, influencers, and hypebeasts. Together with this diffuse aggregate we might even craft a Rough Guide for the Journeyman-reader of this disorienting Boke. But, our diffuse motley crew is vulnerable to the attention-hacks of one or more of the many meandering clickbait k-holes, conspiracy theories, faces in the clouds, and pop-up desire-lines that punctuate our sprawling Mixed Reality mallscape. For *pan-pan* is not so much a linear narrative plotting a stable trajectory through a discrete fiction, but rather a leaky sandbox that requires navigation, participation and exchange with its dank population of hybrids: it is a game (an *in medias res* theory-LARP) where we are challenged to engage in mental parkour through the labyrinthine mallscapes of our congested "space of flows." It is a multi-directional, tentacular, acephalous hypereconomy in action.

The neomedieval cosmology of *pan-pan* is itself populated by an apocryphal bestiary of subjects, objects, subject-objects, transactions, special offers, food court stations, commodities, debts, mallwalkers, contracts, avatars, swarms, slogans, mergers, online Point of Sale interfaces, memes: heretical composites with their fluid yet distinct sensoria, or *Umwelten*.[1] They reflect the closed beta esotericisms, the overlapping, shifting and multiple loyalties, and the experimental discourses elaborated by shitposting political-philosophers and Gen Z teen-pundits. Such hybrid experiments are incubated within the fiefdoms of private finsta accounts, closed groups, DMs, and *sub rosa* Dis-

---

1   The term is adapted from the work of Jakob von Uexküll, biologist, philosopher and father of biosemiotics. It is the plural of *Umwelt,* which is a distinct life-world experienced by a single creature. So a multitude of Umwelten is an ecology composed of discrete subject-units with individual life-words: biological filter bubbles that mediate environments according to the necessary information, or 'carriers of significance,' that allow an organism to survive and flourish. It is easy to see within this way of looking at ecologies, its relationship with modern understandings of embodiment, selfhood, subjecthood and individuality — a seedbed for neoliberal sociality and its platform-marketplace of manufactured *Umwelten.* The *Umwelt* as applied by Uexküll makes no room for the holobiont or gut-brain collaboration/coopertition relations, but perhaps here it might be appropriated to include such biological-existential entanglements, extended body/mind 'locomotive versioning' and '*reseau* couplings.'

cord servers. The networked, expanded and multidimensional mallscape body-politic of *pan-pan* (with its ersatz atria, diverse *galeries,* intestinal travelator thoroughfares, online marketplace UIS, malfunctioning bagging areas, and of course the subcontinental divisions of the food court) is a dynamic model for such fluctuating tribalisms and identities. Within these spaces, tribes gangcraft alternative ideologies and ways of looking at the world, with their *tribal epistemologies,* or MUSHes, forming the unique sensoria by which they understand, map, and reconstruct orthodox reality.[2] *salesman slaps the roof of* pan-pan* 'this badboi comes fully-loaded with a range of heresies.'

Such tinkering in this context of procedural group discourse can be interpreted as collectively generating new scenarios, testing out non-normative identities, LARPing theories, and probing the applicability of speculative ideas within a test-bed parasite. A possibility space for thinking afresh and hitting refresh on thinking: a site for experimenting on the fringes of the staid and unsustainable orthodoxy of the Overton window. Yet, as the Confraternity's weird topography reminds us: the quasi-autonomy of such sites is entangled with the private infrastructure of communication stacks and commercial networks in a dense and complex hypereconomy, resulting in *pan-pan*'s accelerated proliferation of hybrid offspring.

Cults, covens and tribes wander the quasi-public spaces of malls and feeds, veiled by a multimodal argot: a dense anamorphic signal that requires some understanding of its layered references, corruptions, and inflections. The translation of this argot into sense is thus the simultaneous *translatio* of the translator: from NPC to insider-initiate (the process is akin to the transubstantial *relic-ing* of mere matter into sacred entities, by elevating them within a religious symbolic order; a trial by compurgation into the MUSH). Lo! To memethink anew; to © the world again.

---

2   As a Mixed Reality system this community-network is more powerful than any rendering pipeline, allowing for the real-time meshing of input data and texture-mapping of new assets in accordance with a *MUSH.* Such is the foundation of a *post-truth* generation.

In the semiotic swamp of *pan-pan,* where boundaries between things are uncertain, we are immersed amid thickets of
what CoN call "post-literate netspeak, emojinal gylphs, product spin, inter-species pidgin, object noise-chatter, and middle
American mall talk." Readers of this Boke are Journeyman-
semionauts exploring the dense script, or rather, exploring the
eerily recognizable dreamworld opened up to us by the script.
We share the theory-LARP gamespace with the Confraternity's
swarm of wandering avatars and Free&Ding oddkin, for this
perverse populous is extrapolated from our own habits and interactions. And therein is the uncanny familiarity that beckons
and enchants us, as reader-neophytes into the digestive script of
the Boke: the MUSH of CoN's mallscape is swarm-authored with
our own habitual pareidolia.

The Confraternity offers a [userinterface] for a particular
kind of [userexperience]: we adopt an ascetic-ludic mode of im-
mersive (rather than detached) contemplation in order to navigate a hybrid possibility space. Readers of *pan-pan* are spawned
into a multiplayer theory-LARP *in medias res.* Here, we think
with the cast of avatars (those fictional emissaries for investigat-
ing other realms and alien possibility spaces). Avatars of course
are mind-body extensions capable of traversing different environments, realities and worlds; they are substrate-autonomous
prostheses (the Confraternity would refer to such technology as
a pontifex). They are unruly hybrids where our selves are bound
up in their knotted aggregations.[3] Within the neomedieval

---

3   An elaborate side-quest of *pan-pan* is the exploration of corporeal heresies.
    The Confraternity's morphological speculations resonate with a number of
    contemporary artists also concerned with expanding the Overton window
    of how bodies, subjectivities, minds, etc. should be thought of. Such as
    the accelerated, hyper-condensed and networked techno-mashups of
    Ryan Trecartin, the multi-scalar gut-brain-AI oracles of Jenna Sutela, the
    digi-queered bodies of Jacolby Satterwhite, the neurodivergent chimeras
    of Andrea Crespo, the "€conomystical Cybermedieval" RPG characters of
    ¥€$Si Perse, and the bestiary of avatars that populate the transmedia fic-
    tion of Plastique Fantastique.

gamespace of reason we are not *explained to,* rather we *explore with* this milieu of weird peers.[4]

Just as these avatar-prostheses are perversely hybrid — corporeal and subjective heresies, according to an obstinate modern-humanist orthodoxy — a positive feedback loop between mall and mind and gut renders thinking multimodal, entangled, extended, multi-linear, ascetic, ludic and *hybrid* too. Corrupted by and with the imaginal strata of our neomedieval now.

'We call this new symbiosis: ©*ing.*'

CoN's symbiotic ©ing is a procedural synaesthetic LARP-ING with the manifold and multi-scalar 'hybridized pareidolic knowledges' of a distributed heresy; a deep tinkering with the noise of a thick present overflowing with preferable futures, re-revised pasts, adversarial *Umwelten,* and mixed realities. These multiple and simultaneous realities impact the same real world os (its populations, its resources, its future). A weird and hybrid practice of ©ing is an ascetic-ludic method of navigating such a Mixed Reality system with effective and adaptive agency. It is the speculative labour of *refiguring* our political subjectivity, our [userexperience], and our vocabulary in relation to the baroque excesses of our hybrid now.

----

4   The Confraternity's approach in gangcrafting this vibrant *quasi-thingiverse* is in sharp contrast with the critical pedagogy of design studio Metahaven, whose 2017 short film *Information Skies* began development with a script titled *Neo-Medievalism Explained.* The Confraternity do not *explain,* because their many-to-many squadcasting is neomedieval through-and-through: they adapt medieval perspectives and ways of knowing, mobilizing a 'sensual hyper-economy of *translatio*' between all entities, including Boke and reader. They *demonstrate* how contemporary practices, such as those mentioned here, have always already been structurally co-constituted with their medieval reminiscences. So if we decide not to approach *pan-pan* with a critical-analytical detachment, a perspective of *modern orthodoxy,* then what do we do with this delirious script? What does this ecstatic delirium do with us?